A GATE OF LIGHT

A SHADE OF VAMPIRE 91

BELLA FORREST

NEW GENERATION LIST

Thayen - Adoptive son of Derek and Sofia
Richard – Son of Jovi and Anjani *(Wolf-Incubus Hybrid)*
Astra – Daughter of Phoenix and Viola *(Daughter-Sentry Hybrid)*
Isabelle – Daughter of Serena and Draven *(Sentry-Druid Hybrid)*
Jericho – Son of Caia and Blaze *(Fae-Fire Dragon Hybrid)*
Voss – Son of Aida and Field *(Wolf-Hawk Hybrid)*
Dafne – Daughter of Lethe and Elodie *(Ice Dragon-Human Hybrid)*

ASTRA

*T*wo days had passed since the Flip. There wasn't a better name for it. Our lives had essentially been turned upside down. Hrista and her clones had taken over the real Shade, and we were stuck in the fake one. Blistering irony aside, at least we were all together again. My parents. My grandparents. My cousins and uncles and aunts. My friends. A handful of Reapers and the seven of the Daughters, too. We were all here. Not yet defeated.

"Only mildly inconvenienced," Lumi had said dryly.

Thayen and I stayed close to one another, always shadowed by Myst and Brandon. The Valkyrie and the Berserker weren't fans of the living, which didn't come as a surprise. Technically speaking, no one was supposed to know they even existed. Regine and Haldor were even worse, keeping their distance from us altogether and only coming out during the so-called night, when the fake Shade forced most of us into a deep sleep, after feeding on our life energy throughout the day.

Whether we liked it or not, rest was mandatory in this strange world.

"Damn this," I muttered as I left the comfort of my bed in the treehouse my friends and I had used as refuge before the Flip. Now I shared it with my parents. It wasn't even midnight yet. While I did feel tired, part of me wanted to fight the fake island's oppression. Besides, my work was nowhere near done.

Leaving my parents behind to sleep, I made my way through the dark redwood forest. I wasn't heading in a particular direction, but rather following a feeling that I had to be elsewhere. My mom and dad were together again, wholeheartedly relieved, but without my mom's abilities, which remained locked under the multiple runes that had been carved on her body. I had found an inkling of comfort knowing that Hrista's HQ had failed to copy me and the Daughters. It was something about our Hermessi roots, apparently, or so we'd theorized, at least, in the early days of the clone attacks. Jericho had gone back to the Black Heights—well, not the real mountains. This wasn't our home, yet we'd had to make it so while we figured out a way to get us back.

Hrista and her clones had stolen our island. There was no telling what she was capable of, especially when flanked by a dozen Berserkers. I wanted to believe that GASP was bigger and stronger, but this scorned Valkyrie had managed to throw us out of our homes almost effortlessly. We had every right to be worried, but until I figured out how to open shimmering portals of my own—Torrhen had let slip that I could during our confrontation—there wasn't much else we could do. The swamp witches had tried. Sidyan, Seeley, Kelara, Nethissis, and even the Time Master and the Soul Crusher had tried. The Daughters had tried. They had all failed.

I found myself standing in a wide clearing. Triangle-shaped purple leaves climbed up the redwoods with their sprawling vines and slim indigo stems. Some were loaded with lilac flowers that spread their sweet fragrance through the night air. The white glow came down from above like a fake moonlight, slipping through the almost- black canopy, blades of pale white slashing through the obscurity and stabbing the mossy ground. My mind was a jumble of incidents and emotions I couldn't quite reconcile.

Sitting down, I crossed my legs and took deep breaths, trying to find myself in the middle of the madness. For two days, I had been trying to open a shimmering portal. I'd already known I could sense them. Hrista had wanted me dead because she knew I could open them, too. But how?

"I should be able to do this," I whispered to myself, allowing the nocturnal darkness to embrace me. The Shadians had tried to find comfort in this place. The similarity it bore to our home helped, but in the end, we all knew this wasn't the real thing. It wasn't our island. *Our* island was under attack, and I dreaded to even imagine what that meant.

I tried to focus, but the fact that my mind kept wandering back to Brandon wasn't helping. It was bad enough we were cut off from the realm of the living, yet my heart kept thumping whenever the Berserker came close. I was happy to see him reunited with Hammer, however. Only now did I see that an essential piece of Brandon had been missing. The Aesir, a glorious black wolf, was an integral part of his being. Even if nothing else had really gone our way, at least Hammer had been returned safely.

I closed my eyes for a long second, trying to find the feeling I had experienced before. A shimmering gash had ripped open here at some point. Faint tendrils of its energy had been left behind, like fingerprints of an era long gone. The Daughters' pink mist from The Shade had picked up on portal residue from up to six months earlier, so it didn't shock me that I could still sense traces myself. I only needed a little to build on. It was something I'd learned after the Flip: if I could find a smidge of energy to latch onto, I could then construct my own layers on top of it and hopefully, eventually, summon a new portal. I'd had to figure most of this out on my own, too, and I wasn't even sure it would work. Maybe all I needed was just my own power. No one else could teach me. This stuff didn't come with a user manual.

Slowly but surely, my nerve endings expanded like corn popping in a hot iron pan over a blazing fire. *Pop. Pop. Pop.* Sensations came to life, one by one, until I was one with the universe and directly plugged into the atoms of the cosmos. The best I could describe this process was like an in-depth meditation, though I wasn't yet sure how I'd gotten to it. My instincts had never steered me wrong before, however. I'd ridden the wave this far, and I knew I was on to something.

I could feel it in my bones.

Every time I tried focusing on the shimmering gashes, every time I fed on the ghost of portals past, my whole being vibrated and followed a quiet, electrifying pattern. My skin tingled, every pore pricking. The current danced down my spine, tumbling and tickling along the way. There it was—the jolt I needed. It was just inches from my reach, and I was desperate to get to it.

Alas, it slipped away. The more I tried, the closer I got. But never close enough. "Damn it," I cursed under my breath, normalcy taking over and dragging me back into the real world. Well, a copy of the real world, anyway.

"You're frustrated," Brandon said, startling me as he emerged from the darkness on the other side of the clearing. He walked toward me, and wisps of it curled off him like black smoke. "The more you push yourself, the closer you will get, and still... you won't reach your destination."

"You seem to know a lot about my power," I replied with a sulking grumble. "Also, you suck at encouragement."

He shrugged. "It was a statement of fact, not an encouragement. Anyway, I've seen something similar before, a very long time ago. Many souls have passed through Purgatory, Pinkie. Souls of hybrids that weren't ever supposed to be born. Life found a way, however—and so did death, for they came to my door, in the end."

Brandon's darkness faded slowly, leaving only his true form, clearer than ever before. The blue fires in his eyes flickered white more often than before, and especially when he looked my way. I'd identified that as a sign of an intense emotional state, though I wasn't sure what emotions were at play here. I knew what emotions I would've liked from him, but I didn't dare wish or even imagine it when I peered into his eyes. His black hair poured down his back in slick, shiny braids with silver threads at the end. The leather of his vest stretched across his torso, his broad shoulders and narrow hips forming an athletic yet elegant frame. The chain links on his shoulders jingled faintly with every step that he took, as did the steel and silver buckles on his knee-length boots, and I was breathless once more.

He was a dominating presence in my life, and I had not gotten used to that yet.

"You've met people with powers like mine before?" I asked, keeping a sullen frown on my face as a means to mask the rapid beating of my heart. Brandon had already admitted to having a soft spot for me, but I didn't know what to do with that, nor what the next step would be. I was permanently nervous around him because I wanted more, and maybe so did he... but neither of us had made a move.

I was stupidly shy. I'd always been like that. Or was I too impatient? No, maybe just overthinking. He'd already told me that Berserkers and Valkyries weren't made for love, yet I was yearning for something I wasn't sure he could even give me. Yep, definitely overthinking, though it was hard not to when the truth was right in front of me. But even so...

Snap out of it, Astra. Be a Daughter, not a chicken!

"Not exactly like yours, no, but hybrids with Hermessi origins. Daughters of other realms, though not precisely pink wonders like you and your mother. Similar creatures with frightening powers, some of whom fell in love with the commoners, the less extraordinary residents of those realms. The fruits of their love were incredible beings with powers that befuddled even their parents," Brandon said, stopping right in front of me. I craned my head back so I could keep looking him in the eyes. "You, however, are a step above any others I've met. There is absolutely nothing common about sentries. Your genetic package is truly out of this world, something I've never seen before. But you do share some similarities with your otherworldly equivalents."

"Oh?" I managed, his gaze hypnotizing me.

"This portal opening talent, I've seen it before, albeit in different formats, but the basis remains the same. I'm guessing that the more you try, the better you'll get at it. However, the secret to succeeding is more about letting go than it is about delving deeper," Brandon said, then casually sat down beside me. We both stared at the clearing and the washed-out moonlight that filled it, turning most of the leaves from a dirty green to an olive yellow. The colors were wrong. Everything about this place was wrong.

I slowly turned my head to look at him. "So, I should just let go? That's your suggestion?"

"It's just an idea, but unless you tell me what it is you feel is missing, it might be the wrong idea," he replied.

For two days, Brandon had been quietly watching my efforts to prove Hrista right—to demonstrate I could indeed open a shimmering portal. The process of discovery was sloppy and painfully slow, though I didn't lack encouragement. My mother, my father, my violet-eyed aunts—my entire family had my back in this. But I'd failed to deliver so far, and it made me feel... inadequate. Frustrated. Yes, Brandon was right, I was frustrated.

"I'm not sure what's missing," I said. "It's just... the urgency of it. We're stuck in this place while Hrista and the clones and some of your brothers are traipsing around on our island, doing who knows what. Every day that we're here is a day that they've won. We know nothing. We're in literal darkness, and I could be the only one who can do something about it." Pausing to breathe in, I felt the sting in my eyes and blinked back tears. "It's all on my shoulders, and my inability to deliver sooner rather than later angers me."

Brandon didn't say anything for about a minute, while I tried to adjust to what I'd just expressed. Saying it aloud had made it even more real. "If you focus on the time you have left, you will never open a portal," he finally replied. "If you channel your energy into the urgency of your situation, only failure awaits at the end of your journey, Astra." Every time my name left his lips, it felt serious. Profound. Of great meaning and importance. I couldn't look away from him, but I fed on his words and his sound reasoning. He was right. The more anxious I got, the worse it would be. No one had accomplished anything with anxiety.

"You think I should just... what, relax?" I asked, my voice quiet.

His lips were closer than I'd thought. I wasn't sure when the approach had occurred, but mere inches of space were left between us as he'd leaned in, and the proximity sent my blood into a frenzied rush through my body, making me feel lightheaded. For a moment, I wondered what would happen if I just leaned in and kissed him. The white flames of his gaze told me I was on the right track here, but my body... failed me. I'd never had the confidence of a sentry. My aunties, Harper and Serena, were fierce, and they always took what their hearts desired. I, on the other hand, had always been more timid. Like a mouse.

"Deep breaths, in and out," Brandon said, his breath warming my face. It was a strange feeling—more of an illusion, really, since he was only concentrated spiritual energy that had taken a physical form. But he felt real. He felt... oh, so real. "Focus on nothing other than the shimmering portal. You can already feel one after it has closed, right?"

I nodded, my brain slowing down.

"I think you just... you just need to put everything else out of your mind," Brandon added, his voice dropping an octave. I hadn't noticed the raspy undertone before, but it made my breath falter. He was so close. His lips so inviting. We were both slipping away, I realized. The reality of our situation was dissipating like watercolors in a glass of water, until nothing but our souls remained.

"That's going to be hard," I mumbled.

"You... have to try," he replied, his gaze dropping. It settled on my lips, and heat burst through me as if I'd just swallowed the sun itself. We were so close.

But I heard Hammer before I saw him. It only took a split second to understand where this moment would end. The Aesir came tearing out of the dark woods and pounced on Brandon, forcing us apart and making him laugh. My cheeks were flushed, and fires burned in my throat, but I giggled too. Ever since they'd been reunited, Hammer had had a hard time letting Brandon out of his sight.

The wolf had the energy of about fifty preschoolers on a sugar rush, and his Berserker was there for all of it. Despite the missed opportunity, I had to admit that seeing them together like this filled me with the kind of warmth I'd rarely felt since this whole clone nonsense had begun.

"I'm sorry about that," Brandon said to me as he playfully tackled the dire wolf. They rolled over in the grass, dried leaves crunching beneath them, but Hammer didn't give an inch. "He keeps butting in..."

At least he'd said it out loud. I would've felt bad to be the one to point out the pattern. Twice now, Hammer had come between us in what should've been private moments. Twice, the Aesir had interrupted something... important. I couldn't fault the enthusiastic creature, but I did wonder if he was doing it on purpose or if it was just a coincidence.

There was a lot I didn't fully understand about the relationship between a Berserker and his Aesir, so I couldn't exclude anything just yet. I only knew that the Aesir were much brighter than their living equivalents. Either way, my lips tingled at the thought of Brandon's, and I knew we'd take things further eventually. Everything was moving fast, but I didn't know how it would end for us. So why not go at lightning speed now and maybe slow down once we survived?

Brandon's laughter filled me with a muted joy, and I smiled as I watched them wrestle. Where were we going with this connection between us? What was our destination? Did either of us even know?

ASTRA

*W*ith Hammer padding around, his pink tongue out and his sapphire eyes scanning the darkness of the forest, I decided to give the shimmering portal another shot, further encouraged by Brandon. At some point, Thayen and Myst joined us as well, though I wasn't sure exactly when. I only knew Thayen couldn't sleep much either, and the Valkyrie had rarely left his side since the Flip.

There was something different between them. A muted warmth. An awareness of one another. Their movements and body language were surprisingly well synchronized. Whatever this was, I hoped it would only bear good things for the both of them. For all her efforts at distancing herself from the living, from *us*, Myst had become an integral part of our team. A friend, even.

No one said a word while I sank into a meditative state. It was the one part I'd gotten the hang of thus far. I could feel their eyes on me as I sat perfectly still, and I fed on their unspoken encouragement. My mind wandered away from the world around us, though I did feel Brandon's hand close around mine. The touch of his skin was electrifying, and for a moment I jumped back to our almost-kiss. What would I have done if his lips had found mine? How would I have reacted if we'd actually kissed? I wanted it, there was no denying that, but...

Ah, the light. Much like in earlier attempts, the light came from the darkness of my closed eyes, enveloping me in a buzzing warmth as if the sun itself had reached out to take me in its golden arms. "Focus on my voice," Brandon said. "I know you can do it, Astra."

"You really don't know what you're doing, do you?" Thayen muttered. I heard Myst thwacking him on the shoulder.

"Shut up. Let him do his thing," Myst reprimanded.

"What is his thing, exactly?" Thayen replied, sounding amused.

Brandon chuckled. "Nah, you're right, I have no idea what I'm doing here. I'm just going with the flow— hopefully something sticks."

I couldn't help but laugh, though I kept my eyes closed, clinging to the sunshine on my skin like a blanket. Basking in it, I exhaled deeply as I tried to block out their voices and the sounds of the forest around me. My mind paced farther away from reality and closer to the memory of a shimmering portal. I needed that memory as the basis for my own passageway. Brandon squeezed my hand.

He was right about one thing. I required focus more than anything. Something to stick to while I built up the energy and the technique to open a shimmering portal. The ability was absolutely and undeniably somewhere deep inside me. I only had to tap into the stream.

"I can, however, surmise that Hrista and Astra's shimmering portal methods differ. Hrista had physical accoutrements," Brandon said. "Specifically, a perfectly round crystal imbued with some kind of energy which she used to open a portal. Also, a clone dies whenever a portal is opened, and I assume it's because a portal consumes an entire clone's life energy. I'm fuzzy on the particulars, but I'll assume Hrista has more clones than there are Shadian originals just for this purpose. Astra obviously doesn't require these exterior elements, since the specific type of energy required is inside her. I feel it now. Hers is the easier way, believe it or not."

"Plus, she always knew when to open them," Thayen said. "Like when we were chasing Richard's clone back in The Shade."

"Ah, Hrista always had comms open with the clones she sent out into The Shade," Brandon explained. "The magic was set up to respond accordingly."

Looking back now, it made sense. But I didn't have another second to dwell on it. The shimmering portal I had last seen emerged before me, like a mouth wide open and filled with diamonds. Its power emanated outward, the air rippling toward me with a peculiar mixture of hot and cold. I reached for it, my spirit desperate to touch it.

"Do you see it yet?" Brandon asked.

"Yes."

"Can you reach it?"

I'd done this before a couple of times, and I'd told him all about the experience from beginning to end. Having the details, he was able to guide me. He was no expert, but he was the closest thing I had to a mentor in this; he'd gone through more shimmering portals than the entire island's inhabitants put together. "I can try," I mumbled.

"Do it."

As if unchained from my own body, I felt my spirit stretching. I lunged at the portal with a vigorous thrust, the light intensifying into a blinding white before I could feel the shimmer's curious touch. Exhaustion crept up, almost unseen, and I found myself falling, unable to scream. Brandon caught me in his arms, and I was back in the real world, panting. To my surprise, my body had lunged with me, and my feet had briefly left the ground—I'd gotten up and jumped.

Sweat dripped down my temples, tickling my cheeks.

"Are you okay?" Myst asked, watching me with genuine concern.

I nodded slowly. "Yeah. It's not a straight path, I'm afraid. I'll try again."

"Is that wise?" Thayen replied, his brow furrowed. "You must be tired."

"I am. But what other choice do I have? Time keeps marching forward, and Hrista has taken over our island. The sooner I can get us out of here, the better," I said, positioning myself back into a meditative frame: legs crossed, back straight, and palms resting upward on my knees.

Closing my eyes, I took several deep breaths. In. Out. In. Out. Brandon's hands found both of mine this time, holding tightly. "Let me try something," he whispered, and I smiled.

"Okay."

As minutes went by, I experienced a new sensation. A rush of chills burst through me, beginning with my hands. It spread through until every atom in my body was suddenly invigorated, newfound energy pulsating and beckoning me closer to that memory of a shimmering portal. Brandon was giving me some of his spiritual energy, I realized, and the feeling of it coursing through my soul was incredible.

I was light as a feather. Merely an idea floating on the wings of a summer wind.

There it was again. The shimmering portal. I reached out, and this time... this time I felt it tingling my fingertips. I giggled as I ran my hands through the mass of liquid diamonds, trying to understand what it was made of and how I could make one of my own.

"I'm there!" My own voice sounded like a distant echo.

"Hold on to it. What do you see?" Brandon asked.

How could I describe this gaping mouth of raw celestial energy? I couldn't. "I can tell you how it feels," I said. "Warm and cold at the same time. Sharp and soft, too. It's made of everything and nothing at the same time."

"My energy is yours, Astra. Use it," he replied.

As if electrified, I allowed my spirit to record and untangle the cosmic tendrils of wonder that made up this incredible phenomenon. I felt myself getting up again, a sharp current flowing through my legs. My hands were on fire as I imagined myself grabbing onto the edges and opening the shimmering portal wider so we might step through it. I wasn't feeding on Brandon's energy anymore. I'd let go of him.

Myst gasped. "She's doing it!"

I opened my eyes and saw it. Small and thin at first, my hands glowing pink as they ripped the very fabric of this world apart. Brandon stood a few feet back, his blazing blue eyes wide with wonder and... pride, I realized, as he beheld my work. Emboldened by what I'd accomplished, I used the last drops of energy I had left to pull the edges of the shimmering portal farther apart.

My muscles ached. My bones hurt. I'd reached my limits already.

I cried out, unable to hold the damn thing anymore. As soon as I let go, the gash closed, and semi-darkness returned to the clearing. The world stopped vibrating, as did my soul. It was over, but I'd done it.

"Wow," Thayen managed, a grin stretching over his face as he looked at me. "Astra, you did it..."

"I know, right?" I replied, beaming with pride. I couldn't stand anymore, and I didn't even realize it until Myst gasped and the image shifted before me as I fell. Brandon was quick to sweep me off my feet, taking me into his arms. "What's... what's happening?"

He gave me a soft smile. "You're exhausted, that's what's happening. You'll have to stop for tonight, Pinkie. It's time to get you back to bed."

I'd learned the difference by now between his choice of names for me. Whenever things were serious and Brandon needed me to understand the intensity of what he had to say, he used my name. Whenever he was being affectionate or wished to simply take the edge off and play around, he called me Pinkie. I let my head rest on his shoulder, wrapping my arms around his neck as he carried me away from the clearing.

"See you tomorrow, Astra," Thayen said from somewhere behind us.

I might have answered, but I wasn't sure. Melting in Brandon's arms, I didn't think I could keep myself awake for another minute. It didn't matter, anyway. I'd done it. I'd opened a shimmering portal.

This was the confirmation I'd needed—now I knew I could do it again and better. It was no longer a matter of "if" but rather of "when," and that made me look forward to tomorrow. I only hoped I'd open a portal somewhere in The Shade where the enemy wouldn't spot it right away. Brandon's chest felt hard against my relaxed form, his taut muscles firm beneath the black leather. His scent filled my lungs, though I wasn't sure what fragrances adorned his spirit—it was something sharp and vibrant, with only a tinge of sweetness. I breathed him in, glad to be in his arms.

Soon I'd be in my bed. Part of me wished we could stay like this for a while longer, but darkness came over me and silenced the last stream of consciousness I had left. The world of dreams waited.

THAYEN

*A*stra was incredible.

It wasn't the first time that she'd defied the odds—not even close—but this was a whole new level, even for her. I was insanely proud of her, proud of being part of the same family, of having been taught similar values and core strengths. This wouldn't be the last amazing thing she would do, either.

"She did it," Myst said, watching Brandon as he carried Astra off to the treehouse residences. Hammer was right behind them, quiet and ever watchful. It was hard to look away from the creature, a savage but majestic dire wolf that carried a certain timeless wisdom in its Berserker-like gaze. *He may be a beast, but something tells me there's more on his mind than normal beastly things.*

"Yes, she did," I replied, still astonished.

The Aesir were like extensions of a Berserker or a Valkyrie's spirit. Destroying one reduced their masters to mere wisps of deadly, festering darkness—most of whom were attracted to Haldor for some reason. I'd learned that some of Myst, Regine, and Brandon's friends had become Haldor's companions, his to play with for an eternity. Such a fate terrified me, but nothing filled me with more dread than the prospect of being stuck in this place forever while Hrista carried on with her agenda on our island.

"She will be able to hold one open longer the more she practices," Myst muttered after a long and pleasantly peaceful silence—the kind that came after a good meal or during a crimson sunset. Astra's accomplishment deserved this quiet reverence. "I have faith that we will leave this nightmarish land soon."

"Which means Hrista was absolutely right to fear her," I replied. We walked through the woods for a while, tiny figures among the giant redwoods, the fake sky covered by a sea of rustling leaves. There were animals here— animals I'd only caught glimpses of before. Strangely shaped deer and black rabbits with big, violet eyes were just two of the oddities of this alternative island. Nature had found its own way out here. It followed most of the original's pattern, but there were deviations as well. It wasn't hard to spot the difference once you spent a little more time walking around and observing the surroundings. "Astra is dangerous to her and her plans. With her abilities, Astra may be able to get us home."

"Not just that," Myst said, staring ahead at the narrowing path. Wild violets and lilies grew on both sides, their stems stretching outward and casually bending under the weight of their fragranced blossoms. "Hrista controls the Berserkers' access to Purgatory. I believe that's done with the round crystal that Brandon mentioned, though I never saw it myself. I didn't even know Hrista was here until we reached the villa... No one back home knows of what she has been doing, and if Astra can open shimmering portals, it means she can likely control the destination, as well."

"Oh, so the portals don't only connect the real island to the fake one."

She shook her head. "No. I came through a shimmering portal from Purgatory, but I was wrestling a Berserker with 'access' at the time, much like Regine. I wouldn't have been able to come through on my own. Astra could very well alert the forces of Order of what has happened if she can open a portal there. We should absolutely consider that once Astra gets her ability under control, and once the Shadians are safely back in the Earthly realm. We know too little about this place to let over five thousand people stay here for much longer."

"Have you dealt with these passageways before?"

Myst laughed lightly, and it was meant to mock the question but all it did was make me smile, my heart fluttering in my chest. "Valkyries and Berserkers belong in Purgatory. We don't just walk off through a shimmering portal like it's everyday business. That's Hrista's thing, and it's an unacceptable anomaly."

"Okay. That's a no, then," I replied, holding back a chuckle.

"No." Her laughter died as she looked at me. "Every realm functions on some basic principles. I simply observed this phenomenon of passing from one dimension to another and formed an opinion based on patterns. So far, Astra has proven me right on most of my theories, hence my confidence in her ability to do more."

We walked in silence for a while, gathering our thoughts and trying to move away from what we'd just witnessed with Astra. I'd noticed the closeness between her and Brandon. For her sake, I hoped it would lead somewhere good, though I did worry. Like Myst had just said, creatures of Purgatory belonged in Purgatory. If we prevailed against this new nemesis, things would eventually be pushed back into a state of normalcy. That meant the Berserkers and the Valkyries would return to their homes. Where would that leave Astra?

It didn't take a genius profiler to observe her emotions. She had them on display, whether she knew it or not. Astra was falling for Brandon, and Brandon was obviously fond of her too. If they had a chance at something, I wished it for them. Even though reality had a way of biting us when we least expected it. But deep down, I already knew why I wanted it to work between Astra and Brandon; it would spell a positive outcome for whatever this was growing between Myst and me. I wasn't sure of much, but I knew the Valkyrie's impact on me reached deep levels of my being—and not all of it could be attributed to her glorious nature, her splendor as a being of Purgatory. Our connection went far beyond the first impressions of grandeur that she clearly left on anyone who crossed her path.

"Do you regret being here?" I asked, my lips moving before I could stop them. One thought had led to another, it seemed.

Myst gave me a curious look. "What do you mean?"

"If given the chance to do it all over again, would you?"

"Yes," she replied without hesitation. "Stopping Hrista is absolutely paramount."

Her dedication was impressive, but it wasn't what I was trying to figure out. "What about us? The people you've met in the middle of this mess. Would you help us again like you did that day when Haldor came after us with his shadow hounds?"

"Yes." Again, there wasn't a single pause between my question and her answer.

"Good. I'm glad I met you, too," I replied. I would've liked a more detailed answer, something that might satisfy my growing curiosity about her mindset and her emotions, but I had a feeling this was the most I would get from Myst.

"My living days are far behind me. I don't remember much of my life," she said. We stopped under the eldest of the forest's redwoods, a gargantuan tree that was as wide as a building and about as tall as a skyscraper. Its branches were heavy with rich clusters of leaves, its bark reddish-brown and wrinkled with age. The trunk could hold dozens of homes, yet no one had touched it. The residential area was pretty far away. "Life is only a faint memory in the back of my head," Myst added, placing her palm against the hard and rugged bark. "Being around living people feels like a new experience, I'll admit, even though I know it isn't. I'd never left Purgatory since being chosen as a Valkyrie. As the memories of my life faded, it was the only thing I knew. At first, I felt lost and confused and even powerless against such an abrupt change, but once I adjusted, it made more sense. The same can be said about you, Thayen."

"Me?"

"You confused me at first, but now... you make more sense," she replied, the shadow of a smile flitting across her face.

"How so?" I asked.

"I answer to Order, and I function according to the laws of Order," Myst said. "Every being of Purgatory is the same in that sense, and there are thousands, maybe more of us. My powers, my light, everything that I am is a defining feature of the function I serve. I bring glory and brightness, the reward of a life well lived and access to the beyond. Those I'm chosen to guide into that never-ending realm are people of valor and goodness. By contrast, Berserkers are darkness and wrath, a preliminary taste of what is in store for those who have done harm. The balance of the universe and its many dimensions dictates retribution. All of this I understand. Living, however, is a sum total of experiences and emotions and of decisions based on those experiences and emotions. It still feels foreign to me, but I'm beginning to understand why you say or do certain things. Or, better said,

I'm beginning to remember why you say or do certain things."

This was a good time to ask her something I'd been wondering about. "You mentioned your powers, that each Valkyrie and Berserker has a defining ability. Would you mind telling me what yours is? What about Regine's? Brandon's? I know Haldor's is that he's like a magnet to the shadow hounds that serve him."

"It's not my place to tell you about them," Myst replied, the blue in her eyes fading to white for the faintest moment as I inched closer to her. She didn't seem to mind it, either. My body did things without me sometimes. "It's their story to tell, should they choose to do so. But I can tell you about mine."

"Truth be told, I'm dying to know," I chuckled, well aware of how vulnerable and insignificant I was by comparison. I, a mere mortal (albeit gifted with vampiric immortality, but not invulnerable), standing before this marvelous creature of an afterlife realm, a being of light and pure wonder. Simply being able to look at her and talk to her was enough to render me dumbstruck, yet I couldn't stop myself from asking more, from wanting more. "I mean, technically speaking, you already know what my special mojo does..."

She took a step back and slowly turned to face me, one hand resting on the bejeweled pommel of her sheathed sword. I'd taken to calling it Lightbringer. Even Myst had adopted it as its name, previously unaware that she had the liberty to do that. "Just to be clear, I have no control over what's beyond my realm. I cannot disclose anything about it."

"I know that."

"What I can do, however, is project souls from the beyond. I've rarely had to use this ability in Purgatory, except when I was tracing a lineage or when one of us was investigating something. It doesn't really matter. But that's my ability. I can connect to a soul who has already passed through Purgatory, and I can... show their image before me. It allows for communication."

To say that what she'd just revealed was unexpected would've been a gross understatement. The air was knocked out of my lungs as I tried to wrap my head around the concept. "You... you project and speak with dead people, basically," I managed, running a hand through my hair.

Myst nodded once. "Yes."

My heart was already racing, as if it knew exactly what I was about to ask her to do for me. "I've never told you about my parents."

"Derek and Sofia. We've met," she replied dryly, as if I'd just said the silliest thing.

"No, my birth parents. Acheron and Danika, of the Nasani dynasty of Visio," I said. "They died when I was little. Derek and Sofia adopted me afterward."

She stilled, her fiery blue gaze fixed on my face. "You're an orphan."

"I was," I said, sighing. "I don't think of myself that way most of the time—Derek and Sofia are my family now—but my mother... she was a monster. She had my father killed. She would've killed me too in order to preserve her immortality."

Myst sucked in a breath, slowly bringing a hand up to her chest, as if to stop her heart from beating too fast. She didn't have one, biologically speaking—none of the beings beyond the living realm had actual bodies—but the gesture spoke volumes nonetheless.

"Please, don't tell me you wish to see her, of all the people who have died in your world," she murmured, clearly horrified. Ignoring the painful pang in my heart whenever Danika crossed my mind, I chose to focus on Myst's beauty, instead. I was momentarily speechless, mesmerized by the delicate lines of her face, but I managed to shake my head no in response. "Good," she said, "because I have someone better in mind."

Gently, Myst drew her sword and pressed one palm against its blade. Closing her eyes, she shone from within as if light flowed through her veins. Breathless as I beheld her, I barely noticed the luminescent figure that gradually emerged from thin air beside her. Only when his features became clear enough to trigger my most distant memories did I realize what the Valkyrie had done.

My heart broke all over again, but it overflowed with joy, too.

"Dad..." I whispered, my voice gone, my throat burning.

Myst had summoned my father's ghost. The great Acheron Nasani stood in front of me, tall as an oak, smiling as if we'd never been apart for even a second. His spirit shimmered with love, and tears pricked my eyes as I accepted this new reality. My father was here...

THAYEN

"Son? Is that you?"

My father's voice was a soft echo of the past, yet it hit me with the brute force of a tidal wave as I struggled to stand upright. Myst was right beside us, observing quietly, but I saw the blue of her eyes flash white with intense emotion when I glanced at her. "It is me," I managed. "Guess I've changed."

"You're a grown man," he said. "The years have been good to you, my son. You're a handsome devil, huh?" A playful grin came over his face, and I truly recognized him. My father, Acheron Nasani, the young and valiant Lord Supreme with a silver tongue and the adoration of the empire. My mother had always played second fiddle to him as a ruler. Thinking back now, I could easily see why she'd sought to see him gone from this world. Dad was too good.

I exhaled sharply. "I wish I could hug you."

"Where are we? What's happened? How old are you, son? My memory is fuzzy," he replied. He wore the clothes he'd worn the day he was murdered by my Darkling nanny, but the colors were different than I remembered. The high-collared tunic was white velvet covered in swirling leaves of silver embroidery, with matching breeches and light gray hide boots that went up to his knees. His hair was short and soft brown, just like I remembered it, but his eyes drew my attention the most—galaxies of iridescent sparkles swirled within them. I was looking at my father's spirit in its purest form. And he seemed a little... lost.

"What happened to him?" I asked Myst.

"I cannot answer that," she said, offering an apologetic smile. "He knows you. He remembers you because of your blood ties. You're his son, after all. But here in the living realm, even as a projection, Acheron feels out of place and disconnected. Keep talking to him, and he'll ease back into who he was. It takes time, once the soul has been plucked from its place in the beyond."

Shifting focus back to my dad, I realized that everything else about him was unchanged. My memories of him and Mom had faded over the years, but seeing him here now... it was all coming back to me in bright colors, his voice clearer and louder than ever. "Dad... I'm a vampire. It's been twenty years since you—"

"Since I died," he said, his gaze dropping for a moment. I didn't want this conversation to slip into something sad and mournful. Being near him made me happy, so happy I could find my way up to the stars if I tried hard enough. I didn't want us to cry about this. If only I could touch him.

"Do you remember that day?" I asked.

Dad nodded once. "I was not reaped right away. I saw a lot of things I never wished to see... Hm, I remember running a lot, too, from ghouls and... and hiding from Aeternae with scythes. But I snuck around, too. They never got to me. Perhaps I was fortunate."

I wondered what that must have been like. The Darklings were reigning supreme on Visio at the time, with their Knight Ghouls and death magic trickeries. I'd wondered about his spirit after he'd died, but the Time Master had assured me my father had moved on. "You saw it all, didn't you?" I replied, my voice trembling with anger. "The Darklings, their beasts..."

"I also saw you, growing stronger despite the madness. At least you got half of me to keep you going," Dad said, chuckling faintly. "I'm sorry your mother turned out the way she did. My heart broke at the time, but now... it seems so far away."

"It is! It is far away!" I insisted, instinctively reaching out to take his hands in mine. But I only felt the coolness of wintery air when my fingers brushed through him, as though he were made of mist. "Visio has been reformed. Unending was freed. The Aeternae are no more. Balance has been restored, and everyone is happier for it."

"That is good to hear," Dad said, and his expression reflected genuine joy. "I perpetuated our bloody culture because it was expected of me. I was raised to be an Aeternae, and I did not know how to be anything else. But even so, had I known what Danika and the Darklings had been doing for so long..." He paused, taking a deep breath to calm himself. "I should've burned them all alive."

There he was. My father. The great Acheron. I'd missed that side of him the most. The fierce Aeternae. The angry soul who found no mercy for those who went against his principles. I remembered our way of life from my childhood days. Most of the Aeternae had known little to nothing about the Darklings, and never enough to form a coherent opinion or to truly understand what we were at the time. It was part of the reason why the Aeternae had ultimately failed as a society. When suddenly forced to confront the possibility of mortality, they'd turned against Unending. They'd chosen to support the Darklings and to keep the first Reaper buried under the seals.

The memory of those days made me quiver. "What was it about Mom that drew you to her initially?" I asked, choosing to steer away from the harsh truth of my Aeternae culture.

"Well, she was an absolute beauty," Dad chuckled, hands casually resting on his hips. He gazed to the side, momentarily losing himself in the darkness of the redwoods as he remembered my mother. "Danika was a fierce creature. Her presence filled an entire room and made it hard to breathe without her. She carried herself with grace and poise, and she was ready to tear the head off of anyone who threatened her." He stopped for a moment, shaking his head in disappointment. "And I was foolish enough to think she would take all that and invest it into our family. Into you."

"You couldn't have known," I said. "I was blindsided too."

"Yes. But I was your father," he replied, his expression suddenly serious. "I was supposed to protect you, to keep you safe."

"Dad, you did everything you could. Mom fooled everybody." My eyes flickered to Myst. She must be so confused right now.

Myst gave me a curious look. "I take it this is a story you will share with me sometime?"

"And who is this wonderful creature?" Dad cut in, suddenly aware of Myst's presence beside him. He measured her from head to toe with a gleam of admiration in his multicolored eyes, a smile tugging at the corners of his mouth.

"I'm the one who raised you from the beyond," Myst replied, raising her chin. "I am Myst. A Valkyrie of Purgatory."

"Purgatory? Oh wait, that was my judgment. You were there, yes! I remember you now. We've met before," Dad said. "You carried me off, right?"

She couldn't stop herself from smiling. "And you kept asking me to join you."

"Dad," I chided, but I was laughing too. It sounded just like him. My father had never been a womanizer, but he'd always appreciated the impact of a beautiful woman. He'd loved jesting in that vein too. Some in the imperial court had found his comments offensive—but only when they'd been aimed at their wives or daughters. Otherwise, they'd laughed with him, and shamelessly so.

"Your friend, I take it?" he replied, pointing a thumb at the Valkyrie. I nodded once more. "I have to tell you, kid. I am proud to see you've chosen to aim above your level. It's impressive." He looked at Myst. "My son is a good man. A fierce man. A noble man. I don't need more than a minute here with him to know it. I hope you know it too."

She didn't respond right away, and I held my breath for a few seconds. Dad eyed me with a mixture of curiosity and amusement, but when Myst spoke again, he listened intently.

"Thayen is one of the strongest spirits I have ever come across," she said. "An army of Berserkers will not break his soul. His body, yes. But not his soul. His soul has the power of the entire universe crammed inside it. And I am fortunate and honored to consider him an ally."

Dad shot me a grin. "I think she likes you."

"How are you?" I asked, my cheeks burning as I proceeded to move the conversation away from yet another difficult subject. He had been away for so long and was unaware of so many things, it was hard for him to know when to stop with his playful jests and devilish innuendos. In that respect, he was just as I remembered him, and it filled me with a familiar warmth. My Aeternae family was twisted and gone, but my father's spirit had braved the unknown and had found his way back to me. "How have you been? What is it like for you?"

"I'm fine, son." He then proceeded to give me details of his new existence, but I heard nothing. Only saw his lips moving. He was certainly saying something, yet I wasn't getting any of it. "Wait," Dad muttered, his voice back. "What's going on? I'm talking, but it is silenced... Why?"

Myst rubbed the back of her neck. "There is a control system in place," she said. "The living can never know what the beyond is like. Therefore, if you talk about it, your voice is taken from you. If you talk about anything else, your voice is yours again."

"That is a neat trick!" Acheron replied. "I would have liked to have that handy during my days in court. More than once I yearned to listen to silence instead of the constant whining of councilors and overprivileged nobles..."

"Dad."

He looked at me, serene as a summer's morning. "Yes, son?"

"I love you."

"I love you too," he said. "And looking at you now, I understand how much I miss you. But I do not regret how things worked out. You have found happiness, have you not?"

Smiling, I decided to tell him about the people who had saved me. "Do you remember Derek and Sofia, by any chance? I know it was so long ago, and I'm not sure what rings familiar and what doesn't."

"Derek and Sofia Novak. Yes. I remember them." My father sighed. "I hope they survived that nightmare." "They did. And they adopted me. I've been living in The Shade for two decades now," I said, then told him about the Aeternae losing their immortality and the preservation of vampirism. I didn't go into too many details, unsure of how much time I had with him, but I wanted him to know that things had turned out well in the end. "I'm okay, Dad. I've been lucky."

"You deserve every bit of good fortune that comes your way, my son," he replied. "I only wish I could've been there to watch you grow up and become the man that you are today."

"Me too," I murmured.

Myst cleared her throat quietly and gave me a weary look. "I cannot hold him here for much longer," she said, the glow in her sword weakening.

"It's best if you say your farewells. I'm sorry."

"There is nothing to be sorry about," my father interjected. His spirit shimmered softly in the semi-darkness of the clearing, the white and silver of his garments a little brighter than everything else. But it was his love for me that seemed brightest, pouring from his kaleidoscopic eyes as he looked at me and smiled. "You have an incredible life ahead of you, my son. And there aren't enough words in this world to properly convey how proud I am of who you are, of who you've become."

"I'm just thankful I got to see you one more time." Tears stung in my eyes, but I held them back, unwilling to break down. Not now, not when I couldn't even hug my father. I had to stay strong and keep a straight face. I had to do him proud. "Perhaps we shall see each other again someday."

"Well, I hope so. Just remember, Thayen—every step you take, every mistake, every good or bad or utterly terrible choice you make in this life... it becomes experience, and it teaches you to do better. Remember that, and you will be fine. I'm sure of it."

"Thanks, Dad."

"Myst, if you'd be so kind, I would like to return to wherever you plucked me from before I start weeping like a little girl," my father said, his voice shaking slightly. Myst smiled, and the glow in her sword vanished altogether.

The spirit of the great Acheron Nasani went with it, and I was the orphan prince once more. I knew it wasn't a perfectly accurate description, but I couldn't stop myself from feeling that way in my father's immediate absence. I realized I'd had no idea how much I'd really missed him all this time. My heart ached on a deeper level now, and I knew the pain would never really go away. I would have to live with it.

But it seemed a small price to pay for seeing him again.

The silence settled over the clearing like a heavy quilt of darkness and lost memories. I turned slowly to face Myst as she looked my way. "When you told me your real parents' names and bits about your life on Visio, I remembered I had guided your father into the afterlife. Of course, I'm not normally allowed to say such things, but I suppose this entire situation calls for an exception or two. I would have held him for longer, but I'm tired. My energy levels are not what they used to be. Not in this place, at least. I believe the false island is affecting my kind as well, though not as acutely as the living."

My arms moved before I could say anything. I wrapped them around Myst and pulled her into a tight embrace. My very soul sang in that moment, the close proximity of the Valkyrie having an unexpected effect on me. It mattered, but not enough to pull me away from her. I welcomed the light and the warmth suddenly coursing through my veins. "Thank you," I whispered in her ear. "Thank you for this incredible opportunity. I will never forget it, Myst. Thank you."

She didn't say a word. She didn't move. I would've liked a reaction, but the silence was fine too. Being pushed away would've been infinitely worse. At least this told me the Valkyrie was okay with a hug. I didn't feel a heartbeat, but every atom of her beamed through me for a short while as I clung to this incredible moment. It only lasted a few seconds, but it felt like ages glowing with the promise of bliss.

"My apologies," I said as I stepped back, cold without her in my arms. "I didn't mean to step out of line."

"No, no, it's fine," Myst replied, her eyes burning white. She couldn't even look at me, and I knew I'd rattled her somehow. My heart was still thumping, proof that something was going on between us, but I didn't know where it was going or how to pursue it further. "I'm glad I was able to give you some form of closure with regards to your father, Thayen. I imagine it was important for you to say those things."

"What a power you have," I said, seeing Myst in a different light. I'd already been in awe of her, but this ability raised her to a whole new level. "Bringing souls from the beyond like that..."

She gave me a shy smile. "For a long time, I thought it was a useless thing. My sisters are capable of extraordinary feats. By comparison, I have felt weak. But seeing you and Acheron just now, I realize how wrong I was. You are right to marvel—it is a great power I hold, and you have helped me learn to appreciate it."

I would've liked to do something for her in return. Maybe I didn't have the abilities nor the resources for something as incredible as what she'd accomplished with my father, but there had to be something I could offer. Myst deserved that much as a token of my gratitude—only it wasn't just gratitude I was feeling. There was something else brewing in my chest. Something strong and bright that packed quite a punch.

In the middle of this insanity, I was falling in love, and I wouldn't have had it any other way. No, I rather liked this sensation as it grew inside me. Myst was changing absolutely everything about my existence, almost effortlessly and utterly unwittingly.

SOFIA

hree days had flown past since the Flip, and we were nowhere closer to a way out of this place. As far as progress went, it didn't feel like we'd made much since we'd found ourselves plopped in the middle of a fake Shade. The one good thing that had come out of this insanity was that we'd gotten our loved ones back—my son included. But beyond that, every second that passed was just another second Hrista and her underlings spent on our island, in our home, defiling it with their mere presence.

We knew almost nothing about her ultimate goal, only that everything to this point had been planned. It had gone swimmingly, too—we'd been completely unable to stop it, as we lacked the information and complex knowledge that had kept her ten steps ahead in this sick game.

Settling in the fake island's version of the Great Dome, Derek and I waited for a few of GASP's senior officers to join us for a brief meeting. Each of us had been trying different things—magic, technology, a combination of both—but to no avail. We'd been researching this place and drawing our conclusions, though we were nowhere near done with fully understanding every secret in the fake island. There was still work to be done.

"Thayen is still resting," Derek said as we took our seats at the head of the table. There was a monitor mounted on the glass pane behind us, which was rather ironic as I tried to imagine our clones gathering in this room and discussing their plot to overthrow us. I wondered what kind of use they were making of the real Great Dome now that we were away. "Last night was pretty intense."

"No surprise there. I'm so happy he had that chance, though," I told my husband, and I meant it. Thayen had come to us late in the darkness of night to tell us about his encounter with Acheron's spirit, kindly facilitated by Myst—every time her name was mentioned my heart grew three sizes. What an incredible being she was. Her sister, Regine, too. And then there was Hrista, the complete and horrifying opposite. There was so much that still didn't make sense. "It's been twenty years, and the boy never got to say a proper goodbye. I am so thankful to Myst for giving him that closure."

My husband nodded slowly. "True. I didn't wake him. I figured he could use the extra sleep."

"That was a good idea. It's just us oldies today, anyway," I replied, smiling as I watched Corrine and Ibrahim come through the open door first. "My favorite witch and warlock have arrived."

"You're in a good mood," Corrine chuckled dryly.

I shrugged. "Not really, but I've decided not to take any of this to heart anymore. The impossible has happened, and I need to make my peace with it in order to move toward finding a solution. Which is why we're having this meeting. It's literally the least we can do in the absence of everything else."

"Yet you sound defeated. Your words mention moving forward, but your voice says you're tired," Ibrahim replied as he and his fiercely witchy wife sat next to us at the large, oval glass table.

"I am tired," I said, trying to find my smile again. "But I'm also in survival mode. My only choice is to move forward, not to fall back into despair. We're in this mess, and we need to get out of it. I just don't have the strength to do it with a spring in my step, that's all."

"Focus on the solution, not the problem," Liana said, as she entered with Cameron by her side.

Derek smiled. "Beats despair any day."

"Who else are we expecting?" Cameron asked as they sat next to Corrine and Ibrahim.

I went over the confirmations I'd received through the comms system earlier in the morning. Thankfully, that was still working, along with our Telluris connections, but only within the fake island. Everything else remained beyond our reach. "Claudia and Yuri, Vivienne and Xavier, Lucas and Marion. The Time Master will represent the Reapers who got dragged into this as well. The others are currently still working and investigating various parts of this fake haven. Rose, Ben and their spouses are currently engaged in an in-depth search of the island's north side, in hopes of finding more information, perhaps something that might help us get out or at least send a message beyond this realm. We're hopeful, what can I say…"

We had yet to understand how the whole Flip had worked, but one thing had been clear from the very beginning—it hadn't affected only those with clones made after them. It had affected everyone who had been present in The Shade at the time of the event.

"You're bringing the old gang back together," Liana said, almost smiling.

"The last time that happened, we took a holiday and bumped into Ta'Zan," Corrine shot back. "It must be a sign. We, the first generation Shadians, should consider maintaining a certain distance from one another. Whenever we get together, it's just trouble and trouble and trouble, and then more trouble!"

I wanted to laugh, but the events of the past few days still plagued my mind. The images I'd seen from Isabelle's clone continued to haunt me. Hrista was an enemy like no one we'd ever dealt with before. She came from another realm, and she had one hell of a grudge against us. That connection to the Spirit Bender made her even more frightening, not to mention her Purgatory magic and the numerous tricks she and her clones had used against us thus far.

We were at a disadvantage, and we didn't even have our island to seek refuge on. For the first time, our entire nation had been stranded. That was what truly made this so unprecedented and scary.

Vivienne and Xavier were the last to arrive, and none of those present bore any good news. We had gathered some observations after studying this place: regarding medical equipment and magical paraphernalia, along with a better understanding of how each of those units had been used in the glass house extension; regarding the storage facilities sprinkled along the south-western side of the Vale, hidden between old oaks and redwoods and far from prying eyes; and regarding the Port and the cells beneath, where

Isabelle and the others had been held prior to the arrival of our son's crew.

"How is Isabelle holding up?" I asked after we were done presenting the last of the relevant updates. "Her memories interest me more than anything."

"You're not the only one," Corrine replied, crossing her arms as she leaned back in her chair. "We're still working on her with healing potions, but it's a slow process. Whatever chemicals or magic they pumped her with... it's infinitely more potent than what I found in Voss, Chantal, and Richard's bloodstreams. Isabelle was held here for two months, and I figure she wasn't just left on her own to rot in a cave."

"No, the needle marks on her forearms tell us that much," Ibrahim added, scratching his black beard, which he'd allowed to grow long enough to be braided as it reached down to his chest. Silver threads glistened around the collar of his tourmaline surcoat. It covered him from neck to just below the knees, and it was fastened around the waist with a massive leather belt, its tear-shaped silver buckle briefly catching my eye. "Isabelle was experimented on using different potions and injections. Voss remembers seeing the clones in her cell on a daily basis, poking and prodding her, but she was always too weak to fight them off."

Marion frowned. "Do you think we will ever truly understand what they did to her?"

"Eventually, yes," Corrine replied. "But it will take some time, and I worry that's the one thing we don't have as long as we're stuck here, and Hrista is running loose on our island. I'd say we have to prioritize and stop that madwoman first."

"How do we do that, if we can't even leave this place?" Vivienne scoffed, understandably frustrated by this predicament. "Nothing we've tried so far seems to be working."

"I'm just as stumped," the Time Master cut in. He'd been quiet so far, but that did not come as a surprise. He rarely spoke by nature, choosing to listen and analyze before offering a solution or even the faintest idea of one. "But that makes this no different from when we were on the other side of the problem. The only portals that work here are the shimmering ones. We couldn't open one to take us here, and we obviously cannot open one to take us back, either. On top of that, the Valkyries and Berserkers that were left behind are equally... well, useless, for lack of a better word."

"If I may," Brandon's voice cut through the growing sea of discontented murmurs around the table. He stood in the doorway, clad in black leather and clinking silver, darkness oozing off him like a menacing mist while his eyes burned blue. I'd noticed how close he'd gotten to Astra, and I wasn't exactly surprised. This guy knew how to make an entrance just by being himself. The Berserkers and the Valkyries were incredible entities—I was curious and fascinated, but I didn't dare pursue questions I doubted they'd offer answers for, considering that the Reapers had been just as secretive regarding the afterlife. "While my shiny sisters and I might be useless, I do know of someone who isn't."

Derek raised an eyebrow. "Are you talking about Astra? We're aware that she was Hrista's target because she might be capable of opening shimmering portals, but none of us dare to put any more pressure on the girl. She has been through enough already."

"There's no need for your pressure," Brandon chuckled. "Pinkie does that to herself well enough. She managed to open one a little while ago."

The silence that followed was one of pure awe and frightened astonishment as we exchanged glances across the table. Naturally, none of us had any words left. The one thing we weren't sure we'd see happening any time soon had actually happened. Astra had clearly pushed herself, and I wondered and worried about the toll it might've taken on her. She was only a half-Daughter—I wasn't sure how much magical pummeling she could withstand.

"How is she?" I asked, finally finding my voice again.

"Resting. Exhausted. I think she'll awaken before the night begins," he said, leaning into the doorframe. "She was only able to hold it for a few moments, but she did it. With plenty of practice and support, Astra could very well be the one to get us out of here, just like Hrista feared."

Corrine was intrigued. "Why did you decide to tell us? Surely, Astra would've liked to be the one to break this news to us."

"She's insanely shy about it," he shot back with a grin. There was something dangerous and playful about this guy. He was dark, but the lights in his eyes were bright and powerful. Such a contrast surely had a story to tell. "And you're all so gloomy, sitting here and sulking. Three days have passed, and you're already withered. Imagine my feelings when I was told I'd never see Purgatory again."

Lucas cleared his throat. "How long before Astra can open a portal and hold it for long enough for us to go through?"

"Ah. That... I'm not sure. None of us have dealt with such things before," Brandon replied. "But I'm here to offer a suggestion. And I hope that by the time Astra gets stronger with the shimmering portals, you will have had time to consider it properly. When she opens one, not all of you should go through. We should send a team of scouts through first. Think about it. The Flip used many portals, and while Astra's ability differs from Hrista, I doubt she's able to hold one open long enough to get thousands of people through at once."

That caused murmurs to rise from every occupied seat at the table. I wasn't a fan of this idea, either. "We're all eager to go home," I said. "Why should we spend another minute here?"

"Because you have no idea what you're walking back into," the Berserker replied. As much as it irked me, he had a point. "Hrista has taken over, whether you like it or not, and it's her secretive methods that have gotten her this far. I had no idea what the end game was when she had the clones attack you. Haldor knew more than I did, but even he is still in the dark on other, equally pressing, details of her agenda. Keeping everyone in the dark is how she's kept this going. So if Astra opens a shimmering portal, and by some miracle the whole Shade walks through, there's no telling what will be waiting. Hrista knows that Astra is alive. Do you think she'll just kick back and wait for the girl to waltz through a portal?"

Derek nodded slowly, his lips pressed into a thin line until he spoke. "You think scouting is a safer option?" "You have women and children and innocent lives to protect, so yes," Brandon said. "Like I said, I think Astra's got the potential to do a Flip-like transfer in just one portal, but I doubt she's got the energy in her. She'd probably need help. So, getting everyone back in one go is already a big and crazy challenge. Let's do baby steps and start with a scouting initiative. One small team, led by Astra. If she can take them through to the real Shade, she can then figure out a way to take you all back, once we know what's on the other side. You don't know what Hrista has been doing over these past few days. Frankly, I shudder to even think about it; that conniving bitch is capable of absolutely anything and everything. Scouting things out first is your best option."

"Hrista is not an ordinary enemy," I told Derek, returning to my earlier thoughts.

"And once we know what she's been doing on the island, we'll have more intel for Order, too," Brandon added. "Assuming Astra figures out a way to open a portal leading straight into Purgatory, that is. She and I have already discussed that possibility."

Looking around the table, we seemed to be in agreement. The Time Master stood, his galaxy eyes finding Brandon's. "I will be a part of that team," the Reaper insisted. "You will need a diverse crew with enough magic and skills to survive an attack from entities and creatures of any of the known realms."

"That's fine. I welcome variety in this endeavor, too," Brandon said, a half-smile blooming across his lips. "Hrista is an evil thing, and she's intelligent and prepared. Our objective cannot possibly be about defeating her. I doubt that can easily be done, otherwise I would've kicked her ass long before now."

"What is our objective, then?" I asked, though part of me already knew the answer.

Brandon shifted slowly, giving me his full attention. Just looking at him sent shivers down my spine. "First, reaching The Shade. It's in the realm of the living, and so it will be easier for Astra to open a shimmering portal there. We don't yet know how good she is at controlling her destination, but we have hope. Once we're there, we'll gather information. Ultimately, our priority is getting word to Order in Purgatory that Hrista has gone AWOL. It's our final option. Thing is, it's exceptionally risky for Astra to try and open a shimmering portal directly to Purgatory first, since that's not in the realm of the living but far beyond. I don't know how safe that might be. You have to understand... this stuff hasn't really been tried and retried before."

We all knew it would be anything but simple. Together and separately, we'd been through plenty already to understand that the task ahead would not be easy. *And everyone might not survive...* But something had to be done, and our beloved Astra was the key to our success. Hrista may have already confirmed it, but I felt it deep within my soul.

Derek and I had always said that the future generations would save us eventually. *The children. The children are the future.*

UNENDING

*D*ream, my ethereal sister, had been summoned to carry Tristan and me away from Biriane after the... incident. My bare feet touched the sea of reddish pebbles in Taeral's palace gardens. Each of the pathways was covered with these smooth pellets of lacquered scarlet, and they swirled around the heated pools in the middle like ruby snakes. To my left and right, green and red leaf trees reached for the crystalline skies, skirted by rounded bushes and manicured floral topiaries. This place was an oasis of calm and precision, I realized, and I was infinitely more receptive to the physical world since I'd been put inside a living body.

I was still adjusting to every sensation. Even the people around me seemed different. I was forced to pay attention to the slightest details in their body language, yet I failed to find an explanation as to why I had this compulsion to study everything in obsessive depth. I could only enjoy the ride and adapt. In Tristan's realm, it took three days for the human brain to adapt to fundamental changes in its perception. I did not have a human body, but I comforted myself with the idea that I, too, might need three days to adjust. We'd lost Anunit only yesterday. It was still early.

"This is beautiful," Tristan exclaimed. "I haven't seen the palace gardens in at least a year, if not longer."

"It has been a while since you visited," Taeral agreed, smiling. He seemed taller, though it was only my perception that had changed. It could have been the design of his red velvet jacket with gold-trimmed coattails, tightly closed around his waist and creating an elegant contrast with his black pants and leather boots with gold- brushed strap buckles. He wore a white shirt underneath and the band of gold and rubies on the top of his head. Truly a handsome mix. I could see why Eira had been so enthralled by the fae-jinni king.

Walking beside him, the Water Hermessi child was a vision in dark blue satin, her gown resembling an upside- down tulip with thin gold straps and elegant bodice embroideries that told stories through their motifs. "Now, don't be a tease," she told her husband. "You know Tristan and Unending would've come sooner, but their travels often take them so far away." Looking at me, Eira narrowed her eyes, lips briefly pursed. "You seem... different."

"You can tell," I murmured, fires burning in my cheeks. Yet another sensation for me to grow accustomed to. "My sister was dumb enough to put on a meat suit," Dream said from behind us. From her flat tone, I could almost see Dream rolling her eyes even before I looked back over my shoulder at her. "After the hell she endured on Visio, you'd think she would've had enough of physical restraints."

I turned around to face her fully. "For the umpteenth time, this is different. It was sanctioned by Death, and I'm in complete control of the situation. I can always choose to leave this body and return to my true self."

"Prove it!" Dream shot back, crossing her arms. She smelled of lilies, reminding me of Death and my previous form. It was a fragrance we all carried with us as Reapers. It haunted me, still, like a distant memory.

"You know she can't do that. She will lose this body," Tristan interjected. "It's not an actual suit that she can just take off and then put back on. It's not how Anunit's magic works."

"Or any death magic, for that matter," I grumbled, then gave Taeral and Eira a look. They were clearly stunned, lips parted as if their words had left them altogether. I found it amusing how two beautiful and elegant creatures could look so lost. Once more, I was noticing things I'd considered unworthy of my attention before. Tristan had said it would take some time to ease into it, though he wasn't sure on the particulars since he'd never had to inhabit a foreign body this way. "I'm truly sorry... A few things have changed since we last saw each other, Your Graces."

Taeral raised a hand. "Please, call us by our names. We're still getting used to the titles."

"You're in a living body," Eira exclaimed, virtually squealing with joy. "That's what was different. I couldn't put my finger on it. How did that happen?"

"It's a long and complicated story," Dream cut in, still irked by this entire circumstance. I'd missed the ethereal look about her. I'd had something similar in my Reaper form, though I had never boasted her long, almost white hair, nor her high cheekbones and full lips. I could certainly see her appeal—she was what her name implied, in a sense: a dream. A wondrous vision. Did I miss my Reaper form? Not yet. I would miss my ability to telepathically communicate with my siblings and with Death, but I would have to make do. "But it ends with me being called away from my beloved brother and a world full of scrumptious dreams to occasionally nip from in order to carry Unending and Tristan to a portal point of their choosing, since my sister here is no longer capable of treading the dimensions like a proper Reaper."

The king and queen of the Fire Star exchanged amused glances, but it didn't diminish their curiosity in the slightest. Tristan and I had expected this from the moment we'd decided to come here, but this fae world was the more discreet choice among our GASP-connected options. Sherus and Nuriya were enjoying their retirement in a glass villa overlooking a volcanic lake about five hundred miles south of the capital. The GASP base was a hundred miles east. This had been the better place, considering we knew few people in the palace who'd have questions about my obvious condition.

I had promised Death my discretion regarding the whole Biriane issue. I still wondered where the World Crusher had gone and if my maker would find her, but it was no longer my problem. I'd been given a life, and I had no intention of squandering this incredible opportunity.

"Well, we obviously have a lot to talk about," Taeral finally spoke, resuming our walk through the palace gardens. I welcomed the respite. Tristan and I had tumbled through such chaotic times that taking a moment here felt like a muscle relaxant. "Will you be joining us for dinner before you head back to The Shade?"

"Dream mentioned that something happened there recently," I said.

"I was hoping you might bring us up to speed before we return. We were going to have dinner with Tristan's parents tonight, but if you don't mind, I would love to taste that spice water recipe you got from the Calliope succubi."

"I don't have many details about The Shade, I'm afraid," Dream sighed. "And I was told not to get involved with anything GASP-related while on my retreat with Nightmare."

Again, the king and queen exchanged glances. This time, it was Eira who replied. "Spiced water this afternoon sounds just fine," she said. "And yes, there were some events that rattled The Shade in the past week or so. It's a complicated topic, so we should perhaps get comfortable somewhere..."

I couldn't shake the uneasy feeling that had just gripped me by the throat. Every emotion I had experienced in my pure spiritual form had been intense, almost atomic, but what I was dealing with now was something else entirely. More concentrated, perhaps even more acute, like a sharp knife digging through my flesh. It was impossible to ignore.

"Are you okay?" Tristan asked in a low voice, giving me a worried look.

"I'm fine, my love. Still adjusting," I replied with a faint smile, then shifted my focus back to Taeral and Eira. "Shall we go?"

Dream raised her hands in a defensive gesture. "I'm afraid I can't join you. Death requested that I immediately return to my mission with Nightmare as soon as the two of you are safe," she said, nodding at Tristan and me. I couldn't help but chuckle.

"You're itching to feed on more dreams, huh?"

"Well, that, too... but remember it's not something to be concerned about. We're not hurting anyone," my sister said, offering an innocent smile. "As you know, we've always had excellent control over ourselves, with the exception of when Spirit had us trapped."

"I'm not concerned, sister. I trust you. But thank you for bringing us here," I said, knowing this could be the last time I saw my sister for a while. She and Nightmare had always been separated from the Reaper world, always keeping to themselves and reaching out as little as possible. It just wasn't in their nature to be... sociable. "I hope we'll meet again, soon."

"Maybe when your first child is born, you'll grant me the honor of naming him. Or her," Dream replied. Her words carried genuine fondness, yet they sent shivers down my spine. I had yet to conceive, and I had no idea how that would be or how it would feel. It was nice to see my sister was optimistic about the end result, though.

Before I could say something in return, Dream vanished, hiding herself from the eyes of mortals. I looked to Tristan for comfort, but I found his brow furrowed as he watched me quietly. He was worried, having said as much prior to setting foot in this place. Everything about me worried him now, because I was made of flesh and therefore vulnerable. I found it endearing, if not even a little amusing, but I did not let him see that. Tristan had every right to be concerned about me, his wife. However, I had faith it would turn out well in the end.

Taeral and Eira escorted us to one of the gazebos on the west side of the palace gardens. Here, massive magnolias with gold and white blossoms dominated the entire section, enriched by copper leaf bushes and blood red roses. The occasional gold and white marble statue of fire nymph-like creatures jutted from the manicured grass, their slender limbs arched into dance poses and their lips stretched into smiles. One of the palace staff came over with a big glass pitcher filled with spiced rose water, matching crystal cups, and a platter of assorted pastries from the royal kitchen. Unlike Tristan, I wasn't dependent on blood for nourishment, and I had already fed on a fruit basket upon our arrival. Its memory lingered. Every piece of sweet flesh had made me moan with delight, the flavors mixing on my tongue like nothing I had ever experienced before. I had tasted bliss in the pulp of a red plum.

The Fire Fae king and his queen told us everything that had happened in The Shade with the clones and the disappearances of some of The Shade's young GASP members. My stomach churned as I listened carefully to their account of the events that had unfolded. Thayen, Astra, Jericho, Dafne, and Soph were still missing, as were Viola, Chantal, Voss, and Isabelle. I could only imagine how their parents had to be feeling about the situation.

"But the Daughters and the witches and a few of your siblings have it under control," Taeral added. "The Time Master, the Soul Crusher, Kelara, Sidyan, Nethissis, and Seeley and their ghouls are over there, assisting with whatever they can."

"I suppose Dream didn't tell you that," Eira said.

I shook my head. "She probably didn't know. The twins are famously reclusive, even from their First Tenner siblings. It doesn't matter. We're in the loop now, and we have a clear understanding of what might have happened there."

"Do we, though?" Tristan replied, raising both eyebrows at me.

I nodded. "Clones attacked The Shade, some people went missing, but there haven't been any more doppelganger incursions since. No more shimmering portals, either. In theory, it's safe for us to go there. Realistically, I'm not sure."

"You're worried?" my husband asked.

"I think I am, yes..." Noticing the wondering looks on Taeral and Eira's face, I felt the need to add an explanation. "I'm a living creature now. Tristan is now stronger than I am. Fae genes were used to create my body, but I don't have any supernatural abilities. I suppose I am as close to human as I will ever be, in that sense. Mind you, I can still cast a death magic spell with my scythe, but that doesn't count as supernatural. Natural and supernatural alike refer to life, whereas my ability is anchored in death. Anyway, these are just technical details. In light of this substantial change, let's say, we both agreed to not do anything that might put my body in danger unless there isn't a better option. I was hoping The Shade might be our spot."

"It still can be," Taeral said. "It has been secured, I assure you. We speak to them every few hours, we get messages and updates all the time. I know you must feel a little disappointed, but I can assure you that the island is safe again. They didn't have the support they have now when the clones first attacked."

"You're right," I conceded. "I should give The Shade more credit."

"It's only for you two to just kick back and relax for a while, though, right?" Eira wondered. "I know you enjoy your travels a lot, with or without the Reaper accoutrements, let's say."

I exhaled deeply. "At this point, we're merely looking for a place to live in peace, so that my husband might take his vampire cure..."

"Oh... you want to have a baby!" Eira gasped.

"That's what this was all about, yes," Tristan chuckled softly, his eyes glowing with love whenever they found me. The spiced rose water tasted like a sweet garden of wonders, only faintly spicy—just enough to make the tip of my tongue tingle with delight. But it was the overall effect on my body that made me suck in a breath. It felt like a rush of bubbling water coursing through my limbs and making my nerve endings melt into something superb, only amplified by my emotions as I explained my family-related urges to Taeral and Eira.

"You can't tell us anything about how you came upon a body?" Taeral concluded after a while, putting on a faint half-smile.

"I'm afraid not. I promised Death. Not even Dream is privy to that information," I said. "But it's okay. It's going to be okay... just like I'm sure The Shade will prevail, as well." I spoke with genuine confidence, hoping for the best. The universe had brought me so far and into this incredible stage of my existence—it had to mean something. It had to lead somewhere good. Otherwise, what was the point?

My heart was full of love and positive thoughts. I had pushed every other tendril of darkness away, rejecting anything that might impede the rest of my journey to creating a life with my body and soul.

"So, The Shade is safe. Like, one hundred percent." Tristan reiterated, still on edge about returning home upon hearing the news of the clone attacks. I may have influenced him earlier, unwittingly at least.

"Yes. For the time being, anyway," Taeral said. "We spoke to Derek and Sofia this morning, and they said nothing was out of the ordinary. No new shimmering portals, the Daughters' detection system is in place. The kids are still missing, but we're assuming they're alive and in another realm. It's the only scenario that makes sense."

"They send updates every six hours," Eira added. "The next one is bound to come through soon, but it's likely to contain the same parameters of... normalcy, I guess. In case of an emergency, they know to reach out."

Tristan nodded slowly, though he didn't seem comforted by any of this. "We should go see your parents, at least," I said, "and give them the news. And we can perhaps go stay with Kalon and Esme for a while, on Visio."

"Of all the places, that's where you see yourself starting our family?" he scoffed, making me laugh lightly. It was a beautiful sensation, one I knew I might never get enough of in this current state.

"Kalon and Esme are in The Shade, too," Taeral said. "But you are welcome to return here after you visit them and your parents. The palace is huge. Plenty of room to make our esteemed guests comfortable."

"You are too kind," I replied.

Tristan let out a heavy sigh, leaning back in his chair. "This isn't something we can tell my parents over the comms line. Or even Telluris, for that matter." He was talking about my body, and it filled me with even more love to listen to him speak in such terms. "Esme would never forgive me. She'd hang my ass out to dry."

"Then let's go over there. We'll have dinner with them," I replied.

"But we'll get out at the first sign of trouble," Tristan said. "I'll talk to Derek, make sure someone can keep the portal open for us."

"Well, if you wish. But my siblings are there. Reapers. They can zap us away in an instant," I reminded him. "I really think it will be okay. I'm only mortal, not useless. I can hold my own."

I could still cast some death magic, but my knowledge was limited. My Reaper soul allowed me the ability to wield a scythe. Unfortunately, there was very little I remembered—most of it stuff that Tristan had learned from me in the past twenty years. Stuff I remembered teaching him. My history was a blur, but I didn't mind. I had a life ahead of me to live and so many new things for my soul to absorb.

"It seems like the sensible thing to do," Eira politely agreed, stretching an arm around Taeral's shoulders. "We'll be here whenever you decide to return, ready to welcome you with arms wide open."

It felt nice to be surrounded by such wonderful people wherever we went within the GASP federation. I had never truly paid attention to this aspect before, yet it warmed me up on the inside now. It offered a soft sense of security, like I would never be alone in the world. Having Tristan in my life only made things better, but this overarching sense of a supernatural family made me look forward to every single day of my new existence.

It would be okay. I could feel it in my bones.

UNENDING

$\mathcal{I}$ knew it would take a while for me to truly get the hang of being a living person. I'd never been one before. My soul was a copy of an original that had lived once, long ago, but I was my own consciousness with my own experiences. Taeral and Eira were kind enough to escort us to the portal in a chamber next to their throne room. A lot had changed in this place since they'd ascended to the throne.

Architecturally speaking, the palace was different. With the help of witches and earth fae, Taeral had shuffled the rooms around, widened the corridors, and heightened the foundation of the palace by about a dozen feet—just enough to add more steps at each entry point with wrought iron railings and gilded décor details. The portal chamber had its walls covered in plaques of red garnet, superbly polished to a crimson sheen that reflected the light from the sconce candles. A bronze chandelier had been hung overhead, its swirling arms with leaves and opening blossoms loaded with small oil bowls, their wicks burning amber.

There was a quiet reverence about this place. Like moving between realms was a wonder unto itself. And in many ways, it was. For every mortal who didn't have the witches' magic or the Reapers' powers, treading different worlds was a wondrous miracle. Standing before the activated portal, I felt my heart beating faster. I was glad Dream wasn't here to notice my new body's reactions. She would've poked fun at my mortal weaknesses—I probably would've done the same, had our roles been reversed, as I could still remember the old days when all the First Tenners had looked down upon the living. Passengers through life, we'd called them. Temporary creatures, while the rest of us were practically eternal.

Not anymore. I belonged to the living now.

"Remember, whenever you two are ready, we'll welcome you back to the palace," Taeral said. He clearly meant it, and I was inclined to accept the offer, mainly because I knew they had a summer festival coming soon, an event when the whole of the Fire Star would gather to celebrate the new season. Tristan and I had never managed to stick around during the previous festivities, given our intense travels, but I wanted to just stop, for once, and smell the summer roses.

"You'll have a sprawling apartment close to our private quarters, with direct access to the palace gardens via the outer stairs connecting to the balconies," Eira added, smiling. "It's just one of the many improvements we've made to the building since Tae's coronation."

"There will be a gathering of fire fae clans for the summer festival, right?" Tristan asked, and the king and queen nodded. "Then chances are we'll accept your invitation. I've been meaning to get better acquainted with the fire fae culture. I see no better opportunity than that."

We bid the royal couple farewell and stepped through the portal, knowing that Derek and Sofia were already waiting on the other side. Leaving the Fire Star behind, we walked through the translucent tunnel, crossing fields of stars and cyclamen stardust, spiraling galaxies, and dying red dwarves, bright suns with planetary clusters and throngs of rocky asteroids until we crossed the threshold between the Supernatural Dimension and the Earthly Dimension.

I had never traveled like this before. I'd never needed to. I had to admit, it was extraordinary. In some ways similar to my means of movement across the realms, yet different. Tristan took my hand in his, firmly squeezing as he looked at me, and in that moment the whole universe realigned itself around us. We walked together in loving unison, eager to venture into this new stage of our relationship.

Ahead, the Milky Way stretched out before us, a gargantuan flower filled with white hot stars and billions of planets. Its savagery was beautiful.

Its size undeniable. And I felt so tiny and alive in comparison. "Is this what it feels like?" I asked my husband as we continued our short journey through the translucent tunnel.

"What do you mean?"

"Living. Is this it? This constant deluge of sensations and feelings and emotions... of touches and smells and sounds?"

Tristan laughed lightly. "Yes. It's a perpetual discovery of the world around us, of how things make us feel, of how we perceive ourselves against the backdrop of this vast universe."

"I feel tiny," I said. "A mere speck of dust. It's strange. I've never quantified my existence before. My siblings and I, we... we've always been self-aware, but that was it. Does it not scare you? The thought of all this ending? I'm already terrified." The realization came out loud, along with the painful grip on my heart. The thought of losing this... it horrified me.

"What matters is what we do with the time we are given," Tristan said. "How we make the most of every moment, and I, for one, plan to enjoy every second of it with you. Or thinking about you, or simply loving you, even from afar if we're ever apart."

No wonder I loved this man with everything I had. Regardless of what fate might hurl at him, my husband would rise above, one way or another. He would live voraciously, and he would sip on every drop of bliss that his existence had to offer. The best part? I'd be right there with him, sharing the marvelous ride.

"What do you think your parents will say when they see me?" I asked, my mind wandering back to The Shade as Earth's solar system emerged just ahead, giant marbles orbiting the sun, suspended in pure darkness.

"Well, this is new to everyone, not just you and me. It'll be new to my parents, my sister and Kalon, too."

"Yes. That's true."

He smiled. "But I reckon Mom and Dad will be over the moon. They'll have questions, of course. And they'll be a little annoyed when they don't get the answers they want, but they'll be happy, Unending. Happy that we're happy."

"I hope so. I mean, I know your parents well enough to agree, but *ugh*, is this feeling always going to rear its ugly head?" I groaned, rolling my eyes as I tried to swallow back my anxiety.

"You're nervous. It's perfectly normal!" Tristan chuckled. We stopped just before The Shade's portal, and he put his arms around my waist, pulling me into a tight embrace. We kissed, slowly, taking our time to taste each other, giving our souls a moment to sing together. He dropped a soft peck on the tip of my nose afterward. "This is what life is about. Dealing with these emotions, experiencing everything to the fullest, not knowing what tomorrow will hold and not knowing how we'll handle it. That is the true joy of living. This dive into the unknown, headfirst." He nodded to the portal. "Now, come on, let's go. They're waiting for us."

I allowed him to take my hand and escort me to the mass of shimmering blues and greens framed by rune stones. Beyond, The Shade awaited. "They'll probably welcome the change of pace, considering what they've been dealing with while we've been away."

"Yeah, clones. That was a new one, even for me," Tristan stifled another laugh. "What can I say? We're never bored in this life."

I was coming back to a familiar place, yet it seemed different. My perception of it had changed. The Shade was bigger, a hidden paradise on Earth with giant redwoods and whispering forests and the persistent fragrance of fresh grass hanging in the air. Derek and Sofia Novak were the first to welcome us back, their arms wide open, their smiles as brilliant as the sun they'd hidden with magic above the island.

"Esme will be so happy to see you both!" Sofia exclaimed as she hugged Tristan, then me. Suddenly stiff, she took a step back to measure me from head to toe. "Hold on, something's different... Your skin isn't as pale nor as pearlescent as a Reaper's anymore. Or am I imagining this?"

"You're right," Derek said, equally intrigued, while Tristan and I exchanged amused glances. "Whoa. And your eyes. The galaxies within them are gone. What happened? Something's different, Unending. What is it?"

I'd have thought they might notice the eyes first, but we'd known each other for so long that there were things so casual, so familiar, that they never stood out, even when they vanished.

"I got myself a living body," I replied, smiling. "Unfortunately, I can't share the details of how it happened." Sofia squealed with joy, her eyes beaming. "I'm so happy for you!" She paused, giving me an alarmed look.

"Wait. I'm supposed to be happy for you, right?"

"Absolutely," Tristan interjected. "I'll be taking the cure, and then my wife and I will be trying for a baby or two."

"Or ten," I murmured, trying not to laugh.

We needed a few minutes to decompress as the portal closed behind us, and Derek sealed it with a carved stone disk he carried around his neck. "Sorry, it's protocol for the time being," he said. "Ever since the clone incident, we've had to lock things down here, only allowing certain people to come through or leave."

They guided us to the Great Dome nearby, where a table had been set with pitchers of water and fresh blood, along with glasses and a fruit platter. I went straight for the mango slices—the one taste I simply could not get enough of.

Derek looked relatively well rested despite the madness they'd endured, clad in a white linen shirt and navy-blue jeans—casual attire, I thought, considering the circumstances. Sofia was equally relaxed, the white cotton dress flowing down her elegant figure as it brought out the natural copper highlights in her long auburn hair. It seemed like they'd just come out on the terrace to enjoy a glass of spiced rose water and the sight of a full moon.

"Thank you for letting us through," Tristan said as we sat at the glass table. He poured himself a glass of blood. "I can assure you we're the real deal, but Unending's siblings can verify us if need be."

"I no longer can," I sighed, suddenly missing my Reaper nature.

Sofia shook her head. "It's okay. We actually haven't had any incidents whatsoever since..." The humor faded from her voice. Reality had come back to remind her of what she'd lost, though she'd tried so hard to be warm and welcoming. "Since Thayen and his friends disappeared. The Shade is safe, in that sense. Everyone is verified and accounted for. You're the only ones unmarked."

"The Reapers are out, anyway," Derek said. "They said they'd return in a couple of days. Esme has a way of calling Time, if needed, but other than that, we're pretty much Reaper-less for now."

"That's just as well," I replied. "Personally, I don't think I'm ready to face the rest of my siblings yet." It felt true as I heard myself say it. It sounded odd, certainly, but accurate. "I guess because I'm alive now, I don't feel like I belong with them anymore. Not for now, anyway." Besides, Time and the others would've asked more questions. They would've brought it up with

Death too, and considering the burden I'd placed on her by losing both the World Crusher and Anunit... I really didn't want her to deal with that too.

How ironic. I'd been the angry one in this relationship for quite a while. It had only taken a moment of weakness to turn the tide on myself. Death was out there, fixing my mess, and I was out here, living a life.

Tristan tucked a lock of hair behind my ear. "We're taking it one step at a time, remember?"

"Perhaps deal with your mom and dad first before you take it up with her side of the family, then?" Derek suggested, holding back a smile. There was tension. I could feel it, the uneasiness of this entire situation.

The Shade had been turned upside down by the clone attacks, yet Derek and Sofia were trying so hard to keep going, to live as though their existence hadn't been permanently altered. Their son was missing, along with other GASP members. And Phoenix's wife, Viola. Poor Isabelle had been taken months earlier, and no one had realized it. These doppelganger creatures had wreaked true havoc, and I could only imagine what the Shadians were going through. I certainly didn't wish to experience such things for myself.

"How is everyone?" I asked after they gave us the latest updates—none of which pointed to any more shimmering portals opening since Thayen's disappearance.

Sofia shook her head slowly. "Well, Phoenix has buried himself in work. He's got it worse than everyone else, I think, with both Astra and Viola missing. It's awful, but with his sentry nature, he'd be able to sense if Astra had died. It gives the rest of us hope, as well—it allows us to believe the others are alive too, albeit lost or stuck in some other realm."

"You had some footage from beyond, didn't you?" Tristan replied. "Taeral mentioned the silvery cubes you found in Isabelle's room."

Derek offered a faint nod. "Yeah. Nothing conclusive yet. We don't recognize who or what their leader is. We only identified a female with special powers. It's still blurry in terms of exactly what kind of threat we're dealing with."

"And how are you holding up?" I asked him.

He took a moment to answer, running a hand through his short dark hair. The five o'clock shadow suited his square jaw, but I knew it wasn't an aesthetic choice, but rather the remnant of previously sleepless nights and forgetting himself in the midst of so many worries. Peace had found its way back into The Shade, but it had not been an easy ride. "As well as can be expected, I guess. Sofia and I trust Thayen. He'll find his way back to us, or we'll pull something off and get to him eventually. I take comfort in knowing this will not last forever."

"And, in the meantime, we do what we can on our side of the world," Sofia said, letting out a heavy sigh. "But it's good to have you both here. Seeing you is like a breath of fresh air."

"It might have something to do with my wife's current condition," Tristan replied, a grin stretching across his face. "Seriously though, is there anything we could do to help you?"

Derek and Sofia looked at each other, then shook their heads. "We have Corrine and the witches, Lumi and the swamp witches, the Daughters... and Phoenix and Jovi are hard at work on the technical aspect. We're well covered, Tristan, but thank you," Sofia said. "Just relax, go see your parents. Esme and Kalon are with them, on standby in case GASP might need them. I doubt that'll be the case. We've been in an exhausting limbo since Thayen and his friends vanished."

Moments passed in heavy silence, but both Tristan and I knew that there wasn't much we could do for this realm. I was curious to know more. However, I also had to be aware of my new limitations. We'd already had the talk regarding The Shade. We'd both agreed that if push came to shove and we didn't have any better options to save lives, I'd give up my living body. Until we reached that point, however, I didn't even want to think about it. We'd worked so hard to get here.

"You know where to find us," Tristan ultimately said. "Besides, we've got our comms on too. Unending was given her own on the Fire Star." There was a certain sense of pride in his smile. My body did that to him. My life. These were strange times to be alive, but also wonderful.

We take the good with the bad, my incredible husband had told me mere hours ago. *We take the good with the bad, and we make the best of it all.*

A couple of hours later, we were seated at Ariana and Julian's dinner table. Kalon and Esme had joined us, and the atmosphere was one of joy and celebration. I basked in it, and I certainly enjoyed the food they'd brought to the table. Tristan missed his human days, but he didn't mind me stuffing my face with all the goodness that Ariana had cooked.

As expected, they'd all had questions about my living body, but they would have to be content with the same minimal explanation I'd offered to Taeral and the others. "It doesn't really matter," Ariana had concluded. "What matters is you're among the living now, and that's got to be all kinds of exciting!"

Her cooking was exquisite. The dinner table wasn't loaded, since I was the only creature enjoying the taste of food, but she'd managed to cook plenty from the moment Tristan and I had set foot through the door. None of them had expected me to arrive as a living creature. Blood had been the only dish on the original menu, yet the roasted meal was cooked to perfection, bathed in a savory sauce and sprinkled with herbs. The mini quiches were premade and dwellers of the freezer for quite a while before hitting the oven—nevertheless, they were delicious. For dessert, Ariana had sent Julian outside to the small orchard behind their redwood treehouse to fetch some fresh plums and peaches. They smelled amazing, and I kept brushing my fingers over the peach skin, relishing the feel of its soft fuzz.

Everything about this evening was incredible. Esme was all smiles as she couldn't take her eyes off me. We spoke for hours, going over the events that had led to this moment, both positive and negative. "I'd like to see some of that footage, if possible," I ultimately said. "I'm genuinely curious about what Isabelle's clone recorded from that beyond world." We hadn't been able to think of a better name for it, but Tristan had agreed it sounded accurate enough.

"Time had no idea who the leader was, or what she was," Esme sighed, pouring herself another glass of spiced blood. "Phoenix is analyzing the footage, but I'm sure you could pop by tomorrow and have a look for yourself."

"What about the beyond world?" Tristan asked. "Were there any elements in the videos that might provide clues about the location?"

Ariana raised both eyebrows in an expression I could only interpret as befuddlement. "Honestly? No. We only saw trees and a white villa-style building behind the alleged leader. Redwoods, most likely. At first, we thought that particular piece of footage had been shot in The Shade, but I'm sure we would've heard a horde of clones loudly rooting for our demise."

"Plus, there's no such white villa anywhere in The Shade," Julian added.

"We considered California too, but the sky looked weird," Esme said. "We sent a couple of witches to comb through the entire state with their ample magic anyway, just in case. Hopefully they'll have something to tell us. Otherwise, we're stumped."

Tristan's brow furrowed. "The technology the clones have is odd. Like nothing I've seen before." Derek and Sofia had shown us one of the silvery boxes, though Phoenix hadn't been around to connect it and make it project its recorded data. "I look forward to checking that stuff out again, ideally with Phoenix around, and anyone else who might help us figure out what those boxes are made of."

Julian gave us a cool smile. "You two are supposed to relax and make the most of this new and incredible stage in your lives. The entire island is working on the clone issue. It's not demanding the attention of the entire federation, so don't concern yourselves. I'm serious. Take it easy. It's not your responsibility, and Unending is going through something strange and wonderful."

"Yeah, but—"

"They're right," Tristan said, cutting me off with an awkward smile. "The Shade's got its brightest minds handling the situation. And you— you're all I can think about right now."

Esme laughed lightly. "It's been an annoying stalemate here for days. We cannot exist in a perpetual state of anguish in light of what happened either, so I'm glad you two are here."

"How long will you be with us?" Ariana asked. For the briefest of moments, I saw her stealing a glance at Julian, but he didn't seem to notice. His attention was fixed on Tristan and me, and quite lovingly, too. "Do you wish to take one of our guest rooms, or will you be making use of your own treehouse?"

"Mom, I think they'll need some privacy," Esme replied, then pressed her lips into a thin line. A thought crossed her mind as she glanced at her brother. "You'll be taking the cure, then?"

Tristan nodded once. "As soon as things settle down here," he said. "Unending and I agreed not to rush with our baby-making plans until the situation with the clones reaches a satisfactory resolution."

"Satisfactory resolution?" Kalon chuckled, finishing his glass of blood.

"My words, not his," I shot back with a grin. "You see, I can shed this body and become a Reaper again. I would not be able to return to it afterward, however, so I would only make that choice if absolutely necessary. Therefore, Tristan and I agreed not to rush into having a baby until the clone situation is resolved and everyone is brought back safely, just in case. The issue might prove more complex than anyone expects, so better safe than sorry."

Esme shrugged. "Yeah, I can see where you're coming from. I'd probably do the same. The last thing you'd want is to run across a battlefield, belly the size of an overgrown melon, fighting those wretched clones." It made me laugh. I threw my head back as my whole body shuddered and my abdomen muscles ached sweetly, but I couldn't stop. I could only envision myself with a baby bump, charging after a bunch of clones that looked like the people I knew—granted, such a sight should've been tragic, but in the moment I found it hilarious.

My amusement was contagious, and soon it took over the whole table. There were tears in my eyes, and I wouldn't have traded this moment for anything in the whole wide world. Tristan's arm slipped around my shoulders as the laughter finally died down. "Point is, yeah, you're right, sis. Unending and I will definitely be enjoying ourselves while we're here, but if you need us for anything—and I mean anything—please don't hesitate to ask. Okay?"

"We want to help," I said with conviction.

Esme smiled warmly. "Don't worry. We'll reach out."

"In the meantime, however, excuse me while I dig into this peach," I said, my mouth already watering. I'd been waiting and working my way through two courses already to get to the pulp of this matter. My eyes must've been glistening with the childlike delight I'd been feeling, because it made them laugh again.

And I loved the sound of it.

UNENDING

*T*oward midnight, Tristan and I left his parents' treehouse and slowly walked over to ours, about two hundred yards north and snugly hidden between other enormous redwoods that had yet to be fitted with homes for more Shadians. Ours was the only residence in a hundred-yard radius, and I loved the thought of such extensive privacy.

Above, the night sky gleamed down at us through the occasional gap in the dark green canopy. Birds sang from their perches, their trills dancing on the air and echoing around us as if the forest itself was celebrating us in its own way. My hand fit perfectly in Tristan's as we made our way down the path. It was barely a battered trace snaking through the woods, with tall grass and wildflowers rising on both sides.

"You know, if you think about it, nothing seems different about The Shade," Tristan said. "I mean, look around…"

Indeed, we passed by people coming and going, either from or to the Vale or the Black Heights or Sun Beach, judging by the tans on some of the humans. They were friends and lovers, brothers and sisters, families with children and grandchildren. They belonged to different species, yet they got along perfectly. They went about their evening as though a bunch of clones had never trespassed through The Shade, stealing some of the residents and using never-before-seen weapons of war against the others.

"Like Esme said, there's no point in losing yourself in fear and despair, right?" he added.

Looking at the couple that walked up a neighboring path, I caught a stolen glance. It was a little wary, reminiscent of the look I'd seen Ariana give Julian during dinner. It didn't mean much, not considering how many behavioral details were jumping at me now that I was a living creature. I found it overwhelming and difficult to observe and record everything, and yet I couldn't help it. This was my new nature. "They seem okay," I replied, my voice low as we kept walking.

A deer broke a twig somewhere nearby. I caught its grassy scent and imagined its big brown eyes scanning us through the nocturnal semi-darkness. What a wonderful experience it was to be alive.

"I imagine they will all switch right back into battle mode if they have to, but for now, they're staying calm and trying to go on with their lives," Tristan said, and I nodded my agreement.

"There's no point in giving yourself an ulcer. You used to say that."

"I still do," he chuckled. Our treehouse could be seen again, partially hidden by the other redwoods. "There it is.

Home sweet home."

"It's beautiful," I murmured, seeing it through mortal eyes for the first time.

"No, *you're* beautiful," he whispered against my lips before dropping a swift kiss. My cheeks flared hot for a moment.

"Thank you, my love. But I mean it. This place, it's... it's wonderful," I insisted, taking a moment to absorb my surroundings.

The house had a different, greater value to me now. The siding was built from elegant pieces of dark oak wood brought over from Calliope and renowned for their architectural integrity and resistance. The roof had been covered with slate gray shingles made of *habiri* gum wood from Neraka—a peculiar specimen praised for its elasticity and texture, the latter protecting the interior of the house from virtually any form of nature's wrath. It also made outer sealing an obsolete process. Our treehouse was comfortably warm in the winter without need for much firewood, and exquisitely cool in the summer.

Its windows were wide, the frames painted white against the charcoal wall boards, and Ariana had hung white and yellow daisy curtains in the kitchen. I liked them even more now. I could already imagine myself in the morning, standing up there with a coffee mug in my hand and wondering how my life would continue to unfold. Yes, mortality had a certain magic to it.

Wooden steps had been fitted to spiral the massive redwood trunk, connecting the bottom to the elevated treehouse. Stopping right before we went up, Tristan cupped my face in his hands and kissed me deeply. Time itself seemed to stop as I reveled in the taste of him. The softness of his lips, the slickness of his tongue, these were still new and exhilarating sensations. I'd thought I knew love as a Reaper. I'd thought it was the most intense way to love somebody. But I'd been wrong. Oh, so wrong...

My body responded in ways I had trouble keeping up with, but Tristan knew just what to do, his hands slipping slowly from my face to my hips. He pulled me closer, firmly holding me against his solid frame. My pulse was rolling high, like a tide about to crash into the stony shore in the middle of a summer storm. "The house will come and go—it'll be dirt and dust someday—but you, my love, are beautiful. Living, Reaper... it doesn't matter. I love you either way."

"I love you, too," I said, trembling in his arms. "This feels... incredible."

"Mhm, wait till we get to the best part," Tristan chuckled, whisking me off my feet. He rushed up the stairs, effortlessly bringing us both to the front door. He didn't need to let go of me, instead pressing his elbow down on the door handle to open it. Inside, a faint scent of lavender hung in the air. I'd left planters in every window, and Ariana had promised to water them in my absence. Even as a Reaper, I'd taken a liking to gardening in times of peace.

"Is this the best part?" I asked, my cheeks ablaze and my heart thundering against his. He shook his head as he carried me into our bedroom and settled me on the bed. The feel of the soft linens against my sweaty palms made me smile, as Tristan stood before me, tall and breathing raggedly. "No, this is," I said, answering my own question as I unbuttoned his shirt, revealing the ropes of taut muscle beneath.

My husband's skin was smooth, and I wanted to kiss every inch of it. He was a scholar. A stellar anthropologist who rarely resorted to violence—yet he could absolutely hold his own as a vampire, fiercer even than Esme sometimes. He was a man and a soul with enough strength to move mountains. He had the drive to rearrange the stars themselves, if only someone would give him the magical powers to do so.

But tonight, he was simply my husband, his only task to claim me for the first time as a living creature. We made love between the soft, cool linen sheets. He said my name as we experienced one another, skin on skin, heart to heart, and soul to soul like never before. I cried out his as we climbed the steps to ecstasy, our beings singing and humming, our bodies intertwined and never to be torn apart.

Tonight, Tristan was mine, and I was his, like the bonds of marriage had intended. It felt like a wickedly good start to the life I had envisioned for us. I allowed myself to hope that only the good stuff would follow after this. That nothing the universe would throw at The Shade or at our marriage would damage the exquisite thing we'd just started.

My heart might not be able to bear the disappointment of losing all this, I thought to myself as we held each other beneath the featherdown blanket, our hearts full and our spirits utterly sated. Here, love smelled like lavender.

DAFNE

Four days had slithered past since the Flip. Not much had changed other than the level of my patience. I was anxious and restless, virtually climbing the walls and finding it increasingly difficult to breathe at times. My parents were obviously thrilled to be reunited with me, but our location loomed over our heads like a rotten apple, chunks of it falling onto our foreheads to remind us of our imprisonment.

The Black Heights might look like the ones back home, only they weren't real, and every single Shadian dragon knew it. I could see it on their sour faces whenever they came out of their caves or whenever they had to withdraw there for the night. It was a general feeling, however, applicable to every single Shadian who'd been confined to this place.

At least my parents weren't worried sick about me anymore, and Isabelle had been reunited with her family. She had been gone two months, and they hadn't even realized it.

"Where are you going, honey?" Mom asked as soon as she saw me get up and move away from the small fire we'd built to warm us in the morning. This was the one palpable difference between this island and the real one— these Black Heights were much colder, especially near dawn. I'd noticed the difference before, but seeing my fellow dragons observe it as well reminded me of how far away from home we truly were. It only served to feed my festering anxiety, plus I hadn't seen Jericho in a few days, since just after the Flip. That stung the worst, and I couldn't help but feel bad.

My father had insisted that we stick together, ice dragons with ice dragons, as if their petty feuds with the fire dragons even mattered anymore. They didn't, and the great Lethe knew it, too, but abandoning their otherwise hilarious verbal skirmishes with the fire dragons would've meant admitting that our predicament was truly terrible. Renouncing the normalcy we'd lived with for so long solely because that bitch of a Valkyrie had decided to take over our home and toss us in here would've meant we were giving up. I understood why my father felt the way he did, but I didn't appreciate the divide it created between me and Jericho. Not after all we'd been through together.

"I need some air," I said, my tone flat. It wasn't my mother's fault, yet I couldn't help it. I was being snappy with everybody, and I knew that part of the reason was because I missed a certain fire dragon. I had been working on ways to adjust to this new reality. Then again, ice dragons were naturally averse to change in any form, which should have made me resistant to our predicament, much like the rest of my ice-breathing family, who were constantly grunting and pacing their caves, unable to leave this place. It made me smile, knowing that even though I was technically only half-ice-dragon, I was still more ice dragon than the rest of them put together.

"Are you okay?" she replied, watching me intently as I checked my earpiece, then put it back on. Dad always had his on, and mine had become a source of frustration lately, since Jericho hadn't even bothered to say hello. Sure, I'd been busy with my folks, and he'd been busy with his, but still... I would've appreciated a message, at least. We'd almost kissed, hadn't we? I hadn't imagined that?

I gave her a soft smile, trying to hide my emotions, if only to avoid another conversation about how I needed to be more open with my feelings. "I'm fine, Mom. Just a little stir crazy. I'm only going to stretch my legs since there's no news from the Great Dome about a way of getting out of this fresh hell."

"Your father will be back soon," she reminded me. "Don't stay out too long."

Her attempts at parenting were endearing, especially since I was past the age where such lines were even needed, but I knew this was her way of coping with what had happened. She'd lost me for a while, and she'd only just gotten me back. I didn't even want to imagine the kind of horrors she must have imagined in my absence I was her only child—she'd worked with the witches and the Faulty twins to conceive me. Basically, I'd been so much work, losing me would've broken her beyond repair.

Instead, I chose to go over and hug my mother, and she planted a kiss on my cheek. I felt the whole universe of her love in that kiss, and I welcomed it, knowing that someday I might have children of my own who ran off to visit crazy new places, leaving me to wonder about their safety. Karma did have a way of paying people back. "I won't be long, I promise. Also, I've got my earpiece on if you need me," I told her, then walked out of the cave and into the cold and empty darkness.

The sky was blank and black, that strange light glowing from above though none of us had managed to find the damned source yet. The wind blew through the tree crowns, making the leaves rustle and rattle oddly. It was as if even the made-up nature of this place was working overtime to remind us that we weren't home. That we were prisoners.

"Hrista, you heinous, *heinous* nightmare," I muttered, taking a deep breath.

To the south, I could see the lights of the Vale flickering. The clones' Vale, currently occupied by real humans. To the west, the redwood residences sprawled beneath the lush and trembling canopies, extending for at least a mile or so before the witches' sanctuary—which was nothing but a pretty clearing with Hrista's two-story white villa. I knew Corrine and Ibrahim had begrudgingly kept their distance from that place, choosing to spend their time in constant and relentless analysis of every inch of the glass house extension instead, hoping to find something that might bring them closer to a solution for our infuriating predicament.

Yeah, we were all dying to get the hell out of here.

I could see Caia and Blaze's cave from here, too. My irritation began to take on new and surprisingly big proportions. I was on edge, and knowing that Jericho was somewhere in there... it made my blood pump hotter and faster than ever. The walls I had surrounded my heart with were thawing away, perhaps a little too quickly for my comfort. I was feeling things I had never felt before, and my reactions to Jericho's absence were equally frustrating and confusing.

If I went to him now, I would reveal myself as emotionally attached—or so I thought. It made sense to me. Maybe I was wrong, but my instincts screamed against it. Plus, fire and ice dragons didn't mix. That was a cultural aspect I had repeatedly ignored since I'd met Jericho. Now that my father was back in the picture, I found it harder to set aside. Third, Jericho hadn't said a word in days. If I made the first move, I worried I'd come across as needy. Or desperate. Or worse.

"What's worse than needy?" I muttered, stretching my arms out.

It had been a while since I'd taken flight. I had my combo suit on, of which Soph and I had nabbed two from the armory before we'd blown it up, so all I had to do was pull the special black string on my hip and the fabric would roll away into a collar. I turned full dragon and the collar hung nicely around my neck, ready to be unwound and refitted into the combo suit on my humanoid frame. Until then, however, I had this peculiar sky to myself.

Flapping my wings several times, I reveled in the sensation of my scales shuddering and moving ever so slightly as I stretched and lifted my head. I huffed and puffed, as if I'd expelled an entire bag of dust from the bottom of my lungs. The weight of the entire world had just fallen off my shoulders. The clones were gone, as were the Berserkers and Hrista, the wretched fiend. It had vanished—the trouble, the rage, the impotence against this new and still mysterious enemy.

I was a dragon, and I was ready to fly.

Somewhere in the distance, I heard a familiar sound of wings flapping, but I didn't pay any attention to it. I plunged from the edge of the cave and dropped until I could almost taste the morning dew on the redwood leaves before I soared again. I went higher and higher, past the smoky clouds that were nothing more than an illusion.

I reached for the heavens, though I knew there were no heavens here. I wondered, though... where did this pocket of lies end? Where did the sky end? What if I could just pierce through and find my way back to the real island?

Driven by an intense curiosity, I accelerated. The air grew colder, making my spine tingle. I loved the icy feel of the atmosphere against my scaly skin. Breathing out, I pushed myself higher and higher. The sky could not be my limit. I refused to let this place get the better of me.

And then something hard bumped into me.

It knocked me off my course. I found myself flailing and roaring, suddenly angered and embarrassed by my inability to keep it together. Jericho's roar filled the fake sky, and I turned my head to find him shooting toward me like a massive black arrow with turquoise eyes and ridiculously sharp fangs. He was smiling.

How dare he smile! He just rammed into me! He threw me off my game!

Oh, he was having fun. Entire days of not saying a word, and suddenly he was the king of the skies? Nope. Not a chance. I wasn't going to let this play out that way. I quickly hatched a plan, and I knew exactly where this encounter would end.

Snarling, I lunged at him. It made Jericho growl once more but with a smidge of delight as he flew away from me. We were chasing each other, and he was clearly having a good time. I didn't cut him any slack, though I did enjoy letting him come after me, if only to keep those muscles working. We dashed above the fake island, forgetting about everything else around us.

This dance of dragons would end with a kiss. I knew it. I was determined to make it so, if only to teach him a lesson about playing with me this way. My walls of ice were thawing in his presence, yes, but that didn't mean things would go how he wanted. *No. This morning, our lips will meet, and then I'll leave him hanging and yearning for more.*

Determined to reach my desired conclusion, I dropped into a sudden spiraling motion. Less than a mile ahead, Sun Beach stretched lazily against the dark waters, its golden sands glistening against the fake skylight. That was our destination. That was where I'd win this particularly exciting game that Jericho likely didn't even realize we were playing. Or maybe he did...

I'll show you!

JERICHO

I'd made a mess of things over the past few days, and I'd decided this was my opportunity to make up for it. When it had only been a handful of us in this mad place, Dafne and I had found it easier to spend time together, to grow closer. We hadn't had our families, our friends, or society surrounding us, and things had seemed strange and difficult, but not impossible. In the midst of it all, Dafne had stolen my heart.

But now I had no idea what to do with myself. My fear of being rejected by her had only gotten worse over time, until it eventually threw me off my game completely. Upon reuniting with everyone--plus the Flip turning our lives upside down—I'd drifted away from her, telling myself that we had work to do. That we were stuck here, and there were so many issues to deal with. Things had come between us, and I had failed to stop that from happening.

I'd allowed fate to pull us apart at the worst possible time—just when I'd thought the walls of ice around her heart were finally coming down, ever so slowly. Mom and Dad had no idea about my feelings for Dafne, and judging by the indifference that Lethe had consistently shown toward me, I'd figured he was in the dark, too. Almost four days had gone by since I'd even seen or talked to Dafne, and after so much time spent constantly together, it felt awkward and wrong. The moment I'd spotted her coming out of her cave, I knew this was my shot at making things right. I wanted our dynamic back more than anything.

She's mad at me.

Knowing I'd brought this on myself, I considered it a challenge. Dafne's flight was fierce but graceful. It was hard to look away from her. The sky wasn't the real deal, yet she owned it. Her wings stretched wide, the dark gray skin almost iridescent beneath the fake moonlight. It bounced off her scales, and I caught a glimpse of her stormy gray eyes as she gave me a fleeting look before diving into a sudden descent.

I felt compelled to follow, and she didn't make it easy to keep up. This was a dance of sorts, I realized, as we were going up again, flying around one another like fireworks shooting skyward, mere seconds from exploding. She swerved to her left. I dove right, unwilling to lose her, even for a second. I mirrored her every move, my muscles hard and tight along my dragon bones as I followed her through the sky. Her dragon form was slightly smaller and significantly slimmer than mine, which made her movements graceful and fluid, while mine felt heavy and forced.

Nonetheless, she failed to shake me. We flew together for what felt like ages, the air growing colder as we shot through the sky. Up, then down, then left and right, ever changing and shifting. There was no need for words. We both knew why we were up here. Neither of us wanted to stop, yet eventually we knew it was time to land. I was getting tired. And Dafne's motions had become slower and less agile.

We touched down on the fake Sun Beach. It wasn't as bright as the original, but it still offered an illusion of morning. It felt warm as I shifted, my bones crackling in their return to a human form. I tugged on my uniform belt. In an instant, the fabric and zippers released, stretching and covering me from head to toe. "This is easily one of the best GASP inventions," I said, chuckling lightly. "We got lucky that the clones copied this prototype in the armory, along with the rest of our weapons and stuff. We had yet to receive suits like this before the clone attacks, remember? I was so happy you and Soph snatched us a couple of them before we blew that place up." So many times, we dragons had found ourselves in awkward situations due to the absence of clothes after our transformations. The new uniforms were the ideal solution, and they'd made our lives easier since before the Flip, but only now had I had the time and the patience to truly appreciate this gear. Quite expensive and difficult to put together, but their design was flawless. And I'd always looked good in black.

Dafne shot me a cool grin, standing right where the water lapped at the sandy shore. Only the murmurs of this fake ocean remained in the silence surrounding us, and I found myself staring at this exquisite creature. Why did love sound like such a simple and wonderful thing, when it was way more complicated than advertised? Why did the fear of rejection make someone like me act so irrationally, when all I wanted to do was throw my arms around her?

"It's been a while," Dafne said, the humor fading from her eyes.

There it was. The poke. I'd had it coming, but how could I explain how I'd been feeling? How could I make her understand without projecting weakness? That was the one thing I could never do as a fire dragon. It was deeply embedded within my upbringing. Strength and dignity above all. "We've had our hands full," I replied. "There's so much happening."

She looked at me with an intensity I had never experienced before. I would've given anything to be able to hear her thoughts in that instant, to understand how her mind worked... and how she saw me. But a weight fell from my shoulders when Dafne smiled. "It's been crazy, huh? And with the dragons back together, doesn't it feel even harder to have some time to yourself?"

"Yeah. I take it you've had similar issues?"

"I was mad at you. I thought this would be an opportunity to call you out on being so distant, but standing here now... I've kind of lost that appetite," Dafne said, sighing.

I drew in a long breath, letting it out slowly. She was the most beautiful creature I had ever seen, and I feared I'd never get enough of her. "I did give you reason to be mad, huh? Sorry, Dafne. It wasn't my intention to vanish for days."

"Well, I didn't say anything, either," she muttered. "Thing is, I'm ice. You're fire. Our parents might frown a little."

"Your dad, maybe. He's still hung up on the old school stuff regarding the dragon clans. My dad is married to a fire fae. We're obviously on the more open-minded side of things."

That earned me an instant frown. "Excuse me?"

"Well, Lethe is more of a traditionalist." This was all banter, and she knew it, judging by how hard she was trying to hold back a laugh.

"He married a human!" Dafne retorted. "Besides, we both know what the underlying problem really is, and why neither of us has been able to fraternize with anyone outside our family clusters since the Flip."

The humor dissipated between us, like steam rolling out of a boiling kettle until nothing was left but the harsh reality we were stuck with. Dafne and I looked at each other, momentarily silent as our minds worked in unison. I could almost hear the wheels turning.

"Our dads are full dragons. And they are *both* traditionally educated. Fire with fire. Ice with ice. No mingling with humans or whatever," she added. "But they live in The Shade. They married non-dragons out of love, and we're living proof. What's really keeping the whole fire with fire and ice with ice nonsense going is our current situation. It's how they're coping, by blowing antiquated traditions out of proportion because it's easier to deal with than the reality of our situation."

I blinked several times. "The coherence in that entire argument is astonishing."

"We have literally shared a bed, Jericho. I think we both know what's going on between us, but neither of us can say it out loud," Dafne replied. "On top of that, our parents' dragon nonsense is louder than ever, and I haven't seen you in days. Not even a message. Nothing. Are we really going to let Hrista's mess spoil something so potentially beautiful?"

"You think it's beautiful... whatever this is?" I asked, my voice wavering as I motioned at the narrow space between us. Dafne crossed her arms in response.

"I hope so! Otherwise, what's the point of all this tossing and turning, huh?"

I couldn't help but laugh lightly. "And to think I had to breach a fortress of ice to get to you... what happened?

How are we even talking about this?"

"Hrista happened. That whole situation made me realize that I can't waste any more time. I have no idea what tomorrow will bring or how long we'll be trapped here. I only know that I don't want another second to go by without some kind of clarity between us," Dafne said, raising her chin proudly. "So tell me. Why haven't you said anything since... well, since the Flip? Why have we drifted apart after the troubles we survived together? I don't understand."

"I can't blame you." My reply was followed by a heavy sigh. Dafne was right. There was no point in hiding behind our fears and insecurities anymore. My feelings for her were only getting stronger, regardless of whether I acted on them or not. And she deserved my honesty. "From the moment I saw you, I knew you were different. Extraordinary. Possibly out of my league."

Her breath faded, and she stared at me, lips slowly parting.

"I can't fight this anymore," I continued, driven by a simmering need to take this conversation in a different direction. "I've wanted to tell you for a while, but I was afraid that you didn't feel the same way, that you'd reject me. That fear has kept me constantly on edge, and I thought that maybe if I took a couple of steps back, my feelings for you might fade. But nothing's changed. I'm still very much into you."

Dafne's silence drowned out the lazily lapping waves at our feet, and I felt as though my worst fear, the one I had just admitted out loud, was coming true. I was about to get the it's-not-you-it's-me treatment, which was a weapon I'd often employed. No one had ever had the chance to use it on me.

"I mean, if you don't feel the same, and it's just me, I don't mind," I added, suddenly gripped by the icy claws of panic. "It's cool. I'll be fine. We can even pretend this never happened. Bet your dad will be relieved." I ended up chuckling like a moron until Dafne rolled her eyes and put me out of my misery.

"Jericho, it's mutual."

That was all I needed for the world to make sense again. I stared at her for a long second, trying to take in every detail that had made me fall head over heels with this stupendous creature. Her hair was black and long. Normally, I was drawn to short curls the color of summer wheat. Her eyes were gray and filled with mystery. I'd appreciated sunny skies in a girl's gaze before. Dafne was an ice dragon. A fighter. A cracking whip to either dodge or face fearlessly, and my heart began to accelerate as she closed the distance between us.

In an instant, the entire universe shifted as her lips found mine, and we kissed.

For a moment, I thought we had a real sun shining overhead, filling me with an atomic warmth that spread through my body and set my muscles alight. My pulse raced, but the softness of her lips, the sweetness of her mouth... It was the only element of my existence that I could process. It was like tasting heaven, if heaven was an ice dragon named Dafne.

Her hands cupped my face, and the delicate touch of her skin against mine tore a soft groan from my throat. I pulled my head back only so that I could breathe again, wondering how long it had been since we'd started this. The gray in her gaze was almost black, her heart thudding against mine.

"Whoa," I managed.

"Yeah, you can say that again," she whispered, taking a couple steps back.

Dafne's lips were plump and pink. I doubted I'd think of anything else for the remainder of this day. "Well, at least we both know where we stand, right?" I asked, offering a faint smile. I'd gotten past her frozen walls to reach the very core of her. The heat emanating from within Dafne made me wonder if she was really an ice dragon after all.

"We'll just have to figure out where to go to from here," she said, her gaze dropping slowly to focus on the water rushing across the coarse, faded sand.

Dafne couldn't really be an ice dragon, I thought, ignoring the madness of such a thought when she obviously was an ice dragon. But she'd set my heart on fire. The folly of it was palpable, and I didn't want it to end. We'd fallen, and we'd flown.

We kissed again, and the fake Shade vanished around us once more.

ASTRA

On the fifth day since the Flip, I summoned a meeting of what Thayen and I referred to as "the old gang," which meant everyone who'd come to the fake island first. Myst, Regine, Haldor and Brandon joined Thayen, Soph, Jericho, Dafne, Chantal, Voss, Richard, Isabelle, my mom and myself. We'd chosen the

Port for this conversation, mostly for sentimental reasons, since this was where we'd come through initially.

The empty, vapid night of the fake island was beginning to irk me. It wasn't home. Our home was overrun with monsters, and I had grown tired of dwelling here in post-Flip misery. The lighthouse spun its white beam across the vast emptiness beyond the ocean, then back over the island. I found it strange, since the real island's lighthouse had never worked. It moved in a sullen rhythm, as if the fake island were as upset as the rest of us. It didn't stop it from draining our energy as usual, however. My days were forced into twenty-four-hour patterns that demanded at least one third of that to be allocated to sleep. It did the same to everyone, even the vampires.

"Please, tell me you have some good news," Isabelle said. For days, she had been struggling to remember something useful. But the medication that the clones had pumped into her body had done a horrific number on her short-term memory. "Every day I spend in this place feels like a win for those bastards."

"You may have noticed that Isabelle has been feeling a little cranky lately," Voss grumbled.

"They messed with my head," Isabelle insisted. "You're damn right I'm mad. I demand retribution, and I'm never going to get it if we're doomed to rot in this place."

Soph sighed. "I think we all feel that way at this point."

"Well, then I guess it will please you to hear that—" I paused to look at Brandon for a split second, searching for a hint of encouragement in his smile even as his flaming blue eyes reminded me of that almost-kiss we'd had the other day. *Focus, Astra. Focus!* "—I managed to open a longer lasting shimmering portal."

"Yes!" Thayen exclaimed, practically beaming with joy.

Jericho hugged me, laughing in delight, while Richard squeezed my shoulders and grinned from ear to ear. "You did it!" the wolf-incubus exclaimed, practically jumping out of his skin. I was overwhelmed with tight embraces and kisses covering my face as my fellow Shadians fell all over me, excited and thankful and affectionate.

Brandon was kind enough to gently grip my upper arm and pull me away from the melee of limbs and kind souls, laughing lightly while I caught my breath. "Now give them the bad news, and let's see if they still love you."

For hours, the Berserker and I had been discussing proper ways to tell the original crew about what I'd accomplished last night—that after days of pushing myself, I'd managed to open a shimmering portal and then kept it open long enough for people to go through it.

Mom was the first to notice the sour look on my face. "What's he talking about?"

"I can only hold a portal for about a minute—maybe two, tops—and even then it ends with my nose bleeding," I said.

"Much like how my nose bleeds if I try to glamor a Berserker or a Valkyrie," Thayen observed, almost breathless and wide eyed. Beside him, Haldor scoffed and crossed his arms, the pose making him look even bigger than his usual massive self.

"You're not trying that on me ever again," the Berserker replied. Without his shadows—or better said, with his shadows tucked away and out of sight, which we'd recently learned he could easily do—he was still large and frightening, but the darkness had often made him much more intimidating. I certainly preferred him as an ally rather than a foe.

Myst intervened, keeping the focus on me and not on anything trivial. "Hold on. You said up to two minutes," she repeated my conclusion to bring the conversation back on topic.

"Yes." I added a nod to go with it.

"It should be fine, assuming only a few go through," she said.

My mom was understandably confused, though Myst had already understood where I was going with this entire exchange. "Why just a few?" Mom asked, her gaze darting between Myst, Thayen, Brandon, and me. "How many portals would you need to open to get every Shadian through? Mind you, we're talking about five thousand people, more or less."

"With enough practice and a whole lot of energy, just one. But that might take days, if not weeks," Brandon said. "I'm not sure we have that kind of time, considering that Hrista and her minions are running loose in the real Shade."

"Then why did Hrista need so many portals for the Flip?" Jericho asked.

"She used that crystal ball thing and some combo magic from Purgatory, for sure," Brandon replied. "Astra's mojo is all natural, possibly unlimited or easy to supplement, unlike the aforementioned crystal ball, and therefore subject to slightly different conditions. I'm not an expert, obviously, but I'm following my logic and the little bits of knowledge I did pick up along the way."

I sucked in a breath, bracing myself for the proposal. "I'd like to take a small crew through the shimmering portal first," I replied. "A recon team before we let anyone else return to The Shade."

"Wait, what?" Mom blurted, immediately concerned—not that I could blame her.

"It's why I wanted to confer with you all first," I said, sitting cross-legged in the sand. The others joined me in a wide circle, pensive shadows settling over their faces. Above, the lighthouse's beam shot across the black sky. Looking up, the emptiness sent a painful pang through my stomach. The absence of stars reminded me of where we were, and why I was so desperate to get out of there. "We can't risk the entire Shadian population by all returning at once, especially since we don't know what Hrista and the clones are up to. We don't know if she has sealed The Shade off or if she started a war with GASP. We have absolutely no idea, and we owe it to our people to keep them safe."

"Therefore, a small crew to do some recon, now that Astra can portal us back and forth, should help us prepare for whatever Hrista has done with your island," Brandon interjected, giving Mom a warm but brief smile. "Surely you understand the wisdom of such an approach."

Mom nodded slowly. "I do. Who did you have in mind for the team, then?"

"Brandon, Hammer, and me. The Time Master, too. Myst and Thayen, and that'll make two Purgatory entities who can teleport us across the real island if we have to," I said, then looked at Mom, already seeing the disappointment carving its way through her expression. "You should stay back here with Dad. I can't bear the thought of losing you again. Besides, it's me Hrista wants."

"And you're going right to her!" she shot back, shaking her head. "Absolutely not. No, honey, I'm not letting you endanger yourself like that. Your father won't allow this either!"

"Mom, I'm the only one who can open a shimmering portal. If we do send a recon team through, they have to be able to come back," I reminded her. "Also, let's be honest here. I know you're worried, and I appreciate it... you're my mom, you're supposed to worry about me. But I'm a GASP agent, and I cannot in good conscience run and hide from the trouble that has befallen our island. I must do everything within my power to save our home."

She let out a heavy breath, dropping her gaze for a long moment. It felt like a surrender, though she didn't say a word. I took a second to hug her, love pouring through us both with golden warmth, like the kiss of a burning sun.

"I know you're all grown up and independent," Mom whispered in my ear, "but that doesn't stop me from worrying about you. Astra, I give you my blessing to do whatever it takes to get everybody back home, but by the stars, come back to us, honey. Otherwise, you'll break your father's heart beyond repair. Not to mention mine. I doubt I would survive losing you."

"I love you too, Mom," I replied, holding back tears. I blinked several times, then pulled away and looked to the others. "We'd like to take the dragons, too. Dafne and Jericho. You were both instrumental before, and the real Shade needs you."

Jericho and Dafne exchanged glances, and only then did I notice it. The subtle shift, the familiarity in their eyes. They shared something different, something more intimate. It was subtle and brief, but I liked it. Dafne gave me a stern nod. "You can count on us," she said. "I get Jericho's fire is useful for Myst's light weapons, but I'm not sure how any of my abilities will come into play over there."

"You're a fierce fighter," I replied, smiling. "You helped saved us more than once. I trust you to fight alongside us, and you know the Berserkers and the clones as well as any of us here."

Thayen nodded his agreement. "That will definitely matter later. Okay, so we've got the two dragons, and we've already got Time as the Reaper to join the mix."

"Really?" Richard muttered, frowning like a sullen little boy. "You just skim right past me, huh? Your bestie?

Your partner in crime? Your brother from another mother?"

Voss chuckled and gave Richard a nudge that threw him down almost instantly. Voss wobbled, too, but Chantal helped him stand, laughing lightly, while Isabelle held back her giggles and helped Richard up.

"We're too weak, cuz," Voss said, giving Richard a sympathetic smile. "If I can knock you down just like that, it means your reflexes aren't sharp enough yet to withstand a recon mission in what is now basically enemy territory."

"I don't want to stay here and feel useless. I wasn't made to decorate the world. I was made to protect it," Richard retorted with a dash of the overly dramatic.

"Which is why we need you to stay here with us," Mom interjected. "We do alright on our own, but we're stronger with you by our side, Richard."

Richard was momentarily baffled, struggling with anxiety, disappointment, but also flattery. My mom did have a way of bending him and most other incubi to her will—Safira had often said it was a trait of the Daughters. "Incubi whisperers," she'd called us. Well, my mom and the Daughters, actually. I'd been under the incubus's influence before. That was probably due to my not being a full Daughter but half-sentry—at least that had been Mom's theory, and Safira had not contradicted her. Either way, I was glad the Daughters were immune and at least one of them ready to nudge the wolf-incubus in the right direction.

"I'm inclined to accept your arguments," Richard ultimately replied, keeping his chin up, proud as ever. Thayen patted him on the shoulder.

"You're needed here, Rich. Besides, your parents have just gotten you back. You can't leave them behind again."

"What about us?" Regine asked, both eyebrows raised. "You seem to have your team worked out, you even desire a Reaper to assist you, but there was no mention of me or Haldor anywhere."

"Regine, it's not—" Myst cut in, but her sister wouldn't have any of it.

"What, you're going to tell me I'm needed here, too? Like I'm as gullible as Richard?"

"Hey," Richard mumbled, slightly offended.

The Time Master walked onto the beach, accompanied by his ghoul, a tall slender thing named Aphis. Unlike most of his kind, Aphis carried himself mostly on his hind legs, preferring to come across as more Reaper, less ghoul. He barely ever made a sound, and whenever I looked into the black pools of his eyes, I could almost feel the coldness of his existence. A string of decisions had led him to this point, but most had not been his choice. The Time Master had rescued Aphis from the Knight Ghoul ranks of Visio. "A Valkyrie and a Berserker should stick around here to help protect the Shadians," Time said, joining the conversation. "Hrista can still return or send some of her people through to torment or hurt them. While my fellow Reapers are capable of fighting them off, I'm concerned a Berserker might still inflict considerable damage and maybe even loss of life."

Regine gave him a startled look. "You think she would do that? Hrista, I mean."

"Don't you?" Time replied, mildly irritated. "She has spent years building this place and finetuning the clones to replace real Shadians. She clearly hates everything The Shade stands for. We know why that is, too. We helped in the Spirit Bender's destruction. She took over and threw everyone out in return. Of course, I have no trouble seeing her choosing to send her people through just to torment the originals. Hrista is filled with rage. Calculated rage, but rage nonetheless. Surely, you can see that."

Haldor cursed under his breath, the fires in his eyes burning white. "The Reaper's right. Hrista is vicious. I thought my brothers and I were capable of horrible things, considering our nature, but Hrista... She's been working at this for a very long time. Now that I think about it, yeah, I see it too. The possibility that she might send clones or Berserkers through just to mess with the real Shadians."

"What we're doing is recon anyway," I said. "I would never engage her with just a handful of people. But we absolutely have to see what she's planning, how The Shade is faring... we have to know what we'll be walking into."

"Besides, Voss, Chantal, Isabelle, Richard, and I have already dealt with the clones," Mom replied, looking at Regine and Haldor. "We can offer valuable insights and help our Shadians be better prepared in case there is a clone infiltration."

"You'll have Soul, Kelara, Sidyan, Seeley, and Nethissis, too," Time added.

"So, I get to stay back again?" Soph interjected, crossing her arms. I had mixed feelings about her coming along—we were already taking a huge risk with Dafne, Jericho and Richard against the clones, the hostile Berserkers and Hrista. I just wasn't comfortable putting the heiress to Neraka in mortal danger, too. She was more than capable, of course, yet my stomach weighed a ton as I thought about her joining the mission.

Fortunately, Myst was quick to give her a better option. "You need to help keep my sister in check," she said. "Excuse me?" Regine croaked, almost offended, but Myst ignored her, focusing on a rather befuddled Soph. "This will be a recon team. The fewer of us, the better," she added. "I promise you I would be the first to ask you to come along otherwise, but my sister grows restless without me, and I'm sure your parents will feel slightly more comfortable with their only heir staying back once more, at least until we figure out what happened with The Shade."

Soph shook her head slowly. "This doesn't have anything to do with Regine. You just want to keep me out of it." She gave me a sullen look, and it just made me feel worse. I sought Thayen's gaze for comfort, but he seemed equally awkward.

"Myst is right," Regine conceded with a heavy sigh. "I could use you as back up in case something goes off. We can coordinate. You and I, we've already had our share of action, if you think about it." Only then did I realize how the younger Regine had chosen to be the mature one in this conversation. She certainly didn't need a living babysitter, but she understood why Soph would've felt left behind, too. By playing along with Myst's argument, Regine was choosing the middle path of unification, leaving our crew small while strengthening the Shadians' defenses in our absence.

But even with Soph by her side, it didn't make Regine much happier about having to stay back, especially since she had to work with Haldor. If there was one thing that she'd made abundantly clear since day one, it was that she and the Berserker loathed each other. "You'd better not be a pain in my ass," she muttered, crossing her arms as she looked away from him.

"I won't, if you promise to keep that word-salad maker of yours shut," Haldor replied dryly.

Regine gave him a troubled look. "Word-salad maker?"

"He means your mouth," Richard laughed. That earned him a deadly scowl from two Valkyries instead of just one, and I had to press my lips tight enough to prevent a chuckle from escaping.

"You know what? I think I'll be fine to stick around," Soph cut in, narrowing her eyes at Haldor. While he'd been a veritable nightmare as our enemy, he didn't scare her anymore. "I'll look forward to mopping the floor with you if you're not nicer to your light sisters."

It made both Regine and Haldor laugh, albeit for different reasons, but I was simply relieved that Soph would stick with the rest of the Shadian family. Had it been after me, I would've kept the team even smaller for everybody's safety, though I couldn't hold everybody back—case in point, Richard had made it into the crew this time.

"All jokes aside, Astra is on point with this whole endeavor, though, and sticking with a small crew. It's safer for now," Isabelle conceded. "In the meantime, I'll keep working on my memory gaps. Maybe I can recall something useful. But we have to send a recon team through. Like you said, we have to get a good understanding of what our island looks like before we can try to take it back."

Thayen exhaled sharply before bringing up the one problem none of us had truly considered. "Astra managed to convince her mom about this. She's got Phoenix left to get on board, and we each have a set of parents to convince. I suggest we head back and start getting our affairs in order. We have no idea how this will turn out."

I doubted any of them would hold us back on this endeavor. *They wouldn't.* We were fighting for The Shade here, and I knew our parents would offer their support. The problem was that they might offer too much support. The team we'd agreed upon was small but effective. I knew from Brandon that Derek and Sofia would've liked to send more people with us, just to be safe—there were times when emotions got the better of people, overriding even the GASP protocols. Emphasis on "would've liked," though, since they'd already been convinced otherwise by Brandon.

This whole situation was different from what they'd dealt with before, and a million times stranger. We lacked precious information because Isabelle had trouble remembering. I could only imagine how frustrating that had to be for her. Now, after two whole months as their prisoner, she was finally awake and conscious, but her memory loss had persisted. For now, we only had what we'd learned for ourselves, and it wasn't enough to take down Hrista. I briefly looked to Brandon again.

As always, I found a feeling of trust and courage in him. He would be with us every step of the way. And that emboldened me beyond my own strength. Yes, I'd learned to open a shimmering portal and hold it open for a minute or two. It was enough to get a few of us out of here, but it was just the first step in what I believed would be a long, complicated journey back to our beloved island.

THAYEN

"There are plenty of senior agents who could take your place." Phoenix's suggestion was understandable coming from him as a father, but it wasn't realistic, either. Astra let out a small sigh as she gave her father a warm smile. We were already equipped for the mission, having thought it might help the parents adjust to our decision faster. Suddenly I felt hot and uncomfortable with my mom and dad watching me—quietly, but with clear intent.

"Yes, but they lack our experience with Purgatory entities," Astra told her father.

Viola placed a hand on Phoenix's shoulder. "Honey, she has to go, no matter who is on the recon team. She's the only one who can open shimmering portals. Besides, our children have grown a lot in the days that they were away from us. I'd hardly consider them junior agents after what they've endured in this place."

"That's true," Phoenix replied, reluctantly accepting his wife's judgment.

"You've already made up your minds, haven't you?" Lethe replied, a bitter smile persisting on his lips as he looked at Dafne, then at the rest of our crew. One by one, we felt the chill of the ice dragon's gaze, along with the silent promise of the bad things that would happen if we didn't come back with Dafne alive and in one piece. I couldn't blame him.

Dafne hugged her mother, Elodie, then stepped over to her father, taking his hands in hers. "You know we're right about this," she said. "We're the best equipped to spy on those freaks, Dad. We've dealt with them before. We've learned to use some of their tricks, too. Besides, we work well as a team. It's how we survived here before the Flip."

"It is not our intention to fight the clones, the Berserkers or Hrista, but to gather information and help GASP prepare for a proper counter-offensive," the Time Master added. Behind him, Aphis stood dark and silent, his eyes measuring us from head to toe, as if he was becoming acquainted with his new teammates. I had never crossed paths with the ghoul before, as Time had usually chosen to show up on his own, leaving Aphis in a subtle form. "Right now, we don't know what's going on in The Shade or whether the rest of the federation is aware of what has happened."

Blaze scoffed. "So you're just going over there for a quick visit."

"Yes!" Jericho replied, genuinely exasperated. Of every parent we'd had to convince, Blaze and Caia had been the ones with the hardest heads. Mom and Dad had come around relatively quickly, but the fire dragon and fae couple was being downright stubborn.

"And Myst needs you because of your fire power," Caia muttered, visibly dissatisfied at the prospect of her son going away once more. "This is wrong on so many levels."

"Not really," Phoenix replied, his arms crossed and his mind made up. "It's the price we must pay as Shadians and fighters of GASP. As supernaturals, really. Our families, our parents, our children and probably our grandchildren, too. We have no choice but to jump in and go to battle for those who need us. We did it once or twice ourselves, and it made our parents sick with worry. I figure it's only natural that we be put through the same thing now. We can't ask our children to step back when an injustice is committed, simply because we love them too much to lose them."

His words struck a chord in all of the parents present. Dad hid his smile, while Mom fought back tears. In the end, he spoke the truth, and his words achieved the unanimous greenlight that my crew and I had been hoping for. We would've gone either way, but it felt much better to have the support of our parents and loved ones prior to embarking on this new and dangerous adventure.

Silence settled over the group for a good minute as the truth permeated every other concern the Shadians might have had regarding this expedition. It was obvious that this had to be done. Could it have been assigned to more senior GASP agents? Sure. The Shade was full of them, and I had faith in their abilities. But none had interacted with the clones, the Berserkers, or Hrista like we had. If anyone had the experience and necessary knowledge of the enemy, it was us.

"Well, you're already packed up," Lethe conceded, nodding at his daughter. She and Jericho had small bags attached with stainless-steel rings. In these bags, they had a minute amount of invisibility magic, red garnet lenses, and healing paraphernalia in case they needed it. Should the dragons turn, the bags would remain attached through the stainless-steel rings to their collars. Yes, Dafne and Jericho were absolutely packed up and ready to go.

"We have to support them," Elodie told her husband. "It's our duty."

"It is, yes," Blaze sighed, finally reaching the general consensus. He put an arm around Caia's shoulders, and I could almost hear the conversation that the two of them would have later that night. "What can we do to help?"

Jericho smiled. "Just hope for the best. We have already prepared for the worst."

"This is one of those rare instances where I'm glad I'm not alive," the Time Master muttered. It earned him a sly half-smile from Aphis. The ghoul was striking, not only through his preference to stand upright, but also because of his deliberate silence and stolen glances. I could tell there was something different about Aphis, and I had a hard time looking at him like I'd looked at Rudolph—or any other ghoul, for that matter. I just knew, deep down, that this guy would end up surprising us somehow. "Rest assured, all of you, I will do my best to make sure we all return safely," Time promised.

"Thank you," Mom replied. "Soul and the others will work with us on this side of the problem. Unfortunately, none of our communication methods work between this realm and ours," she added and looked at me. "That means that once you step through that shimmering portal, honey, you're completely out of our reach."

"We know that," Astra took the lead. "Which is why we're focusing on recon and not on anything else. We have established clear protocols of nonengagement, per GASP guidelines and hostile territory policies."

Phoenix chuckled, his eyes glassy with tears. "My baby's all grown up and totally mastering the GASP terminology. I'm a proud dad, for sure." It made Viola giggle softly, and it drew smiles from each of us. Fortunately, and despite the dire circumstances, our ability to laugh had survived.

We were going to need it.

"I'm ready," Astra said, breathing out slowly, then looked at me. "We have everything we need, right?"

I nodded once. "Blood supplies. Food. Healing serum. Invisibility capsules. Backup weapons and comms pieces.

The works. We're good to go."

Mom and Dad wrapped their arms around me, holding tight for a while as I absorbed every second of this embrace. I remembered when I'd been only a kid, and they'd brought me over from Visio. The first thing they'd done as my parents, as soon as we'd set foot onto The Shade, was to hug me and promise me that I would always be loved and safe with them. It felt wrong to see Hrista destroy that oath they'd made to their son. She had to be stopped.

The others bid their farewells, while Mom whispered in my ear. "No matter what happens, remember you've got something to come back to, okay? Your mom, your dad, your brother and sister—"

"Who will absolutely be annoyed that they didn't get to say goodbye like you," I shot back with a bitter chuckle, though I understood why we'd had to keep this assembly small and discreet.

"You know we have to operate away from the others," Dad said. "You'll be gone, and yes, we'll get our share of nagging from them, but in the end, they will come to terms with how this went down. It's better this way."

"Mhm, it's better to ask for forgiveness than for permission, right?" I chuckled.

Dad reached out and grabbed me by the back of my neck. He pressed his lips against my forehead. He hadn't kissed me since I was a kid, and it felt nice to feel his affection toward me at such a pivotal point of my existence. I caught a glimpse of Myst watching us. The endearment was there, written all over her face. I could see it. The sight of us warmed her heart, though I wondered how much familial affection she even remembered as a Valkyrie, and whether she missed it.

"You and Astra will lead this team, and you will get what you must from The Shade," Dad said, drawing my focus back to him. His eyes drilled holes into my soul, and I was compelled to listen carefully. "You will alert the rest of GASP as soon as you get out there, by whatever means possible, and you will instruct them to standby until we find our way back to The Shade. Then you will come back to us son, okay?"

"Okay."

Astra hugged her mom and dad, then gave me a confident nod. "I'm ready," she said, though her voice trembled slightly.

"Cool. Let's do this. I'm not a big fan of drawn out, emotional moments," Brandon replied and clapped his hands once with renewed enthusiasm. Hammer, ever his faithful companion, let out a brief howl to express his own excitement about what would happen next—not that any of us had any real clue as to what awaited us beyond this realm. "Pinkie, remember your training."

Astra smiled and put her hands out, palms in a vertical position as she took deep breaths. Her skin lit up white, and the air around her buzzed with a peculiar energy. It only intensified as the minutes ticked by, crackling furiously by the time a ripple emerged in front of her. Clearly, she'd been practicing.

I held my breath.

It looked as though space itself was the surface of a lake, and Astra's magic had just thrown a pebble into it. The ripples multiplied and stretched outward, while our crew slowly moved behind her. Our parents stepped back, their eyes wide as they watched it unfold before them.

Slowly, a white gash appeared across the ripples. It widened, its interior shimmering like an endless sea of diamonds bathed in pure sunlight. It was beautiful and terrifying at the same time. Astra measured her breaths, while Brandon whispered in her ear—encouragements, I assumed—his words must have had a positive effect on her, because the shimmering portal grew taller and wider. Astra's hands clenched into tight fists. She glanced at us over her shoulder.

"We need to go. Now," she said.

One by one, we said our last round of tremulous goodbyes and stepped through the portal. We'd done it before, though not thanks to a true Shadian. Either way, the sensations were identical. The vast, diamond-filled space that glimmered between the fake realm and ours seemed greater than ever. Infinite, actually, and almost blindingly white.

We moved cautiously, putting one foot in front of the other.

"Man, this only gets scarier," Jericho grumbled in front of me.

Brandon chuckled. "Wait till you meet the rest of my Berserker brothers."

"You are optimism incarnate," Dafne retorted.

Behind me, Astra walked in silence. The portal had already closed. I caught her eye briefly. "Are you okay?" "Yeah, I think so. I feel... odd. I don't know why," she said. "I used to be able to feed on shimmering portals opened by Hrista. I guess that's clearly not the case now, since it's *my* energy going into them. I must just be a little tired."

"There it is," the Time Master exclaimed, pointing ahead. A portal had opened, revealing a strange sea of more light. "That's weird."

"The Shade is supposed to be dark, isn't it?" Myst asked.

"Yes," I mumbled, frowning as I tried to make out something, anything, from beyond the portal. "But it could be Sun Beach." Just to be safe, I pulled on my hood and mask, ready to protect myself from what was clearly a bright sun. This was clearly crazy, but our sense of adventure compelled us to proceed. History would not be written by cowards.

But as soon as we stepped through the portal, we knew something was wrong. The air felt different. The light was too bright, and it was everywhere. It took me a while to adjust to the strange view that surrounded us. The colors were wrong.

Grass wasn't green. Flowers were all white, regardless of their shapes. The sky was made of fractured crystals, and I couldn't find a sun anywhere, just an abundance of white light that filtered through the heavens and came down with a wonderful but strange warmth. The air tasted sweet. The wind tickled my face.

We found ourselves atop a hill, but we couldn't see much in the distance. Thick woods rose around us, with tall trees that resembled molten candles. The greenery was gold, the trunks painted chalk white—or maybe that was their natural color. The grass sparkled in shades of soft bronze and copper.

None of this made any sense.

"This feels... wrong," I managed, then looked to Astra. She was stunned, all words gone from her lips as she gawked at our surroundings, trying to make sense of what had happened.

"This isn't The Shade," the Time Master said, alarm marring his otherwise fine features. Even the stars in his eyes were rattled as he glanced my way. Aphis was equally disturbed, the blackness of his gaze stirred by the mystery we'd clearly just walked into.

"I swear I thought about The Shade," Astra blurted, suddenly shaking. "I wanted us to go home, I've opened shimmering portals before. Granted, I never went through any of them, but now... Oh, god, what have I done?"

Brandon and Myst, on the other hand, appeared more pleasantly surprised. Hell, they were both smiling. "You've accomplished something even better," the Berserker replied, Hammer's tail eagerly wagging beside him. "You've brought us to Purgatory."

The revelation hit me like a mallet. It knocked the air out of my lungs, and I froze on the spot, unable to do or say anything. My entire existence had been turned upside down once again. We'd left the fake island thinking we were going to the real one. Instead, we'd ended up in the one place that we, the living, certainly didn't belong, not even for a hot, accidental second.

Our initial plan had just been blown to smithereens. We were in Purgatory.

DEATH

*T*ime, for most, was linear. Even my Reapers perceived it as such. They knew of a beginning, and they expected an end. I, however, experienced time as something fluid. My past, my present, and my future were melted into one another—a swirling soup of things that had happened, things that were happening, and things that had yet to happen. Unlike the living, I did not care for preventing the future from taking something from me, including my own existence. It wasn't my responsibility to stand before the fates and tell them "Not today!" I saw everything, and I floated with it. Through it. Under and over it.

Living in the past, the present, and the future at once could be confusing, even for me. Focusing on a singular thread sometimes made everything more bearable. It anchored me somewhere, and I no longer felt like I was wandering aimlessly in the never-ending expanse of the cosmos.

I kept an eye out for it. My mistakes were still fresh in my mind. The way I'd treated Unending. The way I'd treated all my Reapers, for that matter, even the wretched Spirit Bender. Many people claimed he was my gravest mistake, but I had always disagreed. He'd been a resourceful bastard, yes, but no one could ever be as dangerous as the World Crusher. And to think I had allowed the Soul Crusher to name himself, comfortable knowing his eldest sister would never see the light of day again. The similarity between their names still made me cringe.

"I've made a mess of things," I said. Sometimes speaking words aloud made the statements feel more real, if only for a moment. Nothing was truly linear to me. Not even actions and the consequences that came with them. Everything expanded into a flurry of events that I had to make sense of, to understand and acknowledge.

Unlike the Reapers, I maintained an undying connection to the World Crusher. She wasn't linked to anyone else. Now that she was free, they would not be able to feel her like I could. Tracing her steps from Biriane required a certain amount of concentration. My beloved Thieron lit up white as the scythe, resonating with the faint energy traces World had left behind. All I had to do was follow, though I would need more to get a precise location.

She led me far from her prison, across oceans of sparkling dynasties and an abyss of emptiness, through asteroid fields and along floating rivers of multicolored stardust. The pinks were deep and mesmerizing, electrified by the pure, untamed energy that burned through them, courtesy of the Word. We were so far from the known reaches of the universe, so deep within existence, that I could sense my brother's sleepy presence in everything around us. It wasn't his custom to intervene, and I doubted he would unless I asked. And I wouldn't ask until I was absolutely overwhelmed and unable to resolve this on my own.

Considering how my ego had gotten the better of me before, I wasn't sure where that particular line would be drawn. But the World Crusher was my mess to clean up and no one else's. I had made her, and I had made her too strong—her power nearly rivaled my own. My dread of utter loneliness had clouded my judgment and foresight, the irony of which did not escape me. Taking a deep breath, I tried to envision the path ahead.

I settled on the back of a turbulent comet. Its tail trailed red and purple behind me, furiously sparking and flashing. The light emanating from this magnanimous projectile coursed through me and helped soothe my fragile nerves. I did not like chasing after people. I had not existed for so long to have my leg pulled by lesser beings. And if they thought they could get the better of me, then they were dumber than I'd thought.

"There you are," I muttered, glancing ahead. Swarming across a tumbling asteroid, six Ghoul Reapers huddled together behind a sharp ridge, thinking they could hide from me. I'd allowed my presence to be felt. I'd wanted them to sense me coming. Their fear was my delight. The World Crusher wasn't too far away, but I knew I wouldn't be able to reach her without the ghouls' help, and they were too indoctrinated by her toxicity to leave her be. The Ghoul Reapers followed the World Crusher around, so I only had to follow the Ghoul Reapers. My connection to World was worthless if she insisted on hiding herself from me. I felt her through Thieron, but I just couldn't put my finger on her.

I hopped off the comet, leaving its delicious heat behind. My bare feet touched the rugged asteroid, its surface embedded with cold flakes of platinum that cooled my soles. I heard the Ghoul Reapers scrambling to get away from me. Raising Thieron, I whispered my magic. The pulse exploded outward to raise an invisible barrier around us on a twenty-yard radius. Whenever the Ghoul Reapers tried to breach it, blue light ripples danced across its surface. I heard their muttered curses and whispered concerns. Yes, they knew I'd caught them.

The Spirit Bender had been a bitter being, and I had contributed to his anger by withholding the survival of his species. I'd enjoyed playing with the beings I'd created. Some, I'd only messed with briefly—like Dream and Nightmare's addiction to the dreams of the living. They would never wean off it. Ever. For as long as they existed, the twins would feel the pull of people's dreams. Their souls would demand the nourishment. With others, I'd gone to greater lengths. The Spirit Bender had had it the worst, though Unending—the poor girl—I'd never meant to torment her like this. The ability to grant immortality should have been something wondrous and honorable, but I had forbidden Unending to give it to anyone, and then I'd chastised her for doing it anyway. It had not been my intention at the time. I'd wanted her to use it, and then I'd changed my wretched mind.

Each of the First Ten had suffered at my hands in one form or another, yet they had loved and worshipped me. I had nothing but adoration for them as well, but I also did not care much if they suffered. I lacked a proper grasp of pleasure or joy. The Time Master had once said that I was like a child with a magnifying glass on a bright sunny day, having stumbled upon an ant colony. I caused pain only to see what would happen. That was a shamefully accurate description.

And the Time Master... He felt time as I did, with no actual beginning, middle, or end, and with no power to change anything he saw coming, either. I'd tweaked his ability with that specific limitation. He could go into the future or the past, but only by a minute or two. He could see much farther than that, but his mouth simply refused to open whenever he wished to talk about it. His physical form refused to move whenever he tried to do something about it. Time had tried many times to prevent tragedies from occurring, but he'd eventually given up. He'd learned to keep it all to himself.

I wondered how long it would be before he turned against me. It was bound to happen. Unending was already bitter beyond repair, but at least she was in a body and busy with other aspects of her existence. One less Reaper for me to worry about in terms of a potential mutiny. For now, my focus had to remain on the World Crusher. Of all my creations, she was the most dangerous. She had the power to undo everything in the realm of the living, and she had the will to do it. For the time being, my only fortune was that she wasn't aware of it, though I was certain she'd had plenty of time for in-depth studies during her imprisonment.

"There's no point in hiding," I said, loud enough for the Ghoul Reapers to hear me.

One by one, they came out from behind the black jagged ridge, each warier than the last. The sight of them made me smile, even while they shuddered with a mixture of fear and anger in my presence. They still resembled the Reapers I'd hired to keep the World Crusher from destroying Biriane, but they also looked like the failures who'd helped undo the one element that had kept her from seeking revenge against me for so long. This was what she wanted. Revenge. And I probably deserved it, but the living did not. I owed it to the universe that had made me to try and do something about this.

"You boys are in a heap of trouble," I added, measuring each of the Ghoul Reapers from head to toe. Eneas was still their leader, tall and slender, with black marble eyes and long blond hair. His brothers were like slightly modified copies of him, as only a few differences made them distinguishable from him. Fileas' features were more refined, his physical grace distinctive and unforgettable. His scythe cut the deepest, too. He was the first to speak.

"I think we've earned our freedom."

I nodded to Hadras. The scars of Tristan's handiwork persisted, but he'd healed well. "You're a mess. Thank you, nonetheless. Had you not engaged Unending's husband, I wouldn't have discovered that peculiar ability of his."

"You're telling me you didn't know he could do that?" Eneas shot back, sneering as he crossed his arms and met my gaze in defiance.

"Believe it or not, I can still be surprised," I replied dryly. "As for your freedom, it was fraudulently obtained and therefore invalid."

That earned me furious growls from Filicore and Malin, but Deas wasn't surprised. Instead, he shook his head, the corner of his mouth twitching. "I told you she'd come after us."

"You deceived Unending into setting the World Crusher free. You conspired with my first Reaper, and that, my darlings, borders on unforgivable. You've unleashed potential destruction upon the same universe you were sworn to protect," I said. "How will you repair this catastrophic error?"

The Ghoul Reapers exchanged nervous glances. None dared to challenge what I had just said, because they knew it to be true. I might have been an absolute bitch to keep them locked down on Biriane for so long, but I couldn't leave a bunch of Ghoul Reapers free, either. And I certainly did not want to destroy them, undeserving as they were of becoming such soulless creatures. They were unfortunate accidents, and I wished I had the ability to truly care about them. But I did not. There was no point in saying otherwise.

"When Unending showed up outside the Temple of Roses, you should have sent her away," I said. "But you didn't. You had allied yourselves with Anunit, hadn't you?"

Eneas scoffed. "Why does it matter? It's done. There's no turning back now."

"But there is a way to fix it," I replied.

"We're free. You can't do this to us again!" Filicore snarled, but Malin held him back. His rage was palpable, however. And I certainly deserved it.

I laughed, mockery permeating from my voice. "You must be joking. You're the ones who conspired to release the World Crusher, and that—"

"Excuse me," Eneas cut me off. "You said we'd be free only when the World Crusher was free. That meant never."

"Exactly. You should've accepted the 'never,'" I retorted, unwilling to accept reprimands from anyone, let alone a handful of Ghoul Reapers. They were my doing, in a certain sense. They were like this because I had underestimated the kind of damage World might inflict upon others while in captivity. I did bear responsibility for their condition.

Eneas smirked. "We never consented to being on Biriane forever. We answered your call for help, rose to the occasion and gave it our absolute best. And to reward our loyalty, you locked us there. You never gave us a chance." "I couldn't. The damage was already done. At the risk of repeating myself, you should have accepted your fate,"

I said. It sounded wrong, even as the words left my lips, but I was never one to easily admit my faults or mistakes in front of others, especially in front of lesser beings. There were things about me I would never wish nor be able to change. Whether anyone liked me or not, it did not matter. I offered a dignified end to everyone, but it was an end, nonetheless. Everything else would fade, including one's awareness of my existence. "With that out of the way, however, we seem to be facing quite the conundrum, don't you think?"

Hadras's lips twisted with disgust. "Of your own making, wouldn't you agree?"

"Perhaps. But you haven't exactly been good boys either, or shall I once more bring up the way you deceived Unending into releasing the World Crusher?" I asked, though I already had my answer. It was imprinted on each of their hauntingly beautiful faces. "Good. We're in agreement, then. Something must be done."

Eneas shrugged. "Do you have a solution that doesn't involve dooming us for an eternity? Because we would rather be cast into the nothingness than spend another eon with the World Crusher. Destroy us now, if that is your plan. Otherwise, we'll keep following her, unable to pull ourselves away."

He clearly meant it. There was a sliver of regret twisting in the pit of my stomach, but I ignored it. Maybe I did give a damn, after all. No. I could not allow myself such feelings. After everything I had done and everything else that I was about to do, thinking too much about these things would only grieve me, and the universe needed a sane and functional Death, not one crippled with sorrow. My likeability was always a non-issue since no one could ever possibly "like" Death, but my purpose was ironclad. My sense unwavering.

"You shall be free once I've retrieved the World Crusher," I declared. "You are bound to her. Which means you can sniff the World Crusher out precisely, whereas I can only sense her. I need your help to find her and seal her back where she belongs."

Filicore chuckled bitterly. "You'd better put her on a planet that is already dead, then. You saw what she did to Biriane."

"That is nothing compared to what she will do to the entire universe if she is left to her own devices," I warned him. "The longer the World Crusher is free, the stronger she becomes. The seal served to weaken her, not just hold her down."

"Well, then, it's a pity you can't just destroy her, huh?" Malin replied, his tone clipped. I was responsible for that, too. His fearlessness in throwing such reproaches at me should've caused anger, but I only felt bumbling bitterness, for it was the truth, and I was tired of denying the unpleasant truth of my many shortcomings. "Had you made her slightly more vulnerable, none of us would be here. You found the strength to destroy one of your own before. Tristan told us. You destroyed the Spirit Bender. You could've destroyed the World Crusher too."

I mustered a sardonic, desert dry smile. "But I cannot, so that is not even an option worth mentioning. What say you, then? Will you help me?"

"Do we even have a choice?" Fileas growled.

"I could destroy you and cast you into the nothingness instead. That is an option, since your brother mentioned it," I said. "But I would rather let you be. You've never eaten souls. Perhaps if I pair you with other Reapers you will continue to exist soul-free. I have no reason to destroy you unless you give me one."

Eneas thought about it for a while. None of his brothers spoke. Around us, the universe shifted as the asteroid hurtled through space. Stars danced across the black sky. Once in a while, I caught glimpses of rabid pink and flaming orange stardust. The glimmer of a nearby sun dying. The world would keep expanding, and this dimension would keep thriving—as long as the World Crusher was contained. I could not destroy her, and neither could the Word. The last thing I needed was for him to know about her. He would never forgive me.

It was part of the reason I'd asked Unending for her discretion. I couldn't risk news of the World Crusher reaching Word. I had told him she'd been destroyed ages ago. I'd told Order the same thing. The shame I would feel if my siblings learned about this... It was unbearable to me. I didn't care much about what anyone thought of me, but the Word and Order... they mattered. More than I would have liked to admit.

"And if we help you," Eneas finally replied, "you'll leave us be?"

"On the sole condition that you don't eat souls. So, technically yes," I said.

"It's the word 'technically' that irks me when it comes from you," Filicore grumbled. Of all six, he was the most fearless when it came to speaking to me. As bold as Spirit was, though never as evil nor as selfish. I'd had the fae brothers raised from the dead and turned into Reapers because they had died selflessly to protect their kind. I'd thought an eternity ushering souls into the afterlife might feel like the right reward for what they had done. Instead, they'd ended up as six miserable hybrids, forever stuck between ghoul and Reaper forms, poisoned by the World Crusher.

"None of this is your fault," I conceded. "Aside from your little game with Unending, of course. It would be unfair and hypocritical of me to state otherwise." And I'd been hypocritical enough to last them a thousand lifetimes already. "You have my word on this. Help me catch the World Crusher, help me lock her away again, and I shall let you be, as long as you don't deprive a single soul of their afterlife."

Eneas smiled. "Like you deprived us, you mean."

"Exactly."

"It's a deal," he replied. "We're in."

"You will risk destruction. World will not come voluntarily," I warned them.

"We risk destruction either way," Eneas sighed. "At least, if we work with you, we'll actually be doing a bit of good for this world. Our fates will not have been in vain."

And so it began. The strangest collaboration I'd ever heard of, though not the first of its kind, nor the last: I had enlisted the services of the living. I had dispatched Reapers of my realm too. But the Ghoul Reapers were strangely independent. Their mere existence demanded my respectful approach. An agreement had been reached and just in time, for the World

Crusher's presence burned through me, stronger than ever.

She was nearby, somewhere within this cluster of galaxies. I brought the invisible shield down and motioned for the Ghoul Reapers to go. "Lead the way," I said, and they did. The World Crusher was my mess to fix, yes. But I could not do it alone.

Perhaps this time around I would finally accept that I was unique, but not all powerful nor unbeatable. My own creations had proven that more than once. *Perhaps I should take notice.* In the end, I wished to be able to go back to Unending and show her that I could do better. The future had already shown me that much, so why fight it?

UNENDING

*M*aking love to Tristan was always an extraordinary experience, but now that I'd been given a living body, it was beyond that. It was something I could no longer describe with words of any language; I could only relish every sensation. The feel of his skin against mine, his stubble tickling my face. The taste of him on my lips, the way my heart raced whenever his hands explored me. The sound of his voice pouring into my ear, the strength of him as our bodies came together.

Our souls were already connected. Now our bodies could be too.

"I could cry," I whispered when we descended from the heavens and melted between the soft sheets of our bed. The windows were wide open, and the cool morning breeze swept through, making the flowery curtains dance. "Tears of joy, I mean. I could totally cry."

"I remember a few tears throughout the night," Tristan replied. We spooned beneath the covers, our feet a little cold but our hearts singing in splendid unison. "Nothing makes me happier than seeing you like this, Unending. This is true bliss we're experiencing, and I intend to make the most of it." A moment later, he'd turned us both over. I ended up beneath him, sinking into the mattress and giggling as he showered me with kisses.

Birds sang outside, their melodious trills filling the room as my husband and I could not get enough of each other. He loved my mouth with his, then trailed soft pecks down the side of my neck, peppering the occasional compliment along the way. I liked the way he worshipped me. Having a body had made me strangely self-aware, but not in a negative sense. Tristan had been quick to pick up on the changes in my demeanor, making sure not a moment went by that I didn't know how beloved I truly was.

"See this line here?" he asked, gently tracing my hip with one finger, skin sizzling in the wake of his touch. "It's the same as your physical form as a Reaper. This steep curve that goes down to what is arguably one of my favorite places."

I laughed, and we rolled through the sheets once more. I was on top this time, our fingers entwined as I pulled his arms over his head and kissed him with every drop of love I had in me. Tristan's lovemaking was as diverse as our travels. It could be wild and passionate—and he definitely had a way of making me cry out his name over and over—but it could also be sweet and deliberately slow, which I liked more because it meant I got to enjoy every prolonged second of it.

Judging by how our bodies and souls swayed in the slightly chilly breeze, I could tell we were in for a lazy morning. "I will never tire of this," I told my husband at one point, while he left wet kisses on my bare shoulder. "Tristan, I'm in no rush to lose this body. It's incredible. Everything is... enhanced."

"I've never experienced an existence like yours, so I have absolutely no idea what it was like for you before Anunit gave you this body," he said. "But your happiness is mine, my love. So yes. Let's hold on to the flesh for as long as possible. Maybe we'll find a way to get Death to help us later down the line."

The mention of her name reminded me of the blunder I'd made of the World Crusher's book seal. I sat up, wrapping myself in the blanket. Tristan watched me quietly for a while, waiting for me to respond. I was certain he could tell something was bothering me. I didn't like stepping out of sweet heaven and back into the unpleasant reality, but alas, it had been inevitable. "I wonder how she's faring," I muttered.

"Who, Death?" Tristan asked, then offered a shrug. "I doubt she has much trouble. I mean, she's Death, not some run-of-the-mill Reaper. She made the World Crusher, after all. I trust she'll finally fix that particular mistake, but I'm certain she also wants you to stew a little in the guilt stemming from what happened at the Temple of Roses."

I turned my head to look at him, nodding as I let his words sink in. "You are probably right. Well said, husband.

Eloquent *and* insightful!"

"That's what I thought, as soon as I said it," he laughed. He stood and walked to the bathroom door. What a sight for sore eyes this man was. His tall frame and broad shoulders always made my temperature spike. The way his muscles twitched with every movement made me suck in a deep breath. And the look he gave me as he paused in the doorway made my heart skip a beat. "Would you care to join me?"

A shower with my husband. I would've been a fool to reject such an offer.

An hour later, we were settled on the terrace outside, overlooking the western part of the redwood forest. I caught glimpses of a couple of treehouses, but they were some distance away. We had plenty of privacy in these parts. The birds were still competing for best song of the morning, bouncing from perch to perch. They occasionally stopped to sip the cool dew from the opening hibiscus blossoms I'd been growing in ceramic pots on every balcony and terrace attached to our house.

Tristan had brought out coffee, along with a small porcelain pitcher of milk and sugar on a silver tray. Since he could stomach liquids, he didn't miss an opportunity to have coffee with me. We sipped in pleasant silence for a while, listening to the songbirds and watching the world move below.

I leaned over the sturdy wrought iron edge of the terrace to get a better look, spotting a couple coming from the north, heading west toward the Vale. "You know, this place feels genuinely different," I said, having thought a lot about how I'd been perceiving The Shade since I'd come into a body.

"It's about spatial perception, so I'm not surprised. Your brain is processing the visual information differently," Tristan replied.

"Yeah, but... there's more to it, I think," I murmured. The couple I'd been watching seemed strange. They were holding hands, but there was nothing about them that hinted at happiness or love. If anything, they both looked on edge, constantly looking around. The man glanced up—a Mara, I realized as I noted the Calliope physiognomy. His girlfriend was a vampire of The Shade. I'd seen her before. But the man was startled. Our gazes locked for barely a split second before he yanked the vampire's hand and they walked away, disappearing beyond a cluster of leafy bushes.

Then a young fae crossed the clearing nearby. Chantal. I recognized the silvery succubus shimmer of her skin, a trait she'd inherited from her father, Bijarki. She was as pretty as a summer flower, wearing a short white dress with bold crimson blossoms and crude green leaves imprinted here and there on the smooth fabric of the gently flared skirt. Much like the Mara before her, she looked up at our treehouse.

"More to it?" my husband asked.

"Look down," I told him, and he followed my gaze.

I smiled and waved at Chantal, but she only gave us a faint smirk and kept walking, suddenly stiffer and in an apparent rush to be somewhere. "That's odd," Tristan said, his brow slightly furrowed.

"Right?" I replied. "It's not just me, then."

"Everybody has been checked and accounted for since the clone incident, and the portal is usually closed. It's only opened with Derek and Sofia's supervision," he said. "Maybe they're all on edge? I know I certainly would be if my home were attacked and someone replaced my loved ones with clones."

I gave him a skeptical look. "You think their odd behavior is the result of trauma?"

"What else could it be?"

That was a good question, and it triggered a thought that hadn't occurred to me before. I had been so busy being in love with Tristan, eager to enjoy my new condition, that I hadn't considered the simplest method to double check the situation in The Shade. The living could lie, but the dead were mine for the truth. Except that I'd lost my connection to the Reapers and Death. The downside of having a body.

"Hold on, let me try something." I pressed the call button on my earpiece. A few yards away, more familiar faces moved through the woods. Some wore cold smiles—the devious kind that made me wary. Others were completely lacking in any form of expression. I wasn't sure which worried me more. "Esme, are you there?"

Her voice came through quickly. "Yes. Unending? Is that you?"

"My first time on the comms system," I chuckled. "Listen, could you do me a favor?"

"Anything for you!"

Tristan frowned as he observed some of the people walking right past our redwood. I heard a distant laugh—it held the harsh edge of mockery, rather than the warmth of light humor. I'd learned the difference throughout my years, especially around the Shadians.

"Could you reach out to the Time Master for me?" I replied. "I can no longer connect to my siblings, if you remember."

"Oh. He's not around, but I'll definitely send word," she said.

"What about Sidyan?"

"He's out, too."

"Kelara?"

"On a mission, I think," Esme replied. The more she told me, the tighter my muscles became, my hands balling slowly into fists.

"And the Soul Crusher?"

"I think he was due to come back to The Shade soon enough, but I'm not sure," she blurted. It bothered me.

I shook my head slowly. "Kelara never goes on missions away from Soul," I said, though mostly to myself. "What about Nethissis or Seeley? Weren't they supposed to be around as well?"

"Yes, but they left," Esme sighed. "We're sort of Reaperless for a couple of days. Something ordered by Death, if I remember correctly. You know they don't always share where they're going."

She was right about the lack of transparency, but what mission could Death have for my siblings, considering she was far away, hunting the World Crusher? Something didn't make sense, and my instincts began to flare up like firecrackers. Pop, pop, pop, my mind snapped as I looked to my husband. "Babe, there's something wrong here," I said, after turning my earpiece off. Blood rushed through my veins, perhaps a little too fast. It made me tremble. This was fear. I had never felt fear like this before. It came with the realization that I was vulnerable. No longer the powerful Reaper.

"What do you mean?" he asked.

"I don't know, but it doesn't feel right," I replied, getting up. The taste of coffee was suddenly too bitter. Something was going on, and until we figured out what it was, I could no longer enjoy the perks of being alive. I tried my best to explain every sensation I'd been dealing with since we'd arrived. To my relief, Tristan understood.

He took my hands in his, squeezing firmly. It helped ease some of the shivers. Even the birds had stopped singing, I realized. It was as if nature itself understood something I clearly didn't. "You may have noticed something I wouldn't have because I'm desensitized," he said. "Maybe you're more receptive to everything around you because you're still adjusting to your body. It could very well save both our asses in the end."

"But what are we dealing with? Why are they acting so strangely?" I replied. "If the people are all accounted for..."

"We'll look into it." He stood, looking worriedly around. "For the time being, I think we should go downstairs and stock up on a few things from the safe."

"You mean weapons?"

He nodded. "Might as well be on the safe side."

"You think there are still clones here?"

"I won't exclude the possibility, which means the two of us are in serious danger. But I don't want you to make a radical decision until we confirm," he said. I knew what that meant. He wished for me to hold on to my body for as long as possible.

We rushed downstairs, and Tristan punched the secret code into the safe's number pad. I heard the click of the lock opening, followed by the shuffling of metallic objects and glass. We each had a backpack to fill with a variety of portable weapons—throwing stars, smoke bombs, and short-radius grenades. I fitted a pair of long knives in holsters across my back, leaving my scythe visibly hung from my belt. Tristan had been kind enough to procure me a couple of nicely fitted GASP uniforms to wear. I wasn't a Reaper anymore, technically speaking, but I was still an ally.

"It could all just be in my mind," I said, while Tristan loaded his bag with pulverizer pellets and double-checked a pulverizer weapon before handing it over to me. I'd already slipped about fifty reload units into my backpack. That meant a hundred shots. It was all very unusual for me since I'd always had my scythe and death magic to rely on, but I had seen Tristan and the other Shadians use their weapons so many times. I already knew what every item from my husband's safe did. "Maybe I'm overstimulated and overreacting, I don't know."

"Or you're on to something. Like I said, I didn't like the behavior of some of the people we saw this morning either."

My husband was everything to me, and I was the one who was truly able to protect him—or, I had been, until I'd been given this body. The tables had turned, and Tristan took it upon himself to keep me safe. He wanted me to hold on to this life, to make the most of it and not throw it away for anything. But if push came to shove, we'd both agreed I'd immediately jump out and sacrifice my flesh to be Unending again. *If push comes to shove. You're not there yet.*

"How do we go about this?" I asked. My husband knew The Shade best. If anyone could sneak around unnoticed, it was him. "How do we figure out what's wrong here without setting off any potential alarms?"

I thought about last night's dinner. For a moment, I imagined that Esme and Tristan's parents had been clones all along. Kalon, too. Derek and Sofia. What if we'd walked into some kind of hell and didn't even know it? The mere thought horrified me. Yes, it was too soon to jump to that conclusion. Further study was desperately needed because I couldn't cope with the dread of having fallen into such a heinous trap. I needed to know one way or the other.

"We should get out of anyone's sight, first," Tristan suggested. "South, deeper into the redwoods." He showed me a pair of hi-tech binoculars. "I borrowed these from Phoenix's prototype locker back at the base. These babies will allow me a longer range of vision, since we don't have a sentry friend we can rely on right now."

"Assuming they're all clones, you mean," I murmured, once again horrified by the prospect.

"It's going to be okay," Tristan said, smiling. "We'll figure this out."

A knock on the door startled us both. My husband looked at me first, then calmly proceeded to close the safe and put his backpack on. He kept the pulverizer weapon in one hand, locked and loaded, as he walked over to the door and opened it.

Esme beamed at us both. "Hey, lovebirds! Good morning!"

"Morning, sis," Tristan replied with a broad smile, while I measured his sister from head to toe. She frowned at his weapon.

"What are you doing with that?" she asked.

"Just cleaning it," Tristan replied. I could only imagine what was going through his mind at this point. If this were his sister, I imagined he'd be relieved but deeply embarrassed that he'd basically overreacted by whipping out the big guns. If this wasn't Esme, however... it meant she had been taken. Or worse.

"Cool. So, I was thinking. Since, you know, you and your gorgeous wife are already getting suspicious," Esme said, her matter-of-fact tone a disturbing contrast to her words, "that we might as well get it all out in the open now. It's the polite thing to do."

My blood ran cold.

In an instant, Tristan roared and brought his pulverizer weapon up. Esme giggled as he fired two shots. Nothing happened. Each time, we only heard the clicks. "We disabled every pulverizer weapon on this island," she said. I grabbed my scythe and tried to slash her, but she bent backward out of the way, then kicked me in the stomach. I ended up on the floor, pain searing through my torso from her blow.

I didn't even see how Tristan was subdued, but when I looked up, Esme's clone was on him, his hands bound behind his back. "I'd have given it a few more days," she said. "But I should have known from the looks you were giving us last night that you were on to something. Consider me impressed, since no one else has figured it out."

"You're not going to get away with this," I hissed and scrambled back up. I'd lost my scythe, but I still had two long knives I could work with. As soon as I unsheathed them, Kalon's laughter boomed throughout the entire treehouse. He came down the stairs, while I tried to figure out how he'd gotten in—maybe we'd left a window open or something. I hadn't heard any glass breaking.

"But we already have," Kalon's double said. "Come at us with whatever weapons you'd like. You're mortal, Unending. You're weaker than Tristan now, and... well, look at him."

I did. My husband was furious, a vein throbbing angrily down his temple, but he was helpless. Esme's clone had done a fine job of immobilizing him quickly. That must've been the reason for her ridiculously blunt approach. She'd gone for the shock factor, and it had worked.

"Taeral, can you hear me?" I called out through the comms piece. If the whole island was infested with clones, I couldn't reach any of them. But I could still get to Taeral and anyone else outside The Shade. I wondered where my siblings really were. The clones had copied everyone living, but they had yet to produce doppelgangers of Reapers. It worried me deeply.

Nothing came through the comms system, though.

"You know we would never have allowed you to communicate with the outside world," Esme's clone muttered, shaking her head in dismay as if I'd disappointed her somehow. "Thought you'd be smarter than this."

"Wait, Esme and Kalon were on Visio when this whole clone debacle started," I said, my mind working incredibly fast. "How are you here? How were you made?"

"All that was needed was a bit of hair left behind," Esme's copy replied dryly. "Our originals left plenty of their DNA behind in their redwood cabin. You really aren't as bright as we've been led to believe..." She sounded disappointed.

"Now, now, darling. Be nice. Unending has been through enough," a familiar voice oozed into the living room. I found myself transfixed, utterly paralyzed at the sight of Anunit walking into our treehouse. Only, she looked different. Slightly but fundamentally different, which was an odd observation, but it was the only one that made sense.

"Anunit," I managed, feeling my eyes widen at the sight of her. "I don't understand..."

"That's because you haven't been paying attention," Anunit replied dryly. My hands trembled, making it harder for me to hold on to the long knives. Our pulverizer weapons had been tampered with. Somehow, the clones had hijacked the safe. Tristan's was on the floor. Mine had been left by the safe. Both seemed to laugh in my face. I had been a fool. I wasn't sure I could even perform any death magic that might protect me and my husband. I'd lost my scythe.

"Your eyes," I said, trying to understand why they weren't holding galaxies anymore but wild and peculiar blue fires. I was a complete stranger to this picture, and no one was kind enough to explain things to me. "Your eyes are—"

"Back to normal, thank the stars," Anunit replied, almost laughing. "You have no idea how difficult it is to conceal one's true nature, especially for creatures of Purgatory."

It hit me then, where I'd seen the blue flames before. The golden hair. The slightly shimmering skin I'd initially assumed to be a marker of whatever species Anunit had belonged to prior to dying.

"What's going on?" Tristan grunted, struggling with his restraints. It made Kalon's clone smirk, and I would've liked nothing more than to cut off the bastard's head.

"She's a Valkyrie," I murmured, trying to wrap my head around the monumental deceit into which my husband and I had been pulled from the very beginning. Death didn't know. She couldn't have known. She would've told us. No, Anunit had played us remarkably well. The implications that followed caused heat to burst in my throat, dread clutching my heart painfully—she'd come across as a Reaper to the point where we'd been able to track her as one. The magic and effort required to pull something like that off was unbelievable. "A being of Purgatory."

Anunit grinned broadly. "And Unending gets the prize, it seems."

"She's not a Reaper," Tristan joined my conclusion.

"I never was," Anunit shot back, visibly pleased with herself. "But I made you all believe I was. Death included. It took considerable effort and combined spells, but hey, I pulled it off!" Her good humor didn't mask the horrific situation we found ourselves in. This had been her plan since day one. The quests. The living body. The revelations. It had all been a part of her agenda. Tristan and I had been the marks, and I knew... I knew my body served as a trap.

It broke my heart to finally understand every decision that had brought us here. We couldn't have known. Anunit had played this entire sequence, and our complicated relationship, the strife with Death... Damn, she'd gotten the best of us.

"And for the record, my name's not Anunit. It's Hrista," she said. "The real Anunit is no longer available, I'm afraid. Hasn't been for a very long time. Locked away for the sake of this whole project. The details are pretty boring. And you two are right where you need to be, so I hope you aren't in a rush to go anywhere."

It wasn't a real hope expressed, nor an invitation. It was a statement. A Valkyrie had fooled us, and we were now her prisoners. I had no idea how this would end. I only knew the body I loved and had worked so hard for had suddenly become my prison.

UNENDING

Tristan and I were taken to a cell somewhere deep in the redwood forest. Ironically enough, it was just where he'd suggested earlier as a good hiding place. A structure had been erected here, made entirely of steel and concrete. There were bars on the windows, but I could at least feel the breeze on my face.

"You should make yourselves at home," Hrista said, nodding at the double bed against one wall. There were twin nightstands, a table and two chairs present, along with a trunk of clothes. We also had access to a small bathroom, and I'd already spotted the fruit and blood vial basket she'd left for us on the table. The bitch was thoroughly prepared. "You'll be here a while."

"What's the point of all this?" Tristan asked. "It's obvious you're behind the clone invasion, but how'd you pull this off? Where are the others?" His rage simmered beneath the surface. I couldn't blame him. We were in a truly awful predicament, and I had no idea how to get us out of it. There was so much we still didn't know. "My sister, my parents, what did you do with them?"

"Oh, they're somewhere safe," Hrista replied. "Locked away forever. I needed the whole island, and they never would've gone quietly. I'm not one to support unnecessary bloodshed, however, so here we are." The hypocrisy did not go unnoticed, at least from where I stood, but there was so much she had yet to tell us. I couldn't risk her shutting down, not while I still had a chance to probe for more information.

"But why? What is this all about?" I asked, gripping the steel bars that kept us imprisoned. The walls were covered in death magic runes and other foreign symbols. Naturally, Hrista would've taken many kinds of precautions to keep us submissive while in captivity. "I don't understand why you had to drag me into whatever this is."

Hrista sighed, giving me a look of genuine contempt. I was meant to feel stupid and inadequate, yet I couldn't be bothered. I could only stare at her in disbelief, trying to remember every interaction we'd had, wondering if there had been any signs of such colossal deceit. Something both Tristan and I might have missed. But there was nothing. She'd played us impeccably well. "I needed you off the gameboard, honey. Isn't that obvious? You're Death's first... well, second. You're powerful and capable. I cannot risk you stomping all over my plan. Not after I've worked so hard to turn it into a reality."

Esme and Kalon's clones had retired a couple of steps back, but I could still see their expressions. They seemed in love with one another, and that was pretty much the only genuine aspect about them. They were copies. Frauds. Exquisitely crafted, just like Taeral and Eira had said, but frauds. Tristan had bought their lie from beginning to end, and it was a miracle I'd even noticed the minor discrepancies and fleeting looks. But even after I'd spotted the differences, I hadn't interpreted the details properly. The longer I dwelled on it, the more foolish I felt. This wasn't how it would end. I wouldn't let it.

"Who are you, exactly, and why did you do this to me?" I asked, pointing at my body.

Hrista inched closer, but I saw no hate in her eyes. Just pity. It angered me more than anything else. "I'm the one who's going to tear it all down and prove that the forces of the universe are inadequate and incapable of fueling it any further. The Word. Death. Order. They're terrible. One by one, I will help them prove it."

"You're a foot soldier, just like the rest of us," I replied. "And you're not the first nor the last to think you can do better than them."

"Right. You know one such enterprising soul, don't you? The Spirit

Bender?"

Chills ran down my spine. "How did you know about him? How did you know about any of this? Beings of Purgatory aren't supposed to leave that realm."

"Oh, damn..." Tristan muttered, suddenly realizing something. "Remember... remember on Visio, before he was defeated—Spirit said something about a "her," someone he'd spoken to from beyond the curtain!"

Hrista chuckled. "You're a smart cookie. I like you, Tristan. Even though you betrayed me by trying to capture me after I gave your wife that gorgeous body. Normally, I would've killed you without batting an eye, because I don't generally forgive betrayal. But I need you and Unending alive. I need you both to understand that the entities we worship, they're nobodies. They're frauds with way too much power, and they do not deserve leadership over this world and its dimensions!"

"So, this is just you being pissed off about Spirit, isn't it?" I cut her off, crossing my arms. I couldn't hide my contempt, not when her broken heart was insultingly obvious, now that I'd made all the right connections. "Your lover is gone, and now you're trying to upend the world and the natural order of things? You don't belong here, Hrista. You never will. Give up now and go back to Purgatory. This will end badly for you either way, but the longer you stay in this realm, the worse your demise will be."

"You sound awfully serious, considering you're nothing but a meatsuit now," she retorted, leaning forward. "Let me tell you something, Unending. It takes a certain skill and dedication to pull off what I've accomplished. One by one, the leaders will fall. Death. The Word. Order. Each of them will be revealed as the weaklings that they truly are. We're the gods, Unending. We're the ones with the power, the real power! Think about it! You can make people immortal! One of your brothers can manipulate the flow of time! There are witches in these realms that can build new worlds from scratch! But we're all slaves to the entities that supposedly rule us. How pathetic is that?"

I shook my head, stealing a brief glance at Tristan. "We need law, and we need order. You're too deranged to serve as any form of authority, Hrista."

"And you're never going to leave that body unless you wish to move on into the afterlife," Hrista hissed. I must have struck a nerve, because she'd just revealed a disturbing detail of my condition. I was still shaking, but by gripping the steel bars I'd managed to gradually reduce the tremors. Tristan paced the cell behind me, the balls of his heels thudding gently against the stone floor. He was trying to think of a way out of this mess, though I wasn't sure how that would work. Hrista had played us superbly into this corner.

"This was a trap from the moment you saw me, wasn't it?" I asked, though I already knew the answer. It made her smile.

"I deliberately made myself known to Death. I knew she'd send you after me. You are her strongest, the one they know little about out there. It made sense," Hrista said. "Playing Anunit was easy, if I'm honest. Keeping a straight face while you walked right into it was the only real challenge. This body is your temple. You're sealed in there. You cannot simply renounce it."

"You lied to me."

"Obviously. And you bought it. I can't blame you. You had hope. For that, I do apologize. Think about it this way, though. You're a mortal now, but Tristan could turn you into a vampire. Wouldn't that be cool? You'd still live forever."

"But then she might still die," Tristan snapped.

"And die she will," Hrista shot back with a cold grin. "She will never be a Reaper again. I've combined my knowledge with Spirit's, and I have found a way to send a Reaper's soul right into Purgatory, provided a certain set of conditions are met."

"Let me guess. I've met them," I sighed, lowering my gaze for a moment.

She nodded once. "Yes. Rest assured, it's for the best. I'm keeping you alive because your voice can still reach the entire universe, Unending. Soon you'll understand what it is I'm doing, and why it's important that I do it. We have been tormented by stupid rules and restrictions for too long. You stay in your little square, and I will stay in mine. Heaven forbid I might like you enough to follow you elsewhere... No!" She slammed a fist against the steel bars, and the entire cell shuddered. Clouds of dust fell from the ceiling cracks above. "No. That's not allowed. No feelings. No desires. No fraternizing. No, no, no! Order is making a mess out of Purgatory with her stupid rules... It was so easy to draw the Berserkers out of there. Death is making fools out of each of you on a daily basis. And don't even get me started with the Word, that stuck-up, nonexistent bastard. We could do so much better without them. And I'll make it happen."

"You don't have what it takes to topple the universe, Hrista," I said, trying to stay calm and reason with her. She clearly didn't understand the damage she'd already done to herself. But my words made Hrista laugh, almost hysterically.

"Oh, honey... you've been away for too long. I won't be the one doing the toppling. It'll be you and everyone else," she said. "We'll start with Death. I've already shown you what a self-centered hypocrite she truly is. The lies she has told you. The secrets she has kept. Not to mention what she did to the World Crusher. This is going to be such a fun ride."

Tristan came to my side, glowering at her. "I get it, you've got a bone to pick with Death. I assume it's got something to do with how she ended the Spirit Bender. But what's your beef with The Shade?"

"You were complicit," she growled. "You deserve to live out the rest of your days in misery, unable to ever leave the limbo I've built for you. Well, not you, per se, but your people. I almost thought I wouldn't trap Esme in there, but hey... stupid is as stupid does. You were all so easy to manipulate in one way or another." "The GASP federation won't let you get away with this," my husband replied.

Again, Hrista laughed. "I've already taken over The Shade and they are none the wiser. By the time someone does figure it out, it will be too late. Besides, I didn't bring you down here to share every stage of my ample project with you. I only want you to stay put and survive so that you may see what anyone can accomplish with enough ambition and desire to defeat the gods themselves! Death has already been dealt her crippling blow. The World Crusher is free... and that will prove a massive problem for the Word, too."

It was here that she had me baffled. Part of me already suspected why, but I needed her to say it out loud. "Why?" I asked.

"The World Crusher cannot be destroyed. Not by Death. Not by the Word. I doubt even Order can do anything to her. Death gave her first Reaper way too much power. She'd probably envisioned making herself a partner, but she ended up treating her as a daughter, an underling. And just like neither Death nor Order can kill the Word, and just like neither the Word nor Order can kill Death, and just like neither Death nor the Word can kill Order... they cannot destroy the World Crusher. It's why Death had her sealed in that book. Well, that and the indisputable truth that Death is stupidly sentimental and barely capable of destroying her own creation. Or is it pride? I could never really tell."

Tristan scoffed. "She destroyed the Spirit Bender. We know she can do it if she absolutely has to."

"Not with the World Crusher, she can't," Hrista said smugly. "Anyway, you two lovebirds settle in. Make this your home for a while. Feel free to make some babies too. I can have someone fetch your husband the vampire cure for that. This is the precious Shade, after all. We've found everything here. We've read and seen everything, too, including all that footage Isabelle's clone hid. It was left behind in the Great Dome after the switch. For days, we've been pretending to be the real deal, and no one has figured it out. Even Nova, that undergrown Daughter—she has yet to catch on. You see, without actively searching for her sisters, she won't immediately feel their absence. I have maintained a strict lockdown on this place, but I made an exception to let you two lovebirds back in. Seems like I made the right choice."

"You've been plotting this for a long time, haven't you?" Tristan gasped.

"Heh... You have no idea," she told him, then looked at me with a pitiful smirk. "Enjoy the life I have given you, Unending. It's the only one you will ever have." She took a couple of steps back, the overhead lights casting metallic reflections over her black and white catsuit, split right along the vertical middle. "I will have someone fetch you when we reach the next stage of events. It's going to be a busy week, I'll tell you that much."

She turned around and left, her figure shrinking in the narrow corridor. Kalon and Esme's clones walked behind her, and the silence they left in their wake was too much to handle. I broke down. It was a miracle I had lasted this long.

Tristan took me in his arms and held me tight, but I cried and cried, unable to hold anything in any longer. Hrista had stolen everything from me. My immortality. My powers. My very spirit. She'd locked me inside a body, in a fashion worse than Spirit had on Visio. Death would not be my release. It would only leave my husband alone in this world, while Hrista went on with her sick revenge fantasy.

She'd had her heart broken. She had been disappointed. And just like the Spirit Bender, she was proud and vicious enough to believe she was entitled to a better outcome. I wasn't sure how we were going to beat her, but... "We'll figure it out," Tristan whispered, while my tears trickled down his shoulder. We no longer had our telepathic connection, but we knew each other well enough to understand our common mindset. "We'll figure it out, Unending."

"How? We're trapped here. She doomed me..."

"No. She put limits on you. Death is still out there," Tristan said. "Whatever Hrista is planning, the rest of the world doesn't know it yet. Taeral had no idea. The rest of GASP know nothing about this, for sure, otherwise this whole place would've been surrounded by now. I don't care what Hrista can do as a Valkyrie, she's not limitless."

"Death is," I murmured. "Sort of. We need to get out of here..."

"We need to gather our thoughts, first and foremost," he said.

And he was right. We needed to take deep breaths and collect our thoughts. We needed to go over every event and decision that had brought us here, and we needed to assess all that we had learned so far. There was a way out of this cell. There was a way out of The Shade, too. Death was out there searching for the World Crusher, who clearly had a part to play, too. I would reach her, one way or another. I only needed my scythe back and the handful of death magic I still remembered to help us get where we needed to go.

But Hrista had my scythe. *Damn it...*

ASTRA

"This doesn't make sense." I'd said it before. Perhaps if I said it again it would make sense. But nothing changed. The truth was all around us—bright white and enriched with shades of gold, silver, copper, and bronze. I'd brought our crew to Purgatory, and I had no idea how.

Clearly opening shimmering portals wasn't just about the actual splitting of space and stepping from one dimension to another. It was also about learning to choose where to go, and I had left that part out entirely. No one else had thought it would be an issue, either, but how could they have? We weren't experts in shimmering portals. Hrista was, and she had taken over my island.

"It's wonderfully weird," the Time Master sighed, staring at our sparkling surroundings. The hilltop was covered in a soft layer of coppery grass. A tall forest of odd trees skirted the mound, their bark chalk white and their leaves crunchy and bright gold. Their rustling sounded metallic in the delicate wind. "The sky seems made of diamonds." Aphis, his ghoul, was stunned, his big black eyes getting bigger as he tried to take it all in.

We looked up, breathless for a moment and stunned by the iridescence. A sun wasn't needed here. The sky shone vividly enough to illuminate everything. Myst smiled broadly, a warm familiarity taking over her expression. "It's always daytime in Purgatory," she said. "There are dark places, of course—like where the Berserkers prefer to dwell—but it is always day..."

"I'm so confused. What did I do wrong?" I managed, tears glazing my eyes. As wonderful as this place was, and as much as I would've liked to explore and make the most of being in this unknown and technically forbidden realm, I couldn't. This wasn't The Shade, and every moment we spent away from home, Hrista had free reign to do terrible things. We didn't even know if the rest of GASP had caught on, or if the clones had, in fact, managed to fully replace the true Shadians. Sure, the originals had been marked, but Hrista had The Shade's resources now. How long before it would be too late to stop her? And what was her endgame? These were questions we desperately needed answers to, and I doubted we'd get them in Purgatory.

On the other hand, I did notice the effect this place had on Myst and Brandon. They seemed... different. The Valkyrie appeared brighter, her humanoid features dissolving into solid light. The Berserker grew darker, the black mist seeping through his pores and coming off him in jet-black wisps. These were their true forms.

"You didn't do anything wrong," Brandon said to me. Even his voice sounded a little different. Lower. Thicker. Raspier. I liked it, judging by the pricks that tickled the skin on my back. "You just need to tweak your destination next time."

"How do I do that? I have no idea how I brought us here!" I replied, exasperated. "How do I take us home?"

Thayen placed a hand on my shoulder in a bid to comfort me. "This isn't so bad, Astra. We're in Purgatory. It's the one place that not even Reapers are allowed to enter, yet here we are... Surely, this is better, right?" he asked, looking to Myst.

"Absolutely," the Valkyrie said. "We've been accidentally fast-tracked. We can find Order. We can tell her what happened. I imagine she'll be the first to want Hrista back here and in chains."

Brandon nodded his agreement. "This could prove to be an excellent shortcut. Why bother fighting clones and other Berserkers, not to mention psycho-Hrista, when we can just tell 'Mom' and she can spank the daylights out of that petulant wraith? It sounds like a clear win in my book."

I wanted to believe him. I wanted to agree. But I'd been dying to return to the real island for days now. I missed home and the realms that were most familiar. The normalcy and the good times. I missed the days when I'd just been a Daughter-Sentry and a bookworm, not the one creature whose shoulders carried the responsibilities of today. There was no way of actually returning to those times, but I could still take us to The Shade. Brandon and Myst did have a point, though.

"You saw Order once," I told Thayen. "How did she seem?"

He wanted to reply, but the Time Master beat him to it. "As bored and teeming with self-importance as Death and the Word. My guess is she will not be easy to find." "It's like you've always lived here," Brandon chuckled.

Jericho and Dafne remained mostly speechless, unable to take their eyes off the peculiar nature around us. The golden sheen of leaves was enough to hypnotize anyone—myself included. Except I was too frustrated about the missed destination to be seduced by Purgatory's extraordinary appearance. "Is this what it's like? All of Purgatory, I mean?" Jericho asked after a heavy pause in which the rest of us tried to gather our thoughts.

"Where the Valkyries dwell, yes," Myst said. "Illuminated and vibrant. Glowing and sparkling. It's meant to fill one's soul with warmth and light. Where the Berserkers dwell, it is dark and dangerous, yet just as beautiful. Some parts of this realm are truly breathtaking." She paused and frowned slightly. "Your presence here is wrong on many levels. I mean, it's good that we made it, but Order will not be pleased when she finds out there are living beings present in Purgatory. Granted, there's a good reason for it."

Brandon scoffed. "Don't you see? Their presence is a gift from the universe. The living are responsible for our return. For our spiritual regeneration! Every single spell or affliction we might have suffered outside Purgatory is gone," he reminded her. "It purges everything. It purifies the soul. It's a fresh start for both of us."

And for Hammer, I noticed. The dire wolf's coat was blacker than ever and yet shimmering in the diamond-light. His eyes beamed with sapphire flames, pink tongue lolled on one side of his jaw as he looked around, smiling his wolfish smile. Hammer was enormous, as big as a horse, his back broad with hard muscles beneath the thick coat, his ears flicking at the sound of every movement around him.

"He's doing great," I said, nodding at Hammer. He looked my way, as if thinking about his next move. A moment later, he closed the distance between us and licked the side of my face, his tongue soft, wet, and bristly. It made me laugh.

"I think that's his way of thanking you," Brandon replied, arms crossed as a grin stretched across his face. I ran my fingers through the dire wolf's coat. He didn't seem to mind, so I stayed close to him, honored and pleased to have earned his affection. "I missed this place too. Up to a point, of course," he added, exhaling sharply. "Reaching Order will not be easy. Time here was absolutely right to raise the issue. He was also right in stating that Order is as complicated and as difficult as Death and the Word and every other universal force out there. She will present her own challenges for us to work through. Plus, at least one of us—mainly me—is on Purgatory's most wanted list after Hrista made me skip this place. I'm expecting a crap storm, I only hope it won't affect the rest of you, too."

I understood his concern, but there wasn't time to dwell on it. We were already here, and I didn't have the juice right away to get us out. Besides, we were right where we needed to be.

"What's that?" Thayen asked, gazing out into the distance. A bright spot approached us, a white light that trembled as it got bigger, its outline suddenly clear as it jumped over a jutting bronze root. It was a horse, a beautiful horse with a long golden mane and blue eyes like Myst's. She cried out with delight and relief when she saw the creature.

"My Aesir... White Cloud!"

The Valkyrie and her Aesir were reunited as Myst threw her arms around White Cloud's strong neck and held her tight. He was a gorgeously muscular stallion with a pure white coat. His mane and tail were silky gold threads, and I knew there were wings hidden in his ribs.

"Oh, I've missed you, too," she whispered in his twitching ear. The horse was overjoyed, nuzzling her face with his. Myst climbed onto his back, and he trotted around with beaming pride while she laughed.

Brandon knew exactly how she felt. "They fill your heart with joy," he said, resting his hand on Hammer's head.

Myst got off White Cloud but kept him close, occasionally kissing his rounded jaw. "You look well. I knew you'd be fine without me."

"I'm glad you two are reunited," Thayen replied, smiling.

"Me, too," she replied, but her delight soon faded. "We have some things to figure out though, and I don't think it's safe for White Cloud to stick around for much longer."

The statement intrigued me. "What do you mean?"

"It's a feeling I have. A feeling I haven't been able to shake since Hrista left Purgatory. If White Cloud stays with me in these current circumstances, he'll be in danger. We know Berserkers are still slipping in and out of Purgatory, but we don't know which of them, or where, or when. We only know it's thanks to Hrista," Myst explained. "She used Hammer against Brandon. And now, I wouldn't be surprised if she found a way to use White Cloud against me. Or Axe, Regine's falcon, against her."

"That makes sense. I wouldn't want anyone to go through what I've had to endure with Hammer," Brandon replied, offering a faint and sympathetic smile.

Myst sighed and turned to look at her Aesir. "You're not safe with me. Not for the time being." The horse neighed, clearly upset by her words, but she caressed his head and scratched him behind the ears. "We'll be together again, I promise. For now, however, I need you to go back to roaming through Purgatory. Stay away from the Berserkers. Stick to the light. And I'll come find you when this is over."

It took a while to convince the creature to leave, but in the end, we watched White Cloud give Myst a lick on the cheek and gallop away, his golden mane shimmering splendidly in the warm wind. I could only imagine how Myst felt about all this, but I knew she'd made the right choice. Brandon would certainly stop at nothing to keep Hammer now that he'd gotten his Aesir back. The dire wolf was more manageable though—White Cloud would've stood out, especially against enemy Berserkers from The Shade.

"That was so cool," Jericho muttered, and I noted Aphis nodding his agreement too.

"Don't worry, Valkyrie sister," Brandon said after a long and emotional silence. "You told him the truth. You two will be together again."

"I know." She forced herself to smile, but it only worked when Thayen took her hand in his and gave it a gentle squeeze. The look they exchanged said more than they ever could in words, and I knew in that instant that she'd found comfort in Thayen, much like I had with Brandon. These were odd and complicated emotions we were dealing with, but ignoring how we felt would've only made everything much harder.

After a while, we all reached the same conclusion.

Finding Order was our best way forward. She could fix everything. Or so I hoped. I didn't say it aloud, instead keeping my thoughts to myself for now. We'd expected Death to work out a few debacles for us before, and we'd been the ones to do all the cleaning up in the end—well, not me, specifically, but the previous generation. And if Time and Brandon were right, then we'd have to deal with Order's fickle nature, too—whatever that might entail.

I knew the Word was more or less careless, intervening solely when he felt like it. I knew Death had secrets, and that she'd told the odd lie or two to save face, causing an abundance of trouble before making the world right again. I could only imagine what Order's great flaw would be. Clearly being a force of the universe did not guarantee perfection of any kind. It didn't even imply good reason.

The Time Master smiled, giving himself a moment to take it all in. "It's strange. My realm isn't really mine. It's just a strip of space and time crammed between the world of the living and Purgatory here. This place is incredible. I can't even begin to imagine why anyone would ever wish to leave this place."

"It's Purgatory. It's a sort of limbo," Myst replied. The gold in her armor shone brighter, as did her hair, capturing the diamond shimmers from above. "Nothing ever stays the same. This hill will be gone in a few days. A lake of silver water might take its place, or a mountain. You never know, because things are constantly shifting."

Thayen was the first to understand the symbolism behind this. "Because souls don't normally linger here either.

Purgatory is just a realm they're passing through, right?"

"Passing through, yes, but it's not that simple. A judgment occurs here. A person's deeds are measured against the life they lived. Decisions are made," she said. "Then, when the verdict is spoken, one of us escorts the soul into the beyond. We never go there ourselves."

"I wasn't going to ask," Thayen replied. "I know how sacred the mystery is to you. I wouldn't have asked about Purgatory, either, but... well, here we are. It's not like we can help it."

"No, I understand. It's perfectly reasonable," Myst sighed, looking to the north. There, stony mountains rose with sharp blue ridges covered with white powder. I wondered what it was, since it couldn't be snow. This wasn't the kind of place that produced such natural phenomena. Everything was different here, and even my lungs could tell that this wasn't regular air. It was much richer in... something, though I wasn't sure what, exactly. But it was making me feel slightly lightheaded. I liked the sensation. It made me come alive. "Over there is the last place I saw Berserkers dwelling. We call that place The Blue Mountains. I expect them to dissolve into sand dunes or something at some point. I'm not sure when, since there is no time here."

"Oh, wow," Time said. "That makes some of my skills woefully useless."

Without the flow of time, the Reaper couldn't do much. He had other death magic knowledge that might come in handy, but I wondered how Purgatory would tolerate the deeds of strangers trespassing. It was so quiet and eerily pretty, and it was meant to fill one's soul with light and warmth, but I had a feeling that such sensations were mostly reserved for the dead who crossed over. We, of the living, were being made to feel unwelcome. It made sense. Technically speaking, we didn't belong here.

"And over there," Myst pointed to the south, where a mountain rose proudly and poked a cluster of white clouds. Bubbling water poured down into a narrow stream before tumbling off a cliff into an astonishing cascade. "That's where Edda should be. It was our dwelling place the last time I was here. I assume it's still there, since the mountain has yet to vanish."

"Isn't it... dizzying? For your world, your surroundings to just constantly shift like that?" Dafne asked, her brow furrowed as she tried to digest the concept. "I'm not sure I'd be able to even keep up. It's definitely uncomfortable." Brandon smiled, and it was the warmest I'd seen him look since we'd met. Clearly he thrived in Purgatory, where his power was at full strength and his soul had been cleansed from whatever Hrista may have done to him. "When this is all you've ever known, it's actually quite normal. Personally, I have yet to fully grasp the idea of time." He paused to look at the Reaper. "Sorry, buddy. No hard feelings. I just don't see the point. I've been dead for so long, I don't remember ever experiencing the linear flow of time."

"How does it work, exactly?" I asked, while Hammer stayed by my side. The dire wolf's affection toward me was flattering, and part of me wanted to squeal with giddiness at how cool this felt. "The absence of time, I mean."

"Oh, it's not an absence per se," Brandon explained. "We may have been using the wrong terms to describe what Purgatory is like. Here, there's no future until it happens, and when it happens it becomes the past and the present combined. Everything I'm experiencing now is vivid. Everything I experienced years ago is still happening. In my mind, I'm everywhere and nowhere at once. I am standing here with you, and I'm the equivalent of thirty years ago, roaming the ruby hills with Hammer, taking advantage of a strange day when the diamond sky turned black for no apparent reason."

Jericho raised an eyebrow. "That happens?"

"A lot happens here, and in no particular order," Brandon said, slightly amused. "The colors change. The basic shapes. The positions of mountains and valleys. Right now, I'm here, observing this hilltop, and I'm also a very long time ago, in a strange era when there was nothing for a while. Not a single form of relief. Not a single stream flowing. Nothing. Just a vast and white emptiness, and all of us out in the open, wondering what happened."

"The hiccup," Myst replied with a smile. "Yes, I see it. We were so confused..."

With a better understanding of how the Valkyries and the Berserkers perceived their existence, I realized what Brandon had said earlier. It wasn't that there was no passage of time in a literal sense. It was that time flowed fluidly, and they lived through the past and the present with equal intensity. There was no yesterday, but there was an internal omnipresence where Brandon was ten-years-ago conscious, and twenty and one-thousand-years-ago conscious, but he was also here now. What we perceived as memories did not exist in this place.

"I admit, I'm fascinated," the Time Master replied. "The way you experience your existence is worthy of comprehensive study. Unfortunately, neither Death nor Order would ever allow us to fraternize. I expect we will be separated as soon as possible by the powers that be."

Jericho cleared his throat. "As much as I'm liking this place, Dafne and I are wondering, what's our next step?

Do we find Order? If so, how? Where?"

"Naturally, we have questions," the ice dragon added with a flat smile. She was well within her rights to be impatient. I'd been briefly distracted by the many oddities of this realm, but my focus quickly returned to our main issue. I kept glancing at Brandon, but he didn't seem to notice. He was clearly enjoying himself here.

"Unlike the Reapers and their Death, we do not have a telepathic connection to Order that we might summon. But we can head for the White Hall of Truth," Myst interjected. "Usually, she's there, overseeing the judgment of souls. Once in a while, she might leave her seat for a little while, but she always returns. Otherwise, I am not sure where we could find her without summoning her, and that comes with troubles of its own. Order can be quite complicated and capricious, not always the friendly type."

"We must go to this White Hall of Truth, then," Thayen concluded. We were on the same page, but everything came to a sudden halt as a dozen Valkyries materialized around us. One second, we'd been on our own, figuring out where to go next, then everything shifted into something heavy and unknown. And none of these Valkyries looked friendly.

Hammer growled and bared his fangs, staying close to me. Brandon was frozen, eyes wide and apprehensive as he cautiously looked around, measuring each of the new figures from head to toe. Jericho and Dafne stayed put, following our usual protocol when it came to meeting new and unknown supernaturals. Thayen didn't move, either, while the Time Master and Aphis, his eternally brooding ghoul, stood tall and proud but quiet before the Valkyries.

"Edda," Myst gasped at the sight of the brightest among them.

Consider me impressed! Edda was over six feet tall, rivaling the likes of Thayen and the Time Master. Broad shouldered but elegant, she intimidated through the sheer force of her spiritual presence. "None of you move," she warned, raising a magnificent trident with a silver handle and thousands of round diamonds encrusted into the hilt. Each spike was an alloy of gold and steel, the metal gleaming beneath the white sky. The tips were sharp, and the outer curves had been sharpened to serve as blades. This trident would inflict significant damage, I realized, and it was pointed right at my head. "You're not supposed to be here," Edda said upon a closer inspection of me.

"Do we know each other?" I managed, slightly confused.

"You wouldn't remember," she replied. "You were barely a babe when

I first laid eyes on you."

"Edda, what are you talking about?" Myst cut in, clearly baffled.

The leader of the Valkyries swung her trident around, shifting its focus to Myst's throat. Edda was a spectacular sight to behold, clad in gold and steel armor, similar to Myst's but bigger and richer in decorative details. Mother-of- pearl inlays in the form of stylized lilies adorned her breastplate, and emerald enamel filled the leaf patterns with a delicate sheen. White silk flowed from her shoulders, the cape weighted down by the plethora of diamonds and emeralds and tiny pearls embroidered into its soft fabric. Her golden wings stretched out behind her, each golden feather capturing the light in a peculiar fashion. Yes, Edda took my breath away. Myst was a stunning creature, aesthetically more beautiful than Edda, but the Valkyries' leader compensated through her imposing frame and the craftsmanship that had gone into her armor.

"You're to be taken to judgment," Edda said, her tone clipped and her eyes burning white with anger when she beheld Myst. "You've betrayed your oaths and Order herself."

"Whoa..." Myst murmured, momentarily speechless. Apparently, Edda wasn't up to date with the unfortunate events that had led to our presence here. I tried to speak on Myst's behalf, but one of the other Valkyries brought up her sword—its tip held close to my lips enough to silence me.

Hammer was dying to react, but Brandon kept giving him stern glances, as if to hold him back. The Berserker seemed... tame. "I think we should talk before we start passing sentences around, ladies."

"We've come in peace," Thayen chimed in, but another Valkyrie pointed a long golden spear at his throat, and the vampire lost his words altogether.

"You, Brandon, and you, Myst, are but two of those sought for treason," Edda declared, unmoved by our attempt to explain ourselves. "You and more than a dozen other Berserkers, as well as two Valkyries who remain unaccounted for, are to stand trial before Order. Your existence within Purgatory hangs in the balance. You brought this upon yourselves the moment you left!"

"We didn't have a choice," Brandon tried to explain, his brow furrowed. "I was forced out. Hammer was taken from me and used as leverage. Hrista is up to some—"

"Silence!" Edda shouted, and her voice thundered across the entire realm, heavy and dripping with raw anger. "I will not lend my ear to a treacherous Berserker. Your kind has never had much good to offer, anyway. Perhaps this instance will convince Order that you and Baldur and the whole of your violent clan are worthless and more of a liability than anything else."

Myst took a step forward, unwilling to let things end like this. "Sister, please, you must listen to what we have to say. Time is of the essence, and—"

"Are you hearing yourself?" Edda shot back, almost laughing. "Time? What time? This is Purgatory, Myst.

Time does not affect us here. Time does not matter here. Whatever else you have to say, save it for your trials."

She turned to leave while the other Valkyries closed in on us. Aphis let out a slight growl, but Time gripped his bony wrist and held him back. "Don't," the Reaper hissed. "Let's play nice." He raised his voice for Edda to hear him, while Aphis resigned himself to this apparent fate. I knew the ghoul was pretty much powerless in Purgatory. Most Reapers, too. This wasn't their realm. This wasn't our realm, either... which begged the question—what could any of us still do here, if push came to shove? "Excuse me, Edda. I presume you're a leader among the Valkyries," Time said, with a polite smile. He did have a certain charm about him, and Edda didn't seem to be immune, though she did struggle to keep a straight face.

"And you're a Reaper. Much like the breathers with whom you keep company, you don't belong here," Edda retorted.

"We must address the issue of Hrista and the missing Berserkers with your mistress, Order," Time insisted. "I would appreciate it if we didn't have to do it in the setting of a trial. Death sent me into the field as her envoy. I doubt she'd like to see me get judged for things I did not do."

Edda measured him from head to toe. "Are you not standing here, right now, in Purgatory, before my eyes?"

"Well, yes, but—"

"Then you're here, and you're not supposed to be here. Therefore, you have broken a fundamental law of the universe, and you shall be judged and punished accordingly, regardless of who your master is," Edda replied bluntly, then looked at her Valkyries. "Escort them to the White Hall of

Truth. By force, if you must."

She didn't wait for any of us to contest her decision. She walked away, the trident glinting in the diamond light and the cape pouring down her shoulders like milk, the embroidered gems and pearls clinking and dancing in the breeze. What an astonishing sight to bring such danger to our very existence.

Myst was quick to pass a few instructions around as she surrendered her sword to one of the Valkyries. "Let them take us to Order," she said, raising her hands slowly in a defensive manner. "It is the only way we'll get to talk to her, I'm afraid, now that Edda has found us."

"She's as arrogant as always," Brandon growled. "I'm not getting punished for something I didn't choose to do, okay?"

"Tell that to Order," Myst reminded him, then nodded at him. "Hand over your weapons. Don't make this harder than it needs to be."

Thayen and I exchanged brief glances. Clearly compliance was our best way forward. In the end, this was the outcome we'd desired, though the circumstances weren't ideal. We'd stumbled into Purgatory, and now we had a chance to tell Order about what had happened. We would also be standing trial for the apparent crime of being here, but that was a whole other can of worms I didn't even want to dig into for the time being.

I hadn't heard anything about punishment handed to the living for trespassing in Purgatory, but my knowledge of this realm was still limited. As the Valkyries huddled us together with their weapons and took ours away before escorting us down the hill, I stayed close to Hammer and Brandon. "Are they serious?" I whispered. We were following Edda in an angry procession down a swirling beaten path that ended miles away with a massive white tower speckled with hundreds of tiny windows from top to bottom.

"About the trial?" Brandon replied, and I nodded once. "Oh, yeah. We're a bit screwed."

A "bit" felt like a major understatement.

Alas, the dice had been thrown. The odds had turned against us, at least for this long, uncomfortable moment. It wasn't the end, however. No, we were going somewhere with this. We only had to make sure we all walked out of this place safely and with our souls intact. Hrista had to be stopped, and that was the only thing I could focus on. She was my objective, and Order was a means to that end.

ASTRA

The walk to the White Hall of Truth was painfully long. This place might pride itself on not experiencing the flow of time, but I couldn't exactly enjoy that particular perk. I belonged to the living, and I got bored fast. Edda led the way, not even bothering to glance over her shoulder at us.

Myst had made her angry, I could tell. Edda obviously despised Brandon and the other Berserkers—though I'd noticed a similar attitude from Regine, as well. Myst had been slightly more neutral, but we already knew of the rivalry between these two factions.

It was a feud as old as time, this struggle between light and dark.

The Valkyries flanked us on both sides. Two of them had been tasked with carrying our weapons and bags, but they still had their golden spears pointed at us, the steel tips thirsting for the blood of the living. I didn't dare provoke them—besides, they were taking us to Order. This wasn't the right moment to fight back and demand some kind of autonomy. Myst had made it clear. We had to play by their rules if we wanted anything done, and Brandon had begrudgingly agreed.

As we moved through the landscape, I took in more of its amazing features. It was my only way of coping with the sudden tension that had overtaken our group, and I knew it wouldn't last long. First, the Valkyries took most of my focus. Thayen, Jericho, and Dafne had a hard time looking away, too. Each of these fine creatures seemed to have been poured from a similar mold. Long, golden hair. Furious blue fires in their eyes. Porcelain skin and rose-pink lips. Spectacular armor of gold and steel with precious gemstone and enamel inlays. Long cloaks of white silk and exquisite weapons that fed on the light.

Distracted by everything new, it took me a while to notice how dim Brandon was getting.

Every moment he spent in the presence of these creatures of pure light seemed to weaken him. Even Hammer's glimmering black coat became dull. Both were affected by the Valkyries, but neither made a sound, accepting this temporary fate. I discreetly took Brandon's hand in mine, startling him. He gave me a curious look that gradually softened as I smiled. "It's going to be okay," I whispered. "We're going to get through this."

I had no idea what had come over me, but I decided to just ride this wave and see where it might lead. We were out of better options, anyway. Brandon squeezed my hand before he let go, not wanting any of the Valkyries seeing this brief moment of intimacy between us. "You're irritatingly optimistic," he replied with a dry chuckle, choosing to look away. If prior to Purgatory he'd been brazen and unabashed in manifesting his attraction toward me, Brandon had performed a 180-degree turn since Edda had taken us prisoner.

This shift did not require an in-depth study, however. It was obvious he was doing it to protect me. We were about to stand trial before Order, purely for having set foot in this place. I dreaded imagining what the penalty was for fraternizing with a being from Purgatory on top of that.

"How are you feeling?" I asked him.

He shrugged. "I could do with a little darkness right about now, but I'll be fine."

Ahead, Myst and Thayen were exchanging hushed words. I could barely hear them, but I figured they were talking about Order and the upcoming trials, which we knew nothing about. The Valkyries allowed for discreet conversation but did give the occasional violent glare of death if any of us spoke up. Jericho had been on the receiving end of it a couple of times, and he'd learned to whisper better. He and Dafne were understandably worried, but I had to appreciate their closeness—something had indeed changed between them, and it was nice to see that love could still find a way, even in the midst of this strange and woefully confusing adversity. Maybe everything wasn't yet lost for me, either. My heart was beating a little bit louder for Brandon. That much was obvious. Now I feared being here might bring an end to this growing dynamic of ours. Brandon's abrupt coolness—however protective it might be—did nothing to calm those worries.

"Tell me about the trial," the Time Master said to him. I could almost feel Aphis breathing down my neck, but I didn't mind. The ghoul was faithful and fierce, protective of those he'd been charged with. I knew he'd stop at nothing to keep us safe, regardless of the cost, though I wasn't sure how long he'd last in this realm and against these beings of light. "Is trespassing really a crime here?"

"Oh yes. Before I was made, there was a Reaper who kept trying to get in," Brandon replied. "She caused quite the fuss, according to Baldur. He's my leader. My 'father,' so to speak. He and Edda were around when that happened. Anyway, yeah. Order made it punishable."

"Punishable how, exactly?" Time asked. "Also, what Reaper are we talking about? I assume you would've said if it was the Spirit Bender."

Brandon shook his head. "He never set foot in this place for more than a brief moment, as far as I know. Otherwise we would've been alerted. Hrista was careful, so no. No, another Reaper. Much older. I don't know who. Hold on..." He shouted at the Valkyrie's leader. "Hey, Edda! What was the name of that Reaper who kept coming here?"

"You're brazen as ever," one of the Valkyries on our right chuckled.

Surprisingly enough, however, Edda answered. "The World Crusher was the name she chose for herself. Death's first."

"Wait, but that's wrong," Time replied, his frown troubled. "The first Reaper was Unending."

"Ugh, I see Death still has that obnoxious habit of lying and keeping secrets," Edda grumbled, shaking her head slowly. I didn't need to see her face to understand how she felt. Her voice spoke volumes. "Though, to be fair, I'm not surprised she wanted to keep the World Crusher's existence quiet. That girl had lost some marbles along the way."

The Time Master tried to get out of the formation so he could be closer to Edda, but a couple of crossed spears came up to stop him. He cursed under his breath, then offered a polite nod and stayed behind Brandon and me. "Damn it, Edda, this doesn't make sense. The Unending was Death's first. How could my maker have withheld the existence of another Reaper this whole time?"

"I don't know. The affairs of her realm don't really interest me. It's something you should discuss with her," Edda replied. "But just so we're clear, that World girl? Crazy evil. She was so desperate to get into Purgatory and into the beyond that she started killing people just so she could reap them and cross the threshold with them. If you've never heard of her, I'm guessing it means Death destroyed her or put her away. And you're better off, believe me."

"Yeah, it absolutely sounds like you haven't missed out on much," Brandon muttered. "Whew, talk about villainous temperaments. Oh, this reminds me. Edda!" he shouted, but only to startle her and the other Valkyries. He seemed to enjoy tormenting them in one way or another. They were like children, I realized. The Berserkers and the Valkyries were doomed to a timeless eternity together. They didn't die, and they could only hurt one another for so long. This was just part of their banter. "Hrista is making trouble in the realm of the living. She tossed the people out of the earthly Shade and shoved them inside another dimension. Then she filled said earthly Shade with clones of her own making."

It was an efficient summary, and it earned him a brief over-the-shoulder glance from Edda. "You'll address this with Order during your trial."

"Is that all you have to say to us?" Myst sighed, visibly disappointed. "Is it so easy to just turn against us and treat us like criminals, even though this whole time the purpose of everything we've done has been to come home and warn you and Order about Hrista?"

"Like I said, tell this to—"

"Yeah, I've heard that line before," Brandon retorted, then gave me a tired look. "See? This I didn't really miss. Sure, it's nice to lose track of time, literally speaking, and it's good to be back in the cradle of my true spiritual power, even if these light ladies are slowing me down a little right now, but everything else... and the way issues like this are handled? Nah. Did not miss this level of disdain and incompetence one bit."

Edda raised her trident. "Watch your mouth, Berserker."

"I speak the truth. And I think Myst finally agrees with me," Brandon replied, fearless in his discourse. He looked at me again. "Yes, Purgatory is incredible. Look around!" I did. Between the rolling hills, orchards with white wood and golden canopies grew tall and rich. Strangely shaped fruits that seemed to have been carved out of marble blocks hung heavily, almost touching the ground. Beyond, blue and white mountains rose and pierced the diamond sky, forests of gold trickling down the zigzagging ridges. A river flowed nearby, its sweet whispers reaching my ears every now and then. Ahead, the White Hall of Truth got bigger and bigger—a massive, marble tower that awaited us quietly. "Look around. It's beautiful, isn't it? 'Strange.' 'Peculiar.' I've heard those terms before today. For us, it's normal. Pretty, but normal. After having spent some time in the fake and in the real island, I guess I've got something to compare this to. So, see this incredible place, right?"

I nodded once. Brandon was talking loud enough for Edda to hear him. He was doing this on purpose—he had something important to say. Something he hadn't had the chance to say yet.

"It's the realm where souls come to be judged. Order, the almighty Order: she listens, and she passes the sentences. Justly, one might say. Always justly. But don't you dare do something you're not supposed to! Don't you dare question her authority! Don't even think about stepping outside the square she might have drawn for you. One slip-up, one innocent mistake, and you'll become the villain, the worthless soul in need of punishment."

"That's enough!" Edda snapped, but Brandon wasn't having any of it.

"No, but it's true. It's what we do here, isn't it?" he shot back. "We obey. Blindly. We do our job. And we never ever ask questions or oppose any decision that might be practically insane. Because that is what is happening here. Myst and I aren't criminals. We left Purgatory because we had to. Because we were compelled by our moral compass to do the right thing. Yet here we are, about to be punished for it."

"Brandon, perhaps you should tone it down a bit," Myst warned him.

"Let's just get to the trial," I said, in a bid to do the same.

But Brandon was too angry. "It's rigged, anyway. That's the thing. I'm a Berserker. Order will never look upon me with kindness. Maybe you, dear Myst, will have it better. But me... we both know I'm done for."

Edda reached him in the blink of an eye and positioned the middle tip of her trident up under his chin. He stilled, hands slowly raised to his sides. Hammer's first response was to snap his fangs at her, but I touched the back of his head, and he held back. I wasn't sure why I had such an influence on the Aesir. I'd only followed my instincts, but it worked. We'd figure out why later.

"I don't care how angry you are," Edda said. Our convoy had stopped moving altogether. Even the Valkyries were watching with wide eyes and slightly parted lips. "I don't care what reasons you had. I don't even care what happens to you, Berserker. All I know is that your kind were the first to go missing, and that somehow Regine and Myst got dragged into it. I blame you for anything that might come to pass because you are creatures of darkness and violence. Without Order's leadership, you are mindless beasts. Now shut up and keep walking. We are about to enter the White Hall of Truth. It demands your reverence."

Brandon looked like he wanted to say something more, but Edda's words had cut deep, and he refused to give her the satisfaction of any additional reaction from him. The Valkyries' leader resumed her spot at the head of the convoy, setting the pace for the rest of our journey. Only a hundred yards were left between us and the giant white tower.

From here, we could see the souls lining up to go in through four different sets of double doors. There were hundreds of spirits in four queues, each measuring about fifty yards in length. The lines didn't seem to be getting shorter, either. If one soul went in, another materialized at the end of the queue. "Whoa," I whispered, astonished by the view before us.

"Yeah, don't hold your breath," Brandon replied, his voice trembling slightly. "We'll be joining them before long."

There was ancient history between him and the Valkyries. Things that had happened. Things left untold. And Order could tell the tale— if only I could get to her in a setting that didn't involve a criminal trial. Alas, a criminal trial was exactly what we were getting. Maybe Order would straighten things out once we got in front of her and told her everything that had happened. It seemed like a reasonable outcome. But would she be reasonable?

Brandon's anger didn't seem misplaced, however. He was speaking from experience, and the fact that Myst didn't contradict him made me think he was telling the truth. I'd worried earlier about what Order's faults might be. Death's imperfections and the Word's lack of presence had taught me that not all forces of the universe were flawless.

I had a feeling we were about to find out.

THAYEN

I found it difficult to look away from the queues. The closer we got to joining them, the more hypnotic the view became. The only other thing that drew my focus was the fear so deeply imprinted on Myst's face. Edda and the other Valkyries stayed close, making sure none of us even thought about leaving. One by one, the spirits were being led through enormous, lavish archways and into the great White Hall of Judgment. The façade was polished to an almost metallic sheen. It sparkled beneath the diamond sky, making me squint so as not to go blind. The copper grass crunched with every step that we took—a sound I hadn't noticed before, and the only sound louder than my own beating heart.

"It's the anticipation that really messes with your head," Brandon muttered from behind me. I stole frequent glances at him, if only to reassure myself that my friends were still here, and that I hadn't gotten lost in Purgatory's judicial entrails on my own. Hammer was restless beside him, but the dire wolf didn't dare leave the line. Not when there were two steel and gold spears pointed at his throat. "That's the whole point of judgment. You've got time to stew and really think about your life and your deeds before you see Order."

"This is where the fate of people is determined?" I asked.

Myst shook her head. "This is where people determine their own fate.

That's the thing with Purgatory—it is pure and untainted by any moral concepts of the living world. Here, you feel like you're supposed to feel. If you've done wrong, regardless of the reason, you feel guilty. If you've done good, you feel light as a feather. Order simply takes all that and analyzes your spirit. What comes afterward is not for us to tell."

"But I can guess, considering she has Valkyries and Berserkers to usher the spirits into the next realm," I said.

It was still hard to wrap my head around this, but I'd gotten some training with the Reapers and their dimension. We of the living had spirits bound in physical bodies. We abided by certain laws of physics and magic. The Reapers, the Valkyries, and the Berserkers were spirits with the ability to manifest physical forms, which were in many senses similar to bodies but didn't function in the same fashion. They did not require food nor sleep, but they experienced pain and even felt love, in their own way. So far, these were the only differences I'd been able to process without much effort. Everything else required additional thinking, and that was low on my priority list as I watched the white tower swallow a few more people from the line.

"Either way, you'd better brace yourself," Brandon sighed. "Order will peer right into your soul and see things you do not wish to remember."

"I'm not sure how judgment works on someone like me or Astra. Or Jericho or Dafne, for that matter," I said. "We're of the living. We're not just spirits."

"On top of that, we didn't really do anything wrong," Jericho interjected, his brow still worriedly furrowed. "We didn't plan on showing up here."

"We'll see how Order sees it," Brandon replied. "She can be iffy at times."

I'd heard the same about Death. "Watch your tongue, Berserker!" Edda snapped. "This is your maker you're talking about. Your fate is in her hands. Choose your words wisely."

"You don't scare me. Baldur doesn't scare me. Order doesn't scare me," Brandon shot back, unwilling to yield before the so-called Mother of Valkyries. "I've had enough of you all, so if you decide I'm no longer needed, so be it. I've done my duty. I've done my best to withstand the adversities thrown at me, to protect my Aesir, and to respect the laws of

Purgatory. It's not my fault that Hrista up and left and screwed so many of us over!"

"Perhaps we should try not to argue with the powers that be anymore," Astra suggested. Much like me, she was preoccupied. Terrified would've been too strong a word, but it was still in the ballpark. This was new to us, and definitely strange. We didn't belong here. The judgment... it was too early for us to go through it. None of this made much sense, yet we had no choice but to move forward. "We should focus on the arguments we're about to make, instead."

"What arguments, Pinkie? Do you really think there's a fair trial coming?" Brandon scoffed, crossing his arms.

Being out in the open like this made him weak. There was too much light, the wisps of darkness flying off him too fast, as if wasted by the brightness. "Our arrest makes no sense. The trial won't either. Hrista left, and someone must be held accountable, so Purgatory is looking to blame the suckers who accidentally came back."

There was anger bubbling beneath the surface, a clear indicator of the history between Brandon and this place. He didn't seem eager to share any of it, but his conclusions were heartfelt, and not the result of a momentary lapse in judgment or rushed, shoddy theories. He'd lived through things in this place, things that crippled his trust in the system, and I couldn't help but wonder how that might play out for the rest of us.

I'd hoped our flesh would be key, but I was beginning to doubt such hopes as we approached the doorway. The tension made the air thicker, and every breath that I took filled my lungs and dropped lead weights in my knees. Each step felt laborious, and my thoughts scattered, preventing me from forming strings of coherent sentences.

"Order is fair," Myst told me. "Brandon may have strong feelings about both her and Purgatory, but they are based only on his personal experiences."

"Absolutely, they are. Go on, tell him I'm wrong, and it's just my perception," Brandon growled, unwilling to back down. He calmed almost instantly when Astra took his hand in hers and squeezed gently, whispering something in his ear that smoothed out every crease on his forehead. I welcomed the effect she had on him. Brandon was our friend and ally, and I didn't like seeing him so anxious and displeased with the realm that was supposed to be our salvation.

"Let us speak to Order, per the regulations," Myst said, giving him a faint smile. There was sympathy in her voice. She knew more about him and his plight than any of us, so her patience made sense. "Each of us will go before her, and we'll have our chance to say everything she needs to hear. Everything about Hrista, about what she's done to the realm of the living, all of it. We shall see then if a standard trial is what we will receive."

She seemed to doubt her own words, however. A subtle wavering of her voice gave it away. I doubted Brandon or the others noticed. She had Edda's full attention, though not for the doubt but for the content of her statement. "Tell Order every single detail. I will be listening."

I understood her position now. This was out of her hands. Even as ruler over the Valkyries, Edda reported back to Order. We were here because Order had demanded it. There was no question about this anymore. We were but pawns on a massive gameboard, and Order was playing with us—and, hopefully, not against us.

"You have to believe me," Myst tried to tell Edda, but the Mother turned away.

"Typical," Brandon chuckled bitterly. Edda may have been assigned the motherly title, but she wasn't really the Valkyries' mother, just like the Valkyries weren't really sisters. It was the idea of family that they and the Berserkers had adhered to. "She gives you an inch of understanding, then yanks it all away and leaves you to fend for yourself."

Edda scoffed. "Better be grateful Baldur isn't here to tear you a new one."

"Like he ever could."

Brandon was easily coming across as the troublemaker. The black sheep of this deeply dysfunctional "family," with a strong personality and a mind of his own. He was a contrarian, too, making it hard for me not to smile or even laugh whenever he opened his mouth. He thrived on stirring the pot and making people sizzle. Astra was receptive to that, liked it, even. Edda, not so much.

Everything faded as we stepped into the White Hall of Judgment. Behind us, the queue was as long as it had been. Every minute, another soul was brought from somewhere to wait their turn. The process never stopped. Spirits came and spirits went—the only difference being that they would never come back from where they were sent, not after this. Life had many levels, many realms through which it permeated. Ours was the simplest and most intense, enriched with a body and internal chemical reactions that generated and amplified emotions and states of mind. Death's realm was supposed to be a transient state, a five-minute pitstop for those who died. A single breath's worth of being and no-longer being before the spirit was reaped and sent... here.

"I'm not overreacting if I admit that I'm scared out of my mind, right?" Jericho muttered. His gaze darted all around us, briefly captured by one soul or another.

"No," Dafne replied, her hand tight in his. "This is terrifying."

"If you're living, yeah," Brandon replied with a shrug. He gazed at Astra, carefully analyzing her expression. "It's going to be okay," he told her. "I'm just being difficult and overly dramatic because it's how I like to be in this place."

"Brandon speaks the truth," Edda interjected without looking at us. "He loves being overly dramatic."

I glanced back at the Berserker, chuckling softly.

"Silence," a voice echoed through the hall. From the outside it had seemed huge and imposing, but on the inside, this place was simply magnificent. The walls were covered in pristine marble bas-reliefs of scenes from different worlds and with varied protagonists, from the familiar humanoids of so many realms to the more peculiar ones with wings and talons, horns and claws, thick furs, and animal features. These were snippets of life, I realized. Moments frozen in time and immortalized in the white stone.

There were images of violent wars with archers and chariots and devastating fires. There were conquests of winged men and women with armor and spears. There were births of kings and queens before whom the subjects bent their knees and brought offerings of fruits and flowers and other riches. There were caravans that crossed entire nations. Lines of majestic horses with long manes and dragonfly wings that galloped through immense canyons, ridden by fae-like men with fireballs in their hands. There were weddings and celebrations too. Bits of joy and laughter and love. Every emotion. Every single deed of the living. It had all been registered here in one form or another.

Long strands of silver hung from the domed ceiling overhead. From each, clusters of diamonds captured the white light that blazed through the tall, narrow windows. The light refracted and danced across the bas-reliefs in a dizzying multitude of greens and yellows and pinks. It was an astonishing sight, and for a moment, I did not want to ever leave this place.

"This is the only place in the universe where every single nation meets. On the walls and down here on the floor," Myst explained.

Each line had people from everywhere. Humans of Earth. Fae of the Supernatural Dimension. Druids and incubi and succubi of the In-Between. Daemons and Hawks. Lamias and Maras. Imen. Perfects and Faulties. Even creatures I had never seen before, of worlds yet undiscovered. I should have been scared in this moment, so close to a power that could make or break me, but I was excited. I only wished my parents were here to see it all. To witness this glorious encounter of life from each corner of the grand universe. I let out a heavy breath, and Myst nudged me softly. "It can be overwhelming, I know."

"And then some," I managed.

The voice that had demanded silence boomed through the hall once more, reminding me of our purpose here. "Next," she said, ordering one of the souls at the head of our queue to step forward. He'd been a man of Earth, likely European or North American, judging by his appearance. Order took my breath away.

"I haven't seen her since I was a child. I remember her perfectly though, and still... I'm overwhelmed," I heard myself whisper.

Order was the perfect blend of Valkyrie and Berserker, I now realized. She was a stunning entity with lush curves and rock-cut muscles. Her armor was a mélange of shiny gold and cold stainless steel, tongues of metal weaving around her torso and calves with rhythm. The lobstered shoulders were pure gold and covered with emeralds and amber teardrops, and a seemingly endless cape of white silk poured from her back.

Her hair was spun gold swirling down one shoulder in a richness of curls, while her eyes were the same blue fires found in the Valkyries and Berserkers alike. In many ways, Order resembled her enforcers. I recognized the leather thigh and upper arm coverings as Berserker gear. Everything else had come from the Valkyries. She sat on a massive throne made of glass, sculpted with insanely detailed filigree that required a closer look to understand the design patterns. Yet no one dared to take a single step out of line. Her sword rested against its side, hidden in its bejeweled scabbard. It reminded me of Myst's weapon, though it was a great-sword, much larger than the Valkyrie's.

Order had no need for it here, it seemed, so I wondered what it did. I wondered if it had powers like Thieron. Or perhaps it was just a symbol of authority. It didn't really matter at this point, for her flaming blue gaze was set on the man before her. "State your name," she demanded.

Her voice was sweet, but there was a sharpness to it that compelled the addressed to respond quickly and truthfully. "Eric Dancer," the man said, shaking like a leaf. He'd been a big man, I noted, with broad shoulders and meaty arms. Not necessarily athletic but definitely large-framed. I couldn't see his face from where I stood, but his tone was heavy and gruff.

"Tell me your crimes," Order replied. "I presume you know them."

She certainly knew. That much Myst had whispered in my ear. "She looks right into your mind and learns everything in the blink of an eye," she added. "You cannot hide anything from her."

"I am a man of faults, I admit," Eric tried to say, but Order shook her head.

"Try again."

Eric looked around, hoping for some kind of assistance. All he got were a few burning glares from Berserkers nearby. Their darkness was weakened, much like Brandon's, though never gone. Never impotent. Order's enforcers were always present here, watching over the procession and taking the souls away once the judgment was done. I'd lost count of how many there were, but it didn't matter. I wouldn't be in this realm for much longer.

Or so I'd hoped.

"How much longer is this going to take?" Astra murmured behind me. "Time isn't on our side. Hrista is in The

Shade as we speak, doing who knows what..."

"You forget that time does not exist here," Brandon replied.

Myst glanced back at her. "It's rather difficult to explain, but chances are that little to no time will have passed in the world of the living. Then again, it's also possible that centuries will have gone by. One can never tell with Purgatory. What matters is that we cannot stop this. And we certainly cannot rush it."

"I asked for silence," Order interjected abruptly. "One more word, and there will be a price to be paid."

None of us wished to learn what that would be, so we kept our traps shut. Jericho and Dafne were pale as sheets of paper, while Astra's skin had a familiar pink glow—she was restless and fearful. Of course, she had every reason to feel this way. Unfortunately, there was a protocol to be followed here, whether we liked it or not. I only aspired to see us all survive this moment and move past it. The Shade awaited. Justice was sorely needed.

"I am not sure what I'm doing here," Eric mumbled.

"You are here because you died. Your soul has left your body behind. A Reaper picked you up and sent you over to us. Do you not remember?" Order replied, sounding bored. It was beginning to feel like a bureaucratic nightmare, not the incredible concept of the beginning of an afterlife that transcended every belief and every living dimension out there.

"I do, yes."

"Then, surely, you remember your life and how you squandered it?"

Eric's shoulders dropped. "I did the best I could with what I was given."

"Pray tell, then. Confess your crimes," Order shot back with a dry smile. "Confess them, or I shall speak for you, and I'm sure you have already been advised of the consequences for such refusal to cooperate."

Even I was rooting for the guy to speak up. I doubted anyone here wanted to be on the receiving end of Order's wrath. Looking around, Eric was still hesitant, likely hoping someone or something might step in and stop this. But all he got was an awkward silence. He was defenseless, and this was his judgment. He couldn't escape it.

"I've stolen," he finally said. "My family needed food on the table, and I couldn't provide for them otherwise." Myst sighed. "That's a lie. Even I can tell..."

"Tell the truth," Order said to Eric. "Why did you steal?"

"Because I wanted to be rich and free. Abiding by the system forced upon me since birth... it just didn't sit well with me," he conceded, sounding more confident as he spoke. "I have taken lives, too. Partners I promised to cut in for different jobs, but instead I stabbed them in the back when we took the riches away from others."

I frowned. "What's going on here?"

"You're standing in the White Hall of Judgment, that's what," Brandon replied. "No one can lie for long in here. The air is loaded with magic. It compels you to speak truthfully. It's a slow acting spell, but as you can see, it does the trick."

"I killed five men after I promised that they would get rich if they helped me," Eric added. "Two I killed because they were in the way. Security guards. Men with families. Decent men who didn't deserve what I did to them."

"And what did all of that get you, Eric?" Order asked, the shadow of a smile settling on her magnificent, oval face.

"Poison in my drink. My girlfriend killed me and took my fortune," Eric said.

The ultimate authority of Purgatory threw her head back with lively laughter. I almost laughed with her, the sound of it was so contagious. "Why doesn't that surprise me? Word does have a way of paying people back, I suppose..."

The statement made me think twice. "Wait, the Word?" I asked Myst, keeping my voice low so as not to be heard. Everybody else stood quietly, listening. Behind us, Jericho, Dafne, and Astra were transfixed by the exchange, while Brandon looked bored. He had done this so many times, though he had never stood for judgment himself. I figured the usual mechanics of judgment still bored him, though his demeanor would likely change once Order's attention settled on him as "the accused."

"The way things happen is more or less undetermined," Myst replied with a whisper. "In the realm of the living, that's chaos. Randomness. The unwitting outcomes of cause and effect, nothing more, nothing less. But sometimes, the Word might have input. In those cases, the way certain things happen is predetermined. In situations like Eric's here, there could be talk of karmic sweetness, I suppose. Order believes the Word is often more involved in the governing of the living than he lets on. He just doesn't make himself seen, nor does he seek to satisfy anyone's demands of justice or fairness."

"So, Order thinks the Word might've had something to do with Eric's demise."

"Or he just faced the consequences of his previous actions," Brandon hissed.

"It is poetic, in a way," Order added, completely ignoring us. "But foreseeable. Certainly not a surprise. Truth be told, Eric, your soul... it is ugly and tainted. You feel no remorse for what you have done. If given an opportunity, you would do it all again, wouldn't you?"

"Oh, yes," Eric replied. I could almost hear him smiling, such was the pleasure in his voice as he spoke. "I have lived an incredible life. Beautiful and lush with riches. I ate and drank whatever I wished. I saw all the places I wished to see. I broke many hearts along the way... yes, I would do it again. The stealing, the killing, if only to experience the same joys once more."

Order didn't hold back her contempt. "Figures. Rasmus, take him. The eternity that awaits Eric is one of his own making. He will not like it, but Order is Justice."

A Berserker stepped forward and grabbed Eric's arm. He briefly glanced our way, the blue fires in his eyes turning white for a split-second before he dragged the spirit away and vanished into the ether. Once again, I was reminded that the white flashes were markers of intense emotions. I assumed Eric would receive his just desserts soon enough. "Can't say I feel sorry for him," I mumbled.

Ahead of us, a young fae stepped up to face Order. She seemed scared, her blue eyes wide while her spiritual form flickered with anxiety. I saw the blood on her white dress where a blade had pierced through, rending everything in its path. That was the trouble with the spiritual form. Sometimes, especially in particularly traumatic circumstances, it retained the violence of the body's demise, at least in appearance, after death. I'd only hoped that would fade away upon reaching the afterlife, having wondered if my dad had suffered a similar issue—I'd seen him whole thanks to Myst, of course, so I was inclined to believe that the afterlife did fix things.

"I take it you know Rasmus?" Astra asked Brandon, and he grunted in confirmation.

"Don't be afraid, child," Order said to the young fae in front of Myst and me. "Come closer. I won't bite. Tell me, what happened to you?"

"I was stabbed," she said.

Order sighed softly. "Where do you hail from?"

"The Fire Star."

"And who stabbed you?"

The girl burst into tears, covering her face with both hands. My heart broke for her. "My brother..."

Order breathed out slowly, gazing across the entire hall and analyzing each expression she encountered. For a moment, she noticed me, and the world, the universe, my existence itself stood still. There was knowledge in the two sapphire flames she had for eyes. There was truth. There was my past in its absolute entirety, no detail spared. I saw it reflected in her look, and I knew that whatever conversation she and I would soon have would change me forever. "Killing one's kin is an abominable sin. Regardless of faith and culture, of education and species, the murder of one's sibling is an unforgivable slight. Tell us why your brother did this to you," Order finally spoke again.

"I'm to inherit the family fortune. Well, I *was* to inherit the family fortune. My brother had been disowned for previous, egregious crimes. He'd hoped he would have the castle and the lands upon his return from prison, but when he found me in charge instead, he... could not accept such a fate. He'd thought the letters from our estate handlers were fakes. Bad jokes, he said. When our parents passed away, he thought he'd have it all."

"Your brother spent a decade in prison for a variety of fraud crimes, right?" Order asked, and the girl nodded once. "Well, then... I see he advanced to murder. And not just any kind of murder, either. The worst of the worst."

I couldn't help but wonder what would happen to that guy. Would he be found and arrested? Would a boulder fall out of nowhere and crush him? The world was in dire need of more poetic justice, but I doubted it would come to pass. The universe did not respond to our demands for righteousness nor to our desires. It didn't work like that, and it had taken me years to figure it out. I had also learned not to mess with the natural balance. I could easily tell Taeral about this guy upon my return, but something told me that the almighty Order wouldn't let us remember these moments, anyway. Everything about Purgatory had been kept under a tight lid until now. I doubted she'd relinquish control over that.

"Helga, please... she deserves better," Order said to one of the Valkyries, then smiled at the young fae girl, already knowing her name. "Irin, you will be fine. I cannot say anything about what follows, but I can promise you won't have to deal with that wretched brother of yours ever again."

The fae girl vanished with Helga.

"I don't feel so good," Myst whispered.

I looked at her, and the blue in her eyes had turned white. "What's wrong?"

"I've never stood before her this way. I've never been on trial. Valkyries and Berserkers are chosen before they reach the White Hall of Judgment," she managed.

Suddenly, Order's attention was on us, and my spine stiffened. "Myst. Step forth, please."

Myst gave me a terrified glance, but I couldn't help her. For the first time, she seemed lonely and vulnerable, and I was useless and scared. I would've liked nothing more than to grab her and my friends and get us out of here, but that was impossible. Astra was too tired to open another shimmering portal now, and I doubted Order would let us escape anyway.

Seeing the Valkyrie like this made my very soul hurt. She'd done nothing wrong. I could only hope that Order would reach the same conclusion. Had it not been for Myst, we never would have survived in Hrista's manufactured hell.

"So, it begins," Myst sighed and turned her back on me, facing Order.

The air thickened with a mixture of doubt and anticipation. Even the spirits of the departed, who had no idea who she was or why she had been brought here, watched Myst with fascinated interest. They could clearly tell she was different and shouldn't be here to be judged this way.

I braced myself and decided I would do everything in my power to make sure Myst walked away from this unscathed. It was the least I could offer as my gratitude... perhaps as a token of my affection, too. I could no longer deny it. The Valkyrie had burrowed into my chest and taken hold of my heart.

The last thing I wanted was to lose her to Purgatory.

SOFIA

*D*uring the Flip, the clones had taken plenty of things with them from the fake island, but they had also left a lot behind. That was our conclusion almost immediately on the first day here. It had taken us a while, but we'd managed to comb through most of the island, documenting every find and adding it to a written inventory of objects not of our making.

We'd found settlements that weren't supposed to be there, either, though we hadn't found any clones occupying them. I had wondered why these spots were separated. If the fake island had been meant as a mirror to our home, then the settlements didn't make sense. They didn't belong. Fortunately, Viola and the others from Thayen's initial crew had told us about the rebel clones who'd chosen to live out here. I imagined they'd been taken along for the ride during the Flip, too, forced to leave it all behind.

We'd also begun analyzing the villa that stood in place of the witches' Sanctuary—yet another oddity that didn't fit in an alleged copy of our beloved realm. Nevertheless, the villa was real, and it had been home to Hrista, an entity we knew little to nothing about. With Astra and Thayen's crew gone, there wasn't much else we, the seniors, could do for the time being. Digging into the enemy's past seemed an appropriate response. Unfortunately, as far as this building was concerned, Haldor had been unable to offer much insight. Given that Hrista had been suspecting him of playing the long con, Derek and I had agreed that she would've been careful with what she'd disclosed in his presence. It was our duty to search and study, anyway.

The villa itself was a beautiful structure with wrought iron railings and French windows and an explosion of fragranced flowers wherever it had been possible to plant some. A lot of care and attention had gone into the details of this place. The furniture, the flooring and the carpets, even the wall art and the cashmere throws in the lounge room were meant to make this into something out of an Earthly magazine.

"I think this fake island was used as testing ground more than anything else," Derek said. With everyone else working on other aspects of this false island, my husband and I had decided to handle studying and cataloguing the villa. The Daughters and the Reapers were conferring on ways to defend ourselves in case the clones decided to come back, while Rose and Ben coordinated with the Shadians to make sure we were ready if such an event came to pass. "And I'm not just talking about faithfully reproducing our realm. Think about it. The cabin in the redwood forest. That was literally taken from somewhere on Earth. This villa too... it must belong to a certain place back home. Everything here seems like the result of a test. Like, let's see if we can do this... or that..."

"It could be. Either way, there is a lot we still don't know," I replied. "Personally, I am surprised by how much the clones left behind. If secrecy had been their game prior to the Flip, this is just the complete opposite."

Derek's gaze darkened. "My guess is they don't care anymore. Maybe they expect us to die here, never to leave again."

"I would agree, but then how do you explain Astra? Hrista knew what she could do before any of us did, including Astra herself. We have her to get us out of here. Sure, she needs more practice, but she's accomplished something incredible already."

"Yes. That's true. But what if there is something here that we haven't discovered yet?" Derek replied. "Something that Hrista thought would end us before we'd be able to leave."

The thought had occurred to me, as well, but I hadn't voiced it. There was no evidence to suggest such a possibility. "If she is as sadistically evil as Thayen made her out to be, I'd imagine she'd want to make us suffer. Being stuck here for an eternity qualifies."

"But we're not really stuck here, since Astra is still alive, thank the stars."

I nodded. "True. But maybe that wasn't planned. Think about it. Minutes passed between the attempt to kill Astra here and the Flip. From what Haldor told us, Hrista was on a tight schedule. She missed the window to take out the half-Daughter who can open shimmering portals, but she couldn't miss the Flip, too. It was more important." "In that case, I hope Hrista is restless and miserable right now, knowing it's only a matter of time before we come after her," Derek replied with a cool grin. We were in her bedroom, a large round room with a walk-in closet and an attached study. The wardrobes and drawers didn't yield anything of interest. It was clear she didn't spend much time here. Her attire was a part of the physical manifestation of her spirit and certainly not something that could be stored inside a dresser or on a coat hanger. "We should try the study next," my husband suggested.

We left the bedroom behind and started going through the shelves first, since they covered most of the windowless walls. Hrista had gathered an impressive number of books here from all over Earth. Works of philosophy and human history, masterpieces of fiction and poetry. She'd even developed quite the appetite for high fantasy literature, judging by the titles I had glossed over. "Hrista has spent a lot of her time reading," I said upon noticing the wear on the spines of most of these books.

"Well, that and scheming, of course," Derek muttered as he went through every drawer he could find. Finally, he found something of interest, motioning for me to join him in front of the desk. It was a folder, its covers made of fine leather and with the letter H elegantly sewn in silver thread on the front cover. Inside it, there were several pages of yellowed paper with black and red ink writing, though none of the symbols and texts seemed familiar. "This is an unfamiliar language," my husband said, rather disappointed.

But my breath caught in my throat once I found a page I could understand, since it had Viola's name scrawled in our language surrounded by foreign runes and symbols. "Do you think this could be it?" I asked, though part of me was already hoping the answer might be yes. "The scheme to Viola's blocking runes?"

"I don't see any other reason for her name to be present like this," Derek muttered, checking the paper on both sides. "Regine or Haldor will know, for sure. It's their magic."

We needed this to be Viola's cure, and desperately so. The fact that everything that had happened to Viola had not also happened to Phoenix concerned me—Hrista's magic and trickery seemed to only affect the Daughter, regardless of her sentry connection to Phoenix. We'd yet to figure out why, but at least getting the runes off her would've made everything better. Viola had a certain flair in her power, a deeper insight and way of observing things, and we needed her at full strength.

"Where did we leave those two?" I asked, trying not to smile. Their animosity was amusing, though the current circumstances did not allow for much humor. However, all friction aside, the Berserker and the Valkyrie had been more than reliable from the moment we'd met. While Haldor had caused Thayen and his crew some grief in the beginning, I certainly understood why he'd had to play such a difficult part.

"Searching the woods outside," Derek said, further studying the folder. "There's a lot of stuff we know nothing about in this thing."

I shrugged. "We'll take it all back to them, then. Surely, they'll know what's what."

Derek let out a heavy breath and settled in the chair for a long moment. Running a hand through his hair, he allowed himself a moment of weakness. It was written all over his face that he was worried sick. He hadn't said much since Thayen and his crew had gone through Astra's shimmering portal. We were both concerned, but I'd kept mine mostly to myself, while Derek had said nothing about our son. Finally, he'd gotten to the point where he could no longer take it.

"What if he doesn't come back? What if Hrista..." his voice broke. He couldn't finish that thought. I wouldn't have wanted him to, anyway. It was an ugly and frightening thought, something a mother should never experience, and I'd already experienced enough heartbreak with Ben and Rose.

I caressed his cheek and pressed my lips against his forehead. He shuddered softly under my kiss, and I settled in his lap for a while. "You know damn well our son is a warrior. Much like Rose and Ben before him, Thayen is relentless to a fault. Do you really think Hrista will get him?"

"If he tries to glamor her? I worry that yes..."

"Oh, honey..." I paused, trying to gather my thoughts. He had every reason to be concerned, but neither of us needed this right now. Our best bet for retaining our sanity was to hope for the best. We owed Thayen that much. "He's got Astra with him. You know how protective she is of her family and friends. Let's not forget the dragons. I don't know Dafne as well as I should, but Jericho... Derek, Jericho will burn the whole island down if he has to."

"Hrista has Berserkers on her side."

"Thayen has one of those too, as well as a Valkyrie. Besides, remember what the mission objective is. Recon. They're not supposed to interact with Hrista," I said. Derek had often been my rock, but there were times when he couldn't take it anymore, and it was my turn to comfort him. This was one such moment, and I did not hesitate. "Babe, we'll get him back. I can feel it in the pit of my stomach. It's kind of hard to explain, really..."

"Don't tell me it's your motherly instinct," he chuckled dryly.

But I went with it. "Yeah. That's right. My motherly instinct. You bet your ass. Thayen's our third. We lost Ben a couple of times along the way, but overall we've done a fine job of raising and nurturing kids, Derek. I doubt we'll fail with Thayen."

"We did raise him well," he said, a smile testing the corner of his mouth. "Maybe I'm just overwhelmed by everything."

"Anyone would be overwhelmed," I replied, confident that he was coming back to me now. I could tell from the faint light in his eyes, glimmering brighter with every moment. He looked my way, and I felt it. The connection we'd shared over the years, stronger and more intense than ever.

I kissed him deeply and got up. "We've survived fresher hells than this, my love."

He started to speak, but the sound of voices downstairs startled us both. One male, one female, both angry and booming through the entire villa. Derek and I exchanged glances, then he grabbed the leather folder with its old papers, and we rushed downstairs. We found Haldor and Regine standing in the middle of the lounge area, a large space with sprawling arches of sofas clustered around a trio of mahogany coffee tables with crystal tabletops. It smelled of orange blossoms and cinnamon here, though I wasn't quite sure where the fragrance came from. There were so many porcelain bowls filled with potpourri, it was difficult to identify the source.

But it wasn't the Purgatory beings' presence that brought both Derek and me to a sudden halt down the central stairs coming from the upper floor. No, the three people they had captured and brought inside were the new point of focus.

"What's going on?" I asked.

"What's going on is that Haldor here is the type to beat the answers out of people, but he just doesn't know his own strength sometimes," Regine replied, giving the Berserker a stern look. She pushed the three captives forward, and I realized they seemed awfully familiar. "We found them lurking in the woods outside, spying on you. Well, looking to spy on you. They never made it close enough."

I was confused. "Wait, I know you... Ida, right? Ida Swanson, from the Vale."

"Erm, guess again," Regine shot back, raising an eyebrow.

It didn't take long to connect these particularly awful dots. "Clones?"

"We have a winner," Haldor grumbled.

"I'll show you a winner when I bash your head in," another captive said, though I could see why she was angry. The left half of her face was covered in bruises and cuts, some of her hair caked with dirt and blood. Her arms were battered, too, and dirt was still falling from her clothes. "You brute..."

"Meet Missa," Regine sighed, then pointed at the third young woman. "And Laurel. Three happy little clones who were somehow left behind."

Missa brushed some of the dirt and grass off, cursing under her breath, while Laurel took a deep breath and a couple of steps forward with her hands up in a defensive gesture. "We mean you no harm."

"That's rich, considering... well, everything," Derek shot back.

Missa tried to come closer, but Haldor yanked her by the arm. She nearly fell backward, but Regine stepped in and helped her stand. "See? This is what I mean. You can't control yourself," the Valkyrie snapped at the Berserker. The two seemed to hate each other, yet they made an exceptional team... most of the time.

"I'm not interested in coddling prisoners," Haldor replied.

"How about not breaking the prisoners, then?" Missa muttered, giving him a murderous glance before she put on a friendlier face and looked at me. "I swear, we are peaceful. There are twenty of us in total that Hrista left behind, but it wasn't an accident. We demanded freedom and independence."

I had a hard time swallowing this pill. "How can we believe you, after everything you've done to us?"

"Well, we didn't do anything. Not the three of us, and not the rest of our village, either," Laurel said. "Hrista agreed to let us loose because she couldn't bring herself to destroy us. We are what she likes to call 'non-compliant' since we have free will. She thinks that's a construction flaw."

"Free will is a construction flaw? That is beyond absurd," Derek laughed. "Free will is the single greatest thing that this universe could have given us. Sure, many of us squander or misuse it, but it is ours forever, and that is how it should be."

It reminded me a little too much of Ta'Zan's original treatment of the Faulties, but this was nothing like Strava whatsoever. This was infinitely bigger and more complex. Our enemy didn't even belong to the world of the living.

"Point is, they claim they have intel," Regine said, elbow resting on the pommel of her sheathed sword. She and Haldor didn't really fit into the design of this lounge room, but I was glad to have them around. They were both strong and capable beings, and we had a better edge against Hrista thanks to them.

I worried the clones might be hiding ulterior motives. "How can we trust anything they say?" I asked, giving Ida, Missa and Laurel a wary look. "Clones have invaded us. They've pretended to be us, and now... they've stolen our home from us."

Ida wasn't impressed with my skepticism. "You've got witches and warlocks, Daughters and Reapers, you even have a Berserker and a Valkyrie in your service—"

"Whoa, I serve no one but Order," Regine interjected, but Ida kept going.

"Pipe down, Barbie. Point is... you've got enough mojo and knowledge and power within your ranks to disintegrate us if you find us deceitful," she said. "We have intel, and we want to help. Hrista's world vision is terrifying. We'd rather take our chances with you and your realm."

"This is only the beginning," Missa warned. "Worse things are coming."

It was hard not to take them seriously. The gravity of their words alone was cause for concern. It made sense, too, that this would be merely an unfortunate beginning, and that more trouble awaited us down the line. If we wanted our son and his friends to survive, if we were to get our home and our world back, we would have to step outside our comfort zones.

We would have to take chances. Derek took my hand in his. "I think we should at least listen to what they have to say."

And listen we would. We weren't exactly overloaded with other options, anyway.

ASTRA

"Myst. What do you have to say for yourself?" Order asked when the Valkyrie stepped up, raising her chin slowly ahead of judgment. I had spotted the look of fear on Myst's face earlier. I knew this wasn't where she wanted to be. She didn't deserve such scrutiny, but like Brandon had said, it was already happening.

I only hoped that he would be proven wrong, and that Order would be fair in her assessments. Staying close to the Berserker, I found muted comfort in his close company, the darkness oozing off him and strangely soothing me with lazy chills down my back. The more time we spent together, the weirder our reactions got. At first, my internal light had made Brandon take a step or two back, but only because it was a natural response. Gradually, however, he'd become accustomed to my glow. At first, his darkness unsettled me, until I realized that it was Brandon who had that effect on me, not just this singular trait.

"Where should I begin?" Myst replied with a tired shrug.

"That is your choice. But tell me the truth," Order demanded, her golden brows slightly furrowed. A delicate shadow drew itself between them, though the blue in her eyes burned brighter than ever.

Edda watched Myst closely as well, but I didn't see any aggression in her expression, only a tinge of irritation. Leaving Purgatory was clearly a serious crime, regardless of the reason. But I wanted to see Myst prevail in this situation. We had so much work to do in the realm of the living, and I doubted we'd get far without her.

"Hrista went missing," Myst said. Every single spirit in the White Hall of Judgment was watching her. Every Valkyrie and Berserker, too, though most among the latter kept stealing glances at Brandon. I would've given anything to hear their thoughts, since their expressions yielded absolutely nothing. "I searched for her, high and low. Through the shifting mountains and across the silver dunes. In the Berserkers' woods and caves, too. All over Purgatory, but I could not find her."

Order cocked her head to the side. "What about her Aesir?"

"Whisper vanished, too," Myst replied. "Even now, I have no idea where he is, though I did find Hrista..."

Edda shook her head. "You left Purgatory." It drew a discrete twitch of Order's mouth. Humor, perhaps, because the interruption clearly hadn't bothered her. I tried not to interfere, for this was not my realm. Not my rules. Edda knew better.

"Hrista left first!" Myst snapped. "It took countless spells and asking around among my sisters and my darker brothers to figure it out. By the time I understood why I couldn't find her, something even stranger was happening. I saw Berserkers sneaking around, ignoring the wandering souls that they were supposed to collect and bring here for judgment."

From what I'd learned so far, our arrival as spirits in Purgatory was not calculated nor expected in any way. We'd simply appear in the middle of this vast wonder of a place, with no sense of direction. The realm would immediately analyze and read our souls without us even realizing it. We'd spend a while like that, wandering aimlessly, until one of Order's forces would come find us. Here, a Berserker could be in five places at once. There were millions of them. Valkyries were just as gifted and just as many. There wasn't a lack of manpower, but they weren't dealing with an abundance, either. Then again, time didn't flow here, so there was no rush.

"They were sneaking around, whispering, always making sure they weren't followed," Myst continued, while both Order and Edda listened with interest. She'd caught their attention. "But I kept watching them, until I saw what they were doing. They were coming in and out of Purgatory through shimmering portals that I had never seen before. I kept a tally of who came and went for a while, then noticed some weren't returning at all. In the meantime, Hrista was still missing, so I thought she might have slipped through one such portal. I worried because none of this was normal."

Edda scoffed. "Yet you didn't come to me with any of this."

"At first, I thought Hrista was just acting out, still reeling from the Spirit Bender's demise," Myst replied, giving her Mother a stern glower. "You knew, too. I see it, now."

"It wasn't exactly a secret," Order shot back. "Continue, Myst. And Edda, stop interrupting her. Myst deserves to be heard."

"At some point, I saw more Berserkers going through a shimmering portal, so I decided to keep an eye out for one of them, in particular. I figured that if I followed him out of Purgatory, I might figure out what they were up to." She paused to take a deep breath. "I look back now, and I realize I should have come to you much sooner with these concerns, but I worried that Hrista might've been hurt or worse." According to the Valkyrie and the Berserkers I'd met, "worse" meant becoming a shadow hound in Haldor's crew. "So, I decided to raise the issue with you, Edda. For that, however, I felt like I needed irrefutable evidence. I picked a fight with a Berserker just as he was about to slip through a shimmering portal. It got rough really fast, but I was determined to take him down. He caught me on the wrong foot, and we ended up tumbling through the shimmering portal. I found myself in the fake Shade, this strange place full of living creatures... and both the Berserker and the portal were gone. I had no way of coming back."

She went on to tell them about the time she'd spent in Hrista's realm, feeling her presence but never being able to find her. She told them about the clones and the peculiar blend of technology and Purgatory magic that had been used to build their weapons and devices. She told them about the Berserkers and the overall strangeness of the fake island. By the time she brought the story back to me and my ability to open shimmering portals, it wasn't difficult to tell that both Order and Edda were utterly astonished.

Around us, there were plenty of jaws that had dropped, everyone now gawking at me as if I were the weirdest creature they had ever come upon. My cheeks burned, and I inched closer to Brandon, hoping he might shield me from all the attention. I didn't like being such a presence in so many minds.

"We were actually trying to get to the real island," Myst ended her account of the events leading up to this moment. "I was glad... thrilled that we'd made it back here, instead. I know you can do something, that you can stop Hrista. And she really must be stopped."

Order raised a hand to silence her. No one said anything for a while, and a mild gremlin of anxiety worked its way through my stomach, gnawing and chewing restlessly until Order spoke again. Her voice echoed all the way up to the domed ceiling, making the bejeweled clusters tinkle gently as they moved on their silver strings.

"Be honest, Myst. If you were to go back and do everything again, is there anything you would change with regards to how you acted and when?" the ruler of Purgatory asked.

The Valkyrie looked at her and Edda first. She gave Thayen a lingering glance next before she smiled and shook her head. "No. Everything I have done, faulted or not, has led me back to you. Back home. And if there is anyone who can bring Hrista to justice, I know it in my heart to be you, Order."

The Time Master and Aphis had been particularly quiet until now. Hammer growled at Aphis, and the ghoul growled back, suddenly drawing attention from Myst and Order. Edda was the first to point an angry finger at the Reaper. "Keep that monster under control. We have the power to destroy him, if we must."

"Why would you?" Time replied, raising an eyebrow. "He's done nothing wrong."

"It's just playful banter between an Aesir and a ghoul, what's the big deal?" Brandon chimed in, equally undisturbed. I was inclined to agree. Unlike the rest of us, the ghoul and the dire wolf didn't have the patience nor the mental complexity to grasp the difficulty of our situation. They tended to respond to threats and delights better than anything else.

"You, Berserker, need to shut your mouth. Nobody asked you," Edda retorted.

It made my blood boil. "All you've done is treat us with contempt, from the moment we arrived," I cut in. "We haven't done anything to you. We're not even responsible for this. Hrista, one of yours, is to blame, and she's the one we're trying to take down. She took our home from us, so pardon me if none of us has the patience to jump through these hoops!"

"Astra Hellswan," Order said, and my blood froze. "Let me finish with Myst, and I'll get to you in a moment.

Edda, please, be quiet. Your anger is misplaced."

The Mother of Valkyries gritted her teeth, but she took a step back and remained silent. Myst cleared her throat as she looked up at Order. "You can do whatever you want. My soul is at peace because I know I've done everything in my power to be on the side of light and justice. Had I been able to return from the fake island on my own to warn you, I would have. I made do with what I was given."

"So, you really wouldn't change a thing?" Order replied, slightly amused.

Myst shook her head. "No. Nothing. Everything I have done, every decision I have made... it brought me back to you. I'm not sure I would've made it home otherwise."

"In that case, I accept your reasoning," Order said. It surprised even Edda, but she didn't object. "You are cleared of any wrongdoing, Myst, daughter of Purgatory. You are welcome back into our realm, with full rights and privileges restored. I believe your Aesir will be very happy to see you."

Myst laughed lightly, though there was a hint of sadness in her voice. "We've already been briefly reunited. Thank you." She bowed before Order and moved to the side, joining a rather sullen Edda. She gave her mother a slight nudge, managing to conjure a weak smile, and it hit me then. Edda was just playing the part of a hard ass. She was pleased to see her "daughter" cleared, just like the rest of us.

"Brace yourself," Time said, his voice low. I glanced over my shoulder and found his galaxy eyes fixed on me. In front of him, Jericho and Dafne appeared just as worried. "Order will speak to you next. Remember, there's nothing we can hide from her..."

"Just be you," Brandon whispered, and I gave him a smile. It was the only thing I could do until I heard my name on Order's lips again.

"Astra Hellswan. Step forth, please."

She didn't follow a queue order this time. But she'd been good to Myst. Correct in her decision. I dared hope she'd show me the same courtesy. I bowed politely and raised my gaze to meet hers. "It's an unexpected honor, but an honor, nonetheless," I said.

"So, you can open those shimmering portals like Hrista," Order replied, getting right down to business as she leaned back in her gilded throne.

"Yes. Though I have only recently become aware of it, as Myst has already told you."

"Do you know why?" Order asked, and I shook my head. "I imagine Hrista might've had a theory or two..." "She said it had to do with my Daughter and Sentry genes. It is a unique mixture that resulted in my ability.

Since she never got a chance to study me—not that I would've let that evil bitch anywhere near me—I cannot take her assessment at face value. I'd rather hear your opinion," I replied. It made her laugh.

"Hrista may have been on to something," she said. "Your Daughter nature stems from the Hermessi—either life or death or both, depending on who created the Eritopian Hermessi that made you. I'm sure you remember that whole Ritual shindig with Brendel and the likes. We heard about it all the way here." Order paused for a moment. "There is also an Oracle gene inside you, passed down from your father, and Oracles are gifted by the Word. One way or another, Death thus meets life inside you, Astra, and so does light, somehow. Don't ask me for the particulars, I'm not an expert on accidental hybrids. A world of possibilities is awakened through your creation. Opening shimmering portals is the tiniest of things you are capable of, my dear, and I hope you have a full life ahead to discover everything in your power."

I couldn't help but glance back at Brandon. He'd been the first to say something similar. He'd felt my power, my true potential, before anyone else. Even my mother and aunts had had no idea of how complex my nature truly was.

"Berserkers and Valkyries feel the strength of your spirit," Order said, as if picking up on my thoughts. "Myst, Brandon, Regine, and Haldor... and especially Hrista, they sense it. They know what they're up against. Given that you're a creature of life and light, your survival instincts will always act as catalysts to unleash the potential inside you."

"So if I wish to tap into my full strength, I must let someone try to kill me? Is that it?" I blurted, annoyed by the concept. It seemed unfair. I'd learned to accept that adversity bred great character and even greater powers, but for once I would've liked to hear someone say there was an easier way to get to the top. Of course, I was more than willing to do the work. It just sucked that I had to.

Order nodded once. "More or less. Survival instincts respond to violence and immediate danger. But you are also capable of surreal planes of concentration and meditation. Sooner or later, you'll find the formula that works best. Whatever it is, you must work at it and never stop. The universe did not plan for you, but I'm certain it is thrilled and curious about you..."

"You speak of the universe as if it were sentient," I murmured, fascinated not only by her words, but by the enormity of this whole encounter. I, a mortal, stood before Order, the ruling force of Purgatory, well past the realm of the dead. A couple of weeks ago I'd found philosophy treaties to be the most challenging among my tasks.

"But it is," Order replied. "It does not need to manifest itself or to speak to you directly, but it is conscious on a cosmic level. It sees and hears and feels everything. Once in a while, it's even intrigued by a special creature. Intrigued enough to demand its full attention. You're too small to understand or feel this, but I resonate with it, much like Death and the Word and other forces under its authority. You've got the universe's attention, Astra Hellswan. I admit, I'm fascinated, but I wouldn't dream of making you feel uncomfortable in any way. You are welcome in Purgatory, though I hope your stay here is as brief as possible. I find you innocent of any charges brought against you prior to the White Hall of Judgment. You're free to leave."

"Thank you," I replied, my mood shifting into a more positive one as I moved away from the never-ending line and stood next to Myst and Edda.

Order smiled broadly as she looked at each of us once more. Myst and I had already provided her with a good opinion. Thayen, Jericho, Dafne, the Time Master and Aphis were still mysteries, and she narrowed her eyes as she read deeper into their souls—or that was my impression, at least. Brandon had warned me that Order's gestures and micro-expressions were not easy to read, or at least were easy to misinterpret. Therefore, any impression she may have given me was not an absolute value.

Everything could change in the blink of an eye, and I realized how painfully true that warning had been when Order set her sights on Brandon next. "Step forth," she told him. "We have a lot to discuss, it seems."

The earlier good vibes began to fade away as Brandon broke from the queue and stood tall before his maker, hands clasped politely behind his back. He had the discipline of a military man, but the mischievous mouth of a rebel. He had the strength of a thousand men, yet the slender, athletic figure of a dancer. Well, the physical manifestation of his spirit had that, at least. I imagined Brandon could've made himself look different, too, but he'd mentioned once that Berserkers and Valkyries usually retained their original forms, mirroring the living creatures they had once been. It was a way to retain their sense of self, Brandon had said.

"You stand accused of many ugly things," Order told him, looking worried. "You left Purgatory. You consorted with Hrista and other Berserkers. You betrayed me and everything you stand for. Tell me, Brandon, is any of this true?"

"Yes and no," he replied calmly, though the fires in his gaze were white.

Right there, in that instant, something changed between him and Order. From the moment he'd said yes and irrespective of the no, his maker shifted uncomfortably in her chair, and I knew this conversation would not end as nicely as Myst's or mine. This conversation would lead to something deeply unpleasant, and I wasn't sure how I felt about it.

The mere thought of any form of punishment against Brandon made me uneasy. It even sent a sharp pang through my heart. Hammer became restless, though he stayed close to his Berserker. I suspected the Aesir knew a little bit more than I did, and he didn't like this, either.

THAYEN

While I had experienced tremendous relief to observe that Order's judgment was, in fact, fair and balanced, something told me it wouldn't go as smoothly for Brandon. I understood why he'd done everything, both good and bad, since before we'd even crossed paths.

Yet as he spoke, as he told Order about the abductions, the sample collections and the many other errands he had to run for Hrista, it became obvious that Order didn't like a single word coming out of his mouth. Brandon had chosen to serve Hrista because she'd threatened to destroy his Aesir—such a fate would've turned the Berserker into a mindless shadow beast, eventually drawn to Haldor, reduced to almost nothing more than hunger and violence.

"You helped Hrista achieve her goals," Order concluded.

A muscle ticked furiously in Brandon's jaw. One quick look at Myst told me she was just as worried. "I had no choice," the Berserker said, his tone clipped. "She had Hammer."

The dire wolf sat on his hind legs, mostly quiet but for the occasional whimper of distress. Order, however, did not seem impressed. "You had multiple choices. You simply picked the one that served you best."

"Yeah, I picked the one that didn't get Hammer destroyed. Not to mention me!"

I was beginning to see why he'd complained about fairness earlier. This certainly didn't seem right, and I doubted my input would do much good. After all, I was just a living creature, a trespasser in Purgatory, a fly in Order's most precious domain. None of this felt right, and the Time Master echoed my sentiments perfectly. "It's not going to end well for him," he whispered.

"What the hell do we do?" Jericho asked.

Dafne sighed. "I'm not sure there is anything we can do. We're virtually powerless in this place. Order could squish us like the tiny bugs that we are."

The irony was glaring, considering that a dragon had said those words. But there was truth in her statement, and not a comfortable one. We couldn't help Brandon, regardless of how much we wanted him to get through this as well as Myst and Astra had. Order wasn't in a forgiving mood anymore. "Brandon, you could have put the wellbeing of others above your own," the ruler of Purgatory said. There was the shadow of doubt in her voice, but the statement resonated clearly across the White Hall of Judgment. The Berserkers were cross, already cursing under their breaths but none dared to speak up. "You knew that what Hrista was doing would hurt innocent people. You chose to be an active participant in that process for the sake of saving your Aesir. That was selfish. Do you deny it?"

"How could it be selfish? I went through a shimmering portal that Hrista opened so I could save Hammer. Once

I was in that foreign realm, the portal was shut, and I was stuck there."

"You left Purgatory," Order insisted, stubborn to a fault. It angered me beyond belief.

"I did it for Hammer! An Aesir, a being of Purgatory that did not deserve to suffer or to be reduced to a mindless shadow," Brandon insisted.

"You did it for yourself," Order replied. "Because you could not fathom your existence altered by the loss of your Aesir. The losses that the Shadians have incurred because of your actions seem to be lost on you. Who knows how many will die because Hrista had your support? I shall ask the same question of your fellow deserting Berserkers, and I know I will get the same answers."

Time scoffed. It drew a frown from Order. "Hold on," the Reaper said, bitterly amused. "So, you're blaming the Berserkers for Hrista's success?

That's inane, to put it mildly. Hrista coerced them all into helping her. Brandon, Haldor, Torrhen, and every other Berserker who's currently with her on the real island."

"He could have said no. He would have been one cog fewer in the machine. He could've chosen to lose Hammer but keep a clean conscience, albeit as a shadow fiend," Order shot back. "Also, I would appreciate it if you held your tongue. This is not your realm, Reaper. Not your judgment, either." She shifted her focus back to Brandon, while some of the souls waiting in line began to quiver in fear. They'd observed mercy earlier with Myst and Astra, but now they could see where this conversation was headed. It made the spirits uneasy. "Brandon, Berserker of

Purgatory, you betrayed the realm, and you betrayed me. It's unforgivable."

"That's a bunch of crap," Brandon spat. "I didn't only help Hrista. I sabotaged some of her operations. I helped Astra's crew along the way. You cannot find me guilty for doing the only things I could do in those circumstances."

"You did what you thought was best. I cannot deny your good intentions," she said. "But it's your actions that have prejudiced Purgatory." Order looked to the Berserkers present. "Seize him."

Astra was furious. "What?! No! Don't!" She moved toward Brandon, but Edda grabbed her by the arms and pulled her back. Order watched with a mixture of amusement and irritation as the half-Daughter burst into a bright pink glow, releasing an energy pulse that threw Edda back and made the other spirits around her wobble for a moment.

"I suggest you don't do anything stupid, Pinkie," Brandon chuckled as the Berserkers moved to immobilize him. Astra reached him in the blink of an eye, and Brandon cupped her face in his hands, briefly pressing his lips against hers. It only lasted a second.

I heard Dafne gasp. Personally, I'd seen it coming. It just saddened me that it had to be this way. The Berserkers tried to get Astra away from Brandon, but she grunted and released another pulse of energy—even stronger than the one before and surprisingly effective. She hadn't been able to deliver such blows back in the real island, yet here, in Purgatory, Astra's powers seemed more... robust.

The Berserkers tumbled across the white marble floor, and Brandon laughed. Edda and Myst were speechless, much like the other Valkyries, while Order watched with a smile twisting her lips. She was amused, and it made me furious. I took my first step toward Astra to try and help her, but Time grabbed my upper arm and held me back. "Don't be foolish," he warned me.

"Pinkie, let it be," Brandon told Astra, whose cheeks were burning red. Her skin glowed intermittently, but it didn't seem to bother him. He'd gotten used to her light, or so I assumed. "It's okay."

"It's anything but okay!" Astra cried out, but Order snapped her fingers, and the half-Daughter froze, eyes wide with horror.

Brandon scowled at his maker. "Leave her be. She's innocent."

"I know," Order replied. "She is also unexpectedly powerful in this realm, and I am not comfortable with that.

Astra will remain immobile for the time being. No harm is being done to her."

This was a thousand kinds of wrong, yet we were all helpless before the queen of Purgatory. She was as powerful as Death, and as important in this universe. The rest of us were tiny drops on a cosmic canvas, too small to even count, yet Astra still stood out with her resilience and power. Order's stunning magic held her back, but it did not stop her from grunting and muttering through trembling lips. "You're wrong..." she managed.

"Brandon, Berserker of Purgatory, you are hereby banned from this realm," Order said, unbothered by the unexpected turn of events. The Berserkers were back on their feet, and they grabbed Brandon, twisting his arms behind his back. Hammer tried to defend him, but he was quickly stunned with a little bit of Purgatory magic. The dire wolf squealed, and the sound pained my heart. "You shall not dwell here anymore, yet you shall not move on," Order added, her tone heavy and firm. "You have not earned the right to walk into the afterlife. We shall see if you ever will."

She snapped her fingers, and a wisp of pure darkness burst from Brandon's chest. He exhaled sharply, eyes wide with astonishment as he tried to understand what was happening.

Edda knew. "The connection to Purgatory has been severed."

"Brandon..." Astra mumbled against the stunning spell, a tear rolling down her cheek. Brandon took a few moments to gather his thoughts, likely studying his own reaction as he tried to figure out what had been done to him. From where I stood, nothing had changed, yet I imagined the Berserker felt it. His brothers moved back, saddened by the rupture that had been caused. They let him be, and Hammer was released from his paralysis as a result. The dire wolf bolted straight to Brandon as he dropped to his knees and nuzzled him with his black nose, then licked his face. "It's okay, boy, it's okay," he told Hammer. A smile tested the corners of his mouth. He glanced up at Order, slowly standing up. "It doesn't matter what you do to me. It's not as bad as what Hrista put me through.

Almost losing Hammer broke me. Banishing me from Purgatory? That's a treat."

"Well, at least you're quick to adjust," Order muttered. Her fingers wiggled on the sculpted armrest of her throne—one of two winged Valkyrie figures that had been blended into the overall structure of gold and white marble. Astra cried out, suddenly released from the stunning magic.

"You're awful!" the half-Daughter croaked, her breath ragged as she tried to recover. No physical harm had been done, but the rage inside her was bubbling, ready to spill over. "You are absolutely awful. Brandon has been loyal and good this whole time. Kind and helpful, too. Perhaps not the easiest personality, but he tries!"

That drew a soft chuckle from the Berserker.

But it angered Order. "You speak to me of goodness in a Berserker? Do you even know who he truly is?" When

Astra didn't answer, she huffed with indignation. "Figures. Why would he tell you?" She looked to Myst. "And you? You never told her? Did you not see that she was falling for a Berserker? Did you not think to prevent such a tragedy?"

I didn't even register the guilty expression on Myst's face until she spoke. "Brandon has been a valuable and reliable ally," she tried to say, but Order groaned and waved her away.

"Spare me!" she snarled and moved her focus back to Astra, while Brandon seemed to shrink and darken behind her. It struck me as odd for him to be so silent, especially after they'd just kissed. He'd certainly had no qualms there. Yet now, the Berserker had lost his vigor. "I select my Valkyries and Berserkers carefully. I study their lives, weighing their deeds against one another. This happens before the White Hall of Judgment, of course, because what is decided here between these walls can never be reversed—my will and my word are absolute. To become a Valkyrie, a spirit must demonstrate their purity. Kindness, acts of valor, and self-sacrifice, these are the things I look for in a being of light. Their soul weighs as much as a feather."

Myst did strike me as the embodiment of such perfection, for it was perfection that Order demanded. I could tell. Edda, Regine, and every other Valkyrie I'd laid eyes upon shared these traits—the pure light, the feather-like allure, the undeniable strength of character. I did not need the senses of a Purgatory creature to observe the truth that was right in front of me.

"And to become a Berserker," Order added, "one must be the worst of the worst. The spirits I choose to become punishers would be the first to deserve a brutal penalty. Murderers, crooks, warmongers, and unrepentant monsters, that's what they truly are. Filthy souls who have taken lives, who have lived in hatred and violence. Brandon brought his empire to ruin. He killed innocent people. Hundreds perished under his blade. And you, Astra, you are naïve enough to think he's good? Why, because he helped you? Don't be a child."

Astra was speechless. She stared at Order, no longer able to look at Brandon. There wasn't disgust I saw in her eyes, though, only a conflict of emotions, like she was trying to process everything she'd just heard. But I could see why Brandon had shrunk. Shame had swallowed him whole. I raised a hand. "Pardon me for asking..."

"Thayen Novak, Nasani prince," Order replied, pursing her lips. "What is it?"

"How long ago did that happen?" I asked. "Brandon's death, I mean."

"We do not measure time here," Brandon replied, his voice tense and barely audible. "But I presume it was ages ago. I no longer remember my life, just faint snippets here and there."

Myst cleared her throat. "Being selected as a punisher is a form of punishment in itself. The Berserkers are doomed to an eternity in Purgatory, unable to ever move on." She gave Astra a brief glance. "In many ways, Brandon has already paid for his crimes."

I was inclined to agree, though I wasn't sure what "ages" meant in this context. How many years were enough to compensate for the lives he had snuffed out? How did we know that Brandon had, in fact, suffered for what he had done? Myst had good intentions, and I understood why she'd chosen to speak up, but I doubted it would be enough to bring Astra back.

Astra had tuned us all out, staring at the base of Order's throne.

"While that is true, only I decide when a price has been paid in full," the queen of Purgatory replied. "Brandon is not a kind soul. He isn't fundamentally decent. Yes, he saved your lives. More than once. But I wonder what the people he killed might have accomplished, if only he'd let them be." It was a good question, but none of us among the living were entitled to ask it, nor could we answer. Only Order had the privilege. "Therefore, banning him from Purgatory is not the worst fate he might endure."

"A perpetuity in a dark and meaningless limbo sounds like a treat," Brandon said, holding back a bitter laugh. "I'll be fine. It's only a peg below a perpetuity in this bright and supposedly meaningful limbo called Purgatory, trust me."

"You can no longer stay here, nor can you move on to worse punishments," Order grumbled. "I suppose you could consider this a win, in a way. Congratulations, Brandon. Your end of the stick isn't as short as I might have thought."

"It's worse," Astra replied, finally raising her gaze. "He won't belong anywhere. He's not of the living, he's not of the dead, either. He's a Berserker banned from Purgatory, forever lost in a sense, never to cross that threshold into the afterlife."

The way she spoke rattled me. Contempt dripped from each of her words, and I wondered whom it was aimed at. Brandon didn't ask, nor did he respond. He chose silence while Astra pointed a thumb over her shoulder at me and the others in our crew. "Now, could you please end this charade and let my friends go? There is still the issue of Hrista that remains unresolved."

It wasn't the reaction that Order had expected. Even Edda was surprised, but the shadow of a smile told me it was a positive response. "I agree. I have wasted enough time on Brandon," Order said, motioning for the Berserker to leave the queue.

Brandon didn't hesitate to join Myst and Edda. Astra didn't move, though, and even Hammer lingered beside her before he padded over to his Berserker. I felt sorry for Brandon. Genuinely sorry. It marked the end of his tenure in Purgatory and the beginning of a very uncertain state of existence. Something told me he'd do fine in The Shade. After all, Mom and Dad were the patron saints of supernatural misfits, and The Shade welcomed everyone. There would be room for Brandon, too, whose powers were still a crucial part of him, darkness his patron forever. He could definitely join us in The Shade... provided we got our home back.

In order to do that, however, we needed Order to come through for us. Doubt nagged me, though I wasn't sure where it had sprung from. I just figured I would've blown a gasket by now after hearing what Hrista had done outside my realm—had I been in Order's impressive leather and steel boots. I would've hit the pause button on the trials and gathered an army to storm the realm of the living and get that miscreant back.

Why wasn't Order doing any of that?

ASTRA

*M*y mind was a sickening blur. Anger, anguish, doubt, confusion. There was a little bit of everything worming its way through my brain and tampering with my ability to process the simplest of emotions. Brandon had once been a monster among men. It didn't matter how many times I looked at him, I couldn't see it. Or maybe I didn't want to see it. Maybe it had happened so long ago that the part of me that had fallen for him chose to be blind.

No, I wasn't blind. His past stood between us now. A big elephant in the White Hall of Justice, and we'd already had so much on our plate. He couldn't even look me in the eyes—if I had been tempted to doubt Order regarding Brandon, well... his inability to meet my gaze proved she'd told the truth. Just because he couldn't remember what he'd done didn't mean he'd never done it. That wasn't how the world worked. He'd done those things. He was capable of those things. I wasn't ready to deal with any of this. Not now. Not when there was so much left for us to do.

My parents were depending on me. My grandparents. My whole family. Our friends and allies. I could not let this fizzle out here, in the heart of Purgatory, while the main issue of Hrista remained unresolved. Gathering whatever courage I had left after I'd dared use my powers against her people, I gave Order a stern look. "You have to help us with Hrista.

You've had your fun with the trials, though they were clearly not needed since you already know what each of us did and why... it's time for you to take action," I said.

Order smiled. "You're quite brazen for a halfling."

"She may be shorter than average, but halfling is a bit much," Jericho said, crossing his arms as he and the others remained in the line of waiting spirits. "Also, she's right. Dafne, the Time Master, Aphis, Thayen, and I... we're with Astra. We have the same motivations. We made the same decisions."

"Truth be told, this was already looking like a farce from the moment she banned Brandon," Dafne replied, raising an eyebrow. It surprised Order to be met with such disdain. It surprised me, too, that my friends had this kind of courage. But it made me feel better, as well, knowing that I wasn't in the wrong. I wasn't the only one who had trouble taking any of this seriously. Sure, Order's power in this place was absolute, but she had not earned my respect.

"I believe you should just leave," Order replied dryly. "You're all cleared and free to go, as more trials against you would be redundant."

That just pissed me off. "Hey. No. What about Hrista?"

Order shot to her feet and threw her arms wide. "Get out!" A violent pulse burst from within her—a lot like mine, strangely enough—and rammed into us.

A split-second later, we had been thrown out of the White Hall of Justice. Thayen, Myst, Brandon, and Hammer. Dafne and Jericho. The Time Master and Aphis. The original gang, reunited away from Order, our plight completely ignored. My blood boiled, and I let a slew of expletives leave my lips as I got up and brushed the coppery brass and silver dust off my GASP uniform.

We'd made it this far, and I wasn't going to leave here without making sure that Hrista got what she deserved. Anything less would've been a colossal failure. Hell, if left unchecked, her crimes might even rival anything that Brandon had committed during his living days. Crap, the thought came back and launched itself with a shudder through my whole being. I still couldn't process the ugly truth.

"I'm not done," I said through gritted teeth as I walked toward the nearest queue of spirits being ushered into the white marble colossus. "She doesn't get to throw us away like old boots."

Anger fueled me as I put one foot in front of the other. Brandon tried to stop me. Almost instinctively, I yanked my arm back and threw a barrier at him—hard enough to hold him back and nearly topple him. I felt bad for a moment, but there was so much I still wanted to tell Order that I was compelled to keep moving.

"Astra, wait!" Thayen shouted after me, but I wouldn't have any of it. Myst didn't even bother, and I wondered why, when the Time Master was already at my side, trying to convince me not to go back in there. "This isn't wise," the Reaper said.

"And just walking away is?" I shot back, shaking my head. "No. We came here to get her help, and she simply threw us out. Hrista is her mess to clean up. Order's! Not ours!"

"While that may be true, pissing off one of the universe's fundamental forces is not a smart move," Time said. "I am powerless here, otherwise I would stop you myself, but I'm hoping you still respond to reason, Astra. She has angered you, I get that. I'm just as pissed off about all of this... but if Order ejected us, we can't just barge back in there and demand her help. We need a plan. Something that will stick."

"Do you have any ideas?" I asked as I almost joined the line.

Edda materialized before me, and I was finally forced to stop. "Don't even think about it," the Mother of Valkyries said. "She will not allow you back in."

"I'll make her!" I didn't really mean it. My frustration was boiling over. Helplessness was not something I wanted to get used to, not even for a minute. I felt like I'd been swimming for days in a certain direction, only to just find out that I'd been pushed in the opposite direction by the current. I'd thought we were going somewhere, and now... now, we were stuck in this wretched limbo, learning truths that would've been best kept hidden.

"Astra, outside this realm, Order is helpless," Edda replied, wearing a faint but sympathetic smile. "She would rather chop off her own head than admit that in front of all those souls. My Valkyries, the Berserkers, the countless spirits she presides over—she would never say it aloud to them, but it's true."

The news hit me like a sledgehammer right in the solar plexus.

"Wait, what?" Time blurted, just as shocked.

"Death is fortunate, for she is tied to the living realm. Yes, she has her own, but it's merely a sheet of space riddled with Reapers and ghouls and souls to reap. She has power in the living realm, and she has power in her domain, too. The Word, on the other hand, has no say in Death's world. And no say in Purgatory or in the afterlife, either. To each, more or less his own, if you know what I mean," Edda said.

"But Death once accidentally created a bunch of Hermessi," I reminded her.

She shrugged. "Consider that a fluke. The forces of this universe may cross paths in one sense or another, but we don't know the exact conditions required for something like that to happen. We don't know how Death acquired the authority to eliminate that much life energy to create Hermessi. Then again, death and life have always been intertwined, in a sense. Order and the afterlife, in general, were always beyond and separate. My point is, Death cannot dictate in the Word's realm, and the Word cannot dictate in Death's realm, either. Hermessi exception aside, please. The same applies to Order. She has all the power here. Beyond, she is but an entity with no place of her own."

"Hold on. Why is Death so special?" I heard myself ask, fascinated by the discrepancy.

"Not that special. Life is death, and death is life, if you think about it. The two are bound forever, intertwined, like I said just now," Edda explained. "But in Purgatory, neither Death nor the Word function. Likewise, Order is—" "Powerless in the realm of the living," I finished her sentence, the gravity of this truth sinking in so fast that I worried I might come apart at the seams.

"She cannot help you. She would like nothing more than to go after Hrista, but she cannot tell you that," Edda sighed, lowering her gaze.

Time scoffed. "She's ashamed."

"What can we do?" Thayen asked, joining the conversation along with the others. Brandon remained at a slight distance, though I could feel his eyes on me. I couldn't just brush off the truth of his past life. It had to be reckoned with. Maybe it didn't define him anymore, and maybe he'd paid the price, like Myst had implied, but... I'd have to address it and deal with it. "We cannot go back empty-handed. If we do reach The Shade when Astra gathers her strength and opens another shimmering portal, I'm sure we won't have an easy time. Hrista might have it locked down, thus making it impossible for any of us to communicate with our superiors."

"That restriction will apply to me, too," Time interjected.

"Either way, we don't really know what we're walking into," Thayen continued, giving Edda a pleading look. "If you could help us with anything at all..."

Myst took Edda's hands in hers. "Mother, please. We cannot let Hrista do this. It's not just Purgatory magic she's using against the living. It's death magic, too. The Spirit Bender taught her some dangerous tricks, and I worry we won't get to Death herself in time."

"Or, even worse, Death might not be enough to take Hrista down," Edda replied, offering a possibility we hadn't yet considered. Now that it had been voiced, however, it was a terrifying realization.

Brandon came over. "Can we talk?" he whispered.

"Now?"

"There is no better time," he replied bluntly and dragged me away from the group, giving Edda an apologetic smile. "Sorry, big mama, we'll be right back. You all talk, we'll catch up in a second."

His demeanor stunned and irritated me but not because it was out of place. No, it was because he wanted to get this big issue between us out of the way, and I didn't feel ready for such a heavy talk. It would've meant bracing for some kind of disappointment in my weary mind, and what Order had just done to us had emotionally drained me.

He walked us both about ten yards to the left of Edda and my crew, placing his hands on my shoulders as we stopped. Hammer had stayed back, too, watching us with his head cocked and blue eyes burning curiously. "You need to understand something," Brandon said. "I meant what I said in there. I don't even remember my life. Most of it is just a blur. I might see my mother's smile sometimes. Or I might hear her voice in a distant dream. Or the laughter of a brother, perhaps, I'm not sure. But the murders I committed... while I do not doubt them, I cannot recall them."

"What am I supposed to do with this information?" I asked him, my voice trembling slightly.

"I don't know. It's just... I've been punishing evil people for as long as I can remember. My darkness is pain and vengeance, and it seeps into the souls of those who feel guilty," he said. "I know how I came to be, I understand the process. Needless to say, I am deeply ashamed and regretful, which is part of the reason why I didn't bring it up before. I most likely did some truly awful things. I wouldn't be able to explain why anymore, but it's unforgivable either way. Evil and murder are unforgivable. So... I don't expect you to just brush it off." Brandon stopped himself, closing his eyes for a moment. When he looked at me again, I had the distinct feeling that he was baring the most vulnerable part of his soul to me. "I have never met anyone like you before, Astra. Your light used to put me on edge, but I can no longer exist without it, somehow. It's hard to explain. You're far above my level. I'm just a Berserker, a former killer who's been paying for his crimes in Purgatory. In a sense, I think you saved me, Astra. That's why Order's decree doesn't faze me as much as it should. It's okay. I'm fine, because I'm hoping you'll allow me to stay by your side."

I stared at him for what felt like forever before I found my words again. "Part of you, you said. What about the rest of you? Why did the rest of you keep this truth away from me?"

"Because I was ashamed," Brandon sighed. "I cannot say that my past defines me, but I'm certain I've carried a few traits over from that life. Whether they're positive or horrendous, I don't know... I only know that when I'm around you, Astra, I find myself striving to be better. Wishing I could be someone worthy of your attention. And your affection."

This wasn't the time or the place I'd thought I would hear such words, yet hearing them filled me with a strange, warm light, nonetheless. It stemmed from the compressed energy between Brandon and me, a vibe we'd been quietly carrying since we'd first met. Neither of us had tried to name it, though we'd both known it was there, growing, feeding on the stolen glances and the affectionate nicknames and the fleeting touches. It had gotten too big and too bright to ignore, and Order's revelations about Brandon had pushed him. He'd feared losing me, and the thought made my heart sing. It was just a tiny song, a murmur of hope and forgiveness.

How could I send him away? How could I hold such a distant past against him, when he couldn't even remember it? Granted, his deeds, whether remembered or not, had still happened. He'd done them. But the person I was clearly falling for had not been defined by them, in the end. I wasn't sure what any of this would mean for us in the long run, but I was certain I did not wish to fight this war without Brandon by my side.

I brought a hand up, ever so slowly, and touched his face. The blue fires turned a brilliant white beneath his long, black eyelashes, his gaze softening on my lips. The kiss he'd given me earlier had realigned everything in my head, switching the order of thoughts, making me dizzy and delighted at the same time. I didn't dare return that kiss now, here… not when I felt so many eyes on us. But I gave him a warm smile. I put every emotion I had in it, and I said things with my gaze, hoping he'd receive the message.

He did, much to my relief. "We'll continue this later, then…"

"We most certainly will," I replied.

"You two done?" Jericho called out, prompting Brandon to stifle a chuckle.

He cleared his throat and gathered his composure, then motioned for me to walk back to the crew, with him by my side. Where I hoped he would always be. "You're an outcast," I said, with still a few yards between us and the others. "What will you do now?"

"Leave Purgatory. But I won't leave you."

"Good." I took a moment to breathe, my pulse still galloping. "What about Hammer? Will he follow you?" "That will be his choice," Brandon sighed. "He wasn't banned. He cannot choose another Berserker, but he can ask Order to send him into the great beyond, if that is his wish. If Order separates us, we will both be fine. Never whole again, not really, but it'll spare me the fate of a shadow beast."

"Or he can come with you, right?" I asked, looking at the Aesir as we approached him.

"He can, but I dare not get my hopes up."

Dafne shot me a broad grin once we rejoined the conversation. "So, Edda has an idea."

"Will it get Hrista to Order?" I asked, giving Edda a stern look.

The Mother of Valkyries nodded. "If you cannot bring Order to Hrista, you can still bring Hrista to Order, yes," Edda said.

And there it was. The simplest solution. The straightforward conclusion. And the craziest damn suggestion I'd heard so far, yet the only viable one. What other choice did we have? Hrista wasn't invincible. She couldn't be. There had to be a weak spot. There had to be an angle we could work to our advantage.

Hrista feared my ability to open shimmering portals. Perhaps what she truly feared was that I could use one to hurl her back into Purgatory.

DAFNE

*I*t was difficult not to resent Order for how she'd treated us.

One of her own was wreaking havoc in the Earthly Dimension, and the queen of Purgatory couldn't even be bothered to tell us that she didn't have the power needed to stop Hrista. That we'd have to bring the rogue Valkyrie back here for Order to be able to do something about that raving lunatic.

Astra and Brandon led the group, while Hammer padded quietly beside the Berserker. Astra was still reeling from the discovery of Brandon's past, but I had a feeling they would overcome it. History shaped us, but we couldn't allow it to define us. That was what my father had taught me, and it was what I believed, as well. Astra looked at Brandon whenever his sights were set on something else. As soon as she glanced elsewhere, Brandon's eyes would find her. It was rather endearing to see them orbiting closer to one another, determined to move past the adversity.

The same could be said about Myst and Thayen, too. Maybe they thought we couldn't see them, but Jericho and I had already placed a bet on how long it would be before they kissed. I gave them a couple of days, considering the silent hunger in Thayen's gaze whenever it settled on the Valkyrie. Jericho insisted it would take them at least a week. He knew the vampire well enough. "Trust me, he's hilariously shy when it comes to women," Jericho had whispered earlier, making me chuckle since the fae dragon was famed for being the exact opposite.

"Are you sure we're going in the right direction?" I asked Brandon.

Edda, who walked with Myst and Thayen right behind the Berserker, glanced at me over her shoulder. "He can feel Baldur. The closer he gets, the stronger the Father's presence. The true and final cut-off from Purgatory will happens when Brandon leaves. Until then, he's still sensitive to his kind."

"Relax, Dafne. I'm sure Brandon has the decency to stop and ask for directions, if needed," Jericho cut in, and it took a considerable amount of effort not to laugh. He'd been cracking jokes since we'd left the White Hall of Judgment, and I knew he was doing this because of how enraging and demoralizing that entire encounter had been.

"And how might Baldur help, precisely?" the Time Master asked. He and Aphis were watching our backs, yet I still couldn't shake the shivers tumbling down my spine. Everything about this place was wrong and mismatched, yet it was breathtakingly beautiful at the same time. It was hard to reconcile such aspects, especially when there were bigger things to worry about. "You said you might know a way to bring Hrista back, Edda, but you have yet to offer details."

The Mother of Valkyries didn't look at us, though I was willing to bet she was smiling. She was a wonder to behold, even from behind. I hadn't given it much thought during Order's trials, but we had some time to breathe and wrap our heads around certain things, and I could truly take Edda in. She was tall and imposing. That stuck with me the most. In that sense, she reminded me of my mother. It had taken the fiercest of women to tame my father's icy heart.

"As you know, the second most powerful beings in Purgatory after Order herself are the Mother of Valkyries— that is, yours truly—and the Father of Berserkers, Baldur," Edda said. "I am hoping that I can get Baldur involved in a recovery mission. I can join you on my own, but I would feel more comfortable with him by my side, as we complement each other."

"Light and darkness," Myst replied. "We may be separate forces, but if we were to combine..."

"Hrista did something similar to herself," Astra said, frowning. "She can control both light and darkness."

Edda sighed. "No one saw that coming, and yes, it's a problem. Which is why I'm counting on Baldur to help us. We don't know what tricks Hrista might have up her sleeve. From what you've told us, she's using death magic, too, and outside Purgatory none of us are as powerful. Perhaps Hrista is a troubling exception for her to do what she has done. Or perhaps she used death magic as an auxiliary power, I'm not sure... but what I am sure of is that we are stronger together. And bringing Hrista back here will not be easy."

"Baldur won't be easy to convince," Brandon warned. "Wait until he hears I was banished."

"What is he like?" Astra asked. It prompted the Berserker to hold back a hefty chuckle, but it wasn't amusement I sensed in his tone. It was dread.

"You'll meet him soon enough."

Around us, the landscape had changed considerably. The copper hills were gone, and the land depressed into a deep valley with reddish tall grass and bountiful orchards with the strangest fruits hanging low from slender branches. The air was dry, smelling sweet—it reminded me of a freshly cut, deliciously ripe peach. "What is this place?" I wondered aloud, mesmerized by the peculiar trees.

Their trunks were perfectly straight and slim, much like aspens. Hundreds of branches shot out from near the ground level and all the way up to the top, about thirty feet high. The leaves were heart-shaped and crimson red, while the fruits were about the size of my fist and covered in a white, snakelike skin. The striking contrast of white and red beneath the diamond sky took my words away.

"Given that we're basically spirits, we do not require food or drink. However, Purgatory does have tastes for us to enjoy," Myst said. "We can still eat. We can still enjoy the cool freshness of a stream." She nodded at the orchard. "Or the sweetness of a white-snake fruit."

I plucked what Myst had referred to as a white-snake fruit from the tree closest to me and turned it over a couple of times. "And this? Is it edible?"

"Yes. Though we've never had living creatures here to taste them," Edda replied. "The spirits like this stuff, but their experience with them is infinitely more intense than ours."

"Or maybe we're just used to the taste," Brandon suggested with a shrug.

Either way, it was a green light to sink my teeth into the white skin. "Ow..." My teeth hurt. "This is hard.

Literally hard. Like a rock. What the hell?"

"Here, like this," Myst giggled and took the white snakeskin fruit from my hands. She smashed it against the tree trunk, and revealed the crimson, juicy pulp. I got half, and Jericho got the other half. For Astra, Brandon plucked a second fruit, inviting Thayen to taste, as well.

"I'm not designed to digest food," the young vampire said.

"This isn't physical food. Everything you see here is pure energy, Thayen," Myst replied. "What you drink and eat here is literally soul food, a wonderful impression, but not something that affects your digestive system."

Convinced by her argument, Thayen welcomed a proper tasting. The fruit was incredible. The pulp was fleshy and rich in water, yet sweet and intense with a sour twist on the tip of the tongue. It was an exploration of flavors, I thought, trying to associate with other fruits I had eaten over the years, both common and rare from different realms of GASP. None came to mind. This was entirely different.

"I feel kind of funny," Jericho muttered, a smile stretching across his lips.

It didn't take long for me to mirror his state. The giggle came over me and wouldn't stop. Brandon, Myst, and Edda were still, watching the rest of us with broad grins as we laughed and laughed and laughed to the point where our abs were aching from the repeated contractions.

"Is this supposed to happen?" I heard myself ask, though my voice sounded really far away. My legs felt soft and mushy, like overboiled spaghetti, and I wrapped my arms around Jericho's neck to stop myself from sinking onto the ground, shapeless and delighted.

"We have no idea," Edda replied. "Like we said, there were never living creatures here to taste the white fruit of mirth."

"The white fruit of mirth? Mirth?!" Astra croaked, lying on the ground on her side, laughing so hard that tears ran down her cheeks. Brandon was right there with her, smiling and holding her in his arms. She pulled herself away and rolled over, her skin glowing pink as she made the most of this sensation.

"This is incredible," Thayen observed, though he was mere inches away from losing it. He kept staring at his hands, turning them over, as though wondering if they were really his or not. The air felt thicker and heavier, or maybe it was just my impression.

"Are you okay?" Jericho's voice made me look up. I was hanging from him like a vine of leafy ivy, subject to the wind and every other force that could impact me, and the fae dragon was laughing, his arms tightening around my waist.

I sighed deeply and managed to find the ground again, the soles of my feet tingling as I pushed myself up on my toes to kiss him. Our lips met, and the entire world disappeared. It didn't matter that people could see us. It didn't matter that we were under the eyes of friends and strangers alike, nor that we'd been bewitched by whatever energies emanated from the white fruit.

Nothing mattered, because in the madness of this moment, in the sweet folly of our disrupted existence, in the heart of the nightmare that had unexpectedly thrown us out of our own homes, Jericho and I had found our way to each other. He'd tugged, I'd pulled, he'd poked, I'd prodded, and finally... we were inching closer and closer. His lips were dangerously addictive. His smile a joy to behold. His strength reassuring. His fire... oh, so exciting.

I had never allowed myself to feel this way for anyone—though I wasn't sure I could actually control such emotions. I'd deluded myself into thinking I could. Well, that lost its virtue, too. It was devoid of meaning, for only one thing had emerged from this storm—the certainty of how Jericho felt about me, and the speed with which I was falling for him.

"You taste like summer," I whispered against his lips.

"And you taste like heaven," Jericho replied. We giggled and bathed in the pure light of diamonds in the sky, hugging and kissing, welcoming the sweet joy of this moment and hoping that it might last forever.

I heard Astra sigh somewhere close by, but I couldn't be bothered to peel myself off Jericho. It felt too good. "I wish we could stay here forever," she said.

"We could, if you wanted to," Brandon replied, his voice soft. Oh, the Berserker was head over heels with our glowing girl, and he'd recently become a free agent, too. I wondered what it would be like for the two of them to be together.

The Time Master's voice cut through the veil of wondrous sensations with a hearty dose of unforgiving reality. "You were banished from Purgatory," he reminded Brandon. "And one of your sisters went AWOL and uber-crazy in the realm of the living. We're wasting precious seconds here."

"You keep forgetting... there are no seconds here," Brandon shot back.

My eyes opened slowly, finding Jericho's fixed on me. Hues of deep blue danced in the turquoise pools framed with jet black lashes. "That's right, there is no time," I murmured, as if waking from a dream.

"But it's all still real," Jericho replied, dropping a kiss on the tip of my nose. "Time is right... We have to keep moving."

I blinked several times just to get the rest of this world back into focus. And just like that, the fun fizzled out, and only the truth remained. We were in Purgatory. We were headed to summon Baldur, Father of Berserkers. And Hrista had stolen our island, among other horrendous things.

"Way to spoil the moment," I muttered, looking at the Time Master, and for the first time since I'd met him, I noticed his ghoul, Aphis, smiling. That was a rare sight.

"Wait, you said earlier that you experience your past and your presence at once," Astra blurted and sprang to her feet while Brandon scrambled to get back up, confused by the sudden change in tone. "How is it, then, that you cannot remember your history as a living creature?"

"None of us remember much from our lives," the Berserker replied. He looked to Edda and Myst for backup. "Tell her. Please."

Astra followed his gaze, and Myst was compelled to oblige. "When we are reaped, we leave our mortal lives behind. The memories begin to fade, ever so slowly. Those who move on get to keep it, but Valkyries and Berserkers, we... we lose it all, eventually. And yes, we experience time differently, that is true. But the memory of life still fades. I believe Brandon when he says he can barely remember, because I can say the same about myself."

"Well, you still have a notion of who you were," Edda said.

"Right. But that is more or less it."

Brandon lowered his gaze. "In my case, it might also be a case of choosing to forget and not wanting the past life to spoil this one. Especially now."

"Come on," Thayen said, breaking the conversation altogether. "Time may not flow the same way here, and the white fruit may be deceptively sweet and wonderful, but we still have work to do. It's been a weird day so far, and something tells me it's about to get weirder."

None of us could object. One by one, we pulled ourselves together and went back to the main trail that crossed this deep valley. Thayen, Edda and Myst stayed close to Brandon and Astra, while Hammer led the way. Jericho, Time, Aphis, and I were last, often looking back to make sure we wouldn't get any unpleasant surprises. This wasn't a good place, and it wasn't a bad place, either, so we didn't know what to expect.

Jericho took my hand in his and gave me a smoldering, dark look. We'd had our fun. And I promised myself that I would do everything in my power to make sure we'd have more fun back home in The Shade, once we'd destroyed Hrista and pulverized the clones. My priorities were shifting, some flocking around Jericho. I didn't mind. I liked the idea of a future with him in it.

My ice was rock solid, but I welcomed his fire with arms wide open. We'd need every ounce of strength against this new enemy.

THAYEN

"Why can't you just teleport us to Baldur?" the Time Master asked after we left the orchard valley behind and braced ourselves for a long walk through a golden desert. There was nothing else around us for miles and miles. Nothing but rippling dunes of gold sand slowly baking in the heat.

Even without an actual sun, warmth permeated throughout Purgatory.

"The Mother and the Father demand that we walk to find them," Brandon said. "It's an ancient tradition. They may find us anywhere in Purgatory, but we must go the distance if we wish to see them."

"That's a little bizarre," Time muttered.

Edda shrugged. "Yeah, we kind of dropped the ball on a few things around here, but with the realm shifting and fundamentally changing every now and then, we lack the stability we'd need to establish better traditions. Our focus is to herd the souls into their respective afterlives, anyway. Everything else here is just... fluff."

I didn't mind the walk. It gave me time to put my thoughts in order. We were slaves to the mechanics of the universe. My only hope was that we wouldn't miss anything important upon our return. Of course, our goal was still getting to the real island. I trusted Astra would come through for us, but she needed a bit more breathing room for now. It had been pretty intense for her, not just in terms of opening and holding a shimmering portal—although to a different destination by mistake—but also as far as her dynamic with Brandon was concerned.

They'd gone through a change, at least from my perspective, a fundamental shift in how they perceived each other. Brandon had been a killer during his living days. A killer ruthless and evil enough to warrant Order's attention in Purgatory. The thought chilled me to the bone, yet I failed to reconcile it with the Berserker walking just a couple of steps to my right. Brandon was not a model of good behavior, nor the most noble entity I'd ever come across—on the contrary. But I still couldn't see him as a murderer.

"What's on your mind?" Myst asked as we walked between the dunes, which got taller with every mile we put behind us. We were following a clear path on a low level, while the desert rose around us with its shiny sea of gold.

"Quite a lot, actually," I replied, almost laughing. "I'm amazed by how much my mind can process at once. But I guess the dominant feeling is disappointment. With Order, I mean. That meeting was... anticlimactic."

"That's putting it mildly," she sighed. "I had no idea until Edda told us, and I am still utterly dumbstruck. Order is powerless beyond this realm, and it just... it doesn't make sense, because the world of the living thrives on... well, on order. On the principle of action and reaction. On species and subspecies. On specific formulas that lead to specific results. On justice for crimes committed. One would think Order herself would thrive in such realms."

"If the forces of the universe were too absolute and all-powerful in every single layer of its endless domain, we'd have a mess on our hands, don't you think?" I asked, noticing I'd earned a faint nod of approval from a half-smiling Edda. "I think things are the way they should be. The Word in life. Order in Purgatory. Death as dual as ever, the beginning and the end of everything, I guess. And I don't know what else there is beyond this realm."

"By that logic, everything is where it belongs. Myself included, here, in Purgatory," Myst replied, and for some reason, it sounded wrong. Well, it sounded right, but I didn't like it. "And Brandon, too. But Brandon has been kicked out. Sooner or later, one of us will have to eject him. Where does that leave him and the alleged order of things?"

For a moment, I stared at her with a mixture of admiration and sheer awe. Her wisdom had enlightened me more than once. She'd carried herself with a whiff of self-righteousness that may have gotten on my or others' nerves at some point, but in the middle of Purgatory, absolutely everything about Myst the Valkyrie suddenly made sense. The glorious attire, the superb sword, the explosion of light coming from within her, the timelessness of her words. Yes, I could see it now.

"Nothing is written in stone," I concluded with a deep exhale, almost losing myself in her eyes. "As long as we have strength in our souls, I think we can pull anything off."

"Your optimism is endearing," Edda snickered, giving me a curious sideways glance. "Myst, this one is definitely special. I can smell the death on him."

I almost blushed. "Oh, you don't know the half of it."

"I kind of do, actually, just by looking at you," Edda replied. "There is death in you. As a vampire, and as a carrier of one of Spirit Bender's soul shards. I told you, I smell it."

"In a sense, vampires are closest to Death's realm," I said, unable to hide the pride that accompanied my statement. "Unending, her first Reaper, or who we *thought* was her first reaper, she's the source of vampirism."

Edda sighed, shaking her head.

That got my attention. "What is it?"

"Nothing. It's just... I'm reminded of how comfortable Death is with lying," she said, then pointed ahead. A forest sprang from the gold sand, with black trees and a sprawling obsidian canopy that stretched for days, enveloping everything beneath it in profound darkness. "Here we are." Edda seemed glad to change the subject.

I would've liked to follow up, but a strange presence emerged somewhere nearby—I could feel it humming in the center of my chest. Whatever Edda was holding back about Death and Unending would have to wait. Baldur came out from the strange forest, and I fell silent.

My throat closed up. Darkness poured off him like thick ink and not in the usual wisps I'd seen on Brandon and the other Berserkers. Baldur was tall and muscular, with long arms and broad shoulders. His hair was a mess of black and indigo blue, braided and tumbling down his back in an imposing mane. His cold eyes cut right through me as they met mine. Leather covered his torso and legs. He wore an ornate breastplate made of silver and steel, tied on both sides with hide strings and covered with mother-of-pearl and watermelon-colored tourmaline inlays. His thigh and calf armor pieces were made from the same material, enriched with runes that glimmered like the sky of diamonds overhead.

Our group came to a sudden halt as Baldur clenched his square jaw and revealed his weapon, a monstrous axe with a long handle made of sculpted bone and wrapped in slick black leather. Its blade shone hungrily and sharp, aching for blood and pain most of all. I never wanted to find myself in its way.

Myst's hand found my wrist and gave it a good squeeze. There wasn't a need for words between us. I knew this meant that she had my back, calmly urging me to let her and the other beings of Purgatory take the lead. Baldur saw me first, though, and he seemed a little too curious for my comfort, so I doubted I'd manage to sail through the incoming conversation unnoticed.

"Hm. Four beating hearts. Plus a Reaper and a ghoul. This is strange," Baldur said, looking at each of us carefully. He narrowed his eyes, for good measure, just to make it clear that he was studying us.

"Baldur, my brother. I come in peace," Edda replied, taking a step forward. "We need to talk. It's important." "Sure, but first... I need to know who this wondrous being is," Baldur retorted, confidently walking toward Astra. Instinctively, I moved to get in front of her, and so did Brandon. Even Jericho and Dafne were about to step in, and Hammer was already restless and growling—but none of us stood a chance.

Myst pulled me aside, while Aphis yanked the dragons back with a low hiss. Baldur waved Brandon and Hammer away like a pair of bothersome flies, a cool grin slitting his face from ear to ear as he beheld Astra. He stopped mere inches from her, taking a deep breath to capture her scent. He groaned softly. "You smell of life and light, little jewel, and I cannot make sense of you."

"She's a Daughter-Sentry," Edda said firmly. "And my guest here."

"Your guest? Don't be ridiculous," Baldur snorted a laugh. "She's an intruder, much like the rest of these breathers, plus the gloomy fellas. Oh, and let's not forget you, Brandon. You're not supposed to be here anymore."

"I take it you heard the news," the Berserker muttered as he picked himself up off the ground. Hammer shook off some of the sand but didn't make another move toward the Father of Berserkers. Astra, the poor soul, stood frozen and speechless and wide-eyed.

"You're exceptional," Baldur said, ignoring Brandon and the rest of us. The leader of punishers was absolutely shameless, and irrevocably smitten. "You're a work of art, a marvel of the universe, a most exceptional accident, Astra Hellswan. And now, you're here, in front of me... within my reach."

He tried to touch her pink hair, but Astra had the sense to pull back. "Whoa, there... do I know you?"

"No, but he's already read your soul," Brandon interjected, his shoulders slumped. "It's part of his power. He just looks at you, like Order would, and he knows everything, though not as deeply as her. Enough to creep you out, for sure."

"Did I allow you to speak? Shush, rogue," Baldur cut him off. "The only reason I haven't ejected you yet is because this wonderful girl seems to like you, which is a terrible shame. I hope to rectify that." He smiled at Astra. "Give me your heart and your body and you will never experience emptiness or sadness or darkness ever again."

Edda scoffed. "Oh, enough with the syrupy garbage. You're the Father of Berserkers. The epitome of darkness. If she lets you do anything to her, she invites shadows that will haunt her forever and probably into the afterlife, as well. Stop it."

"I can't help it. Can you not see how gorgeous she is?"

Baldur was quite the character. And judging by how Myst pressed her lips together so as not to smile, I began to worry. Was the father of Berserkers all bark and no bite? They would've said something prior to this meeting. No, that didn't make sense. Was he insane?

He sure looked like he had at least a streak of madness going on.

"You *are* creeping me out," Astra replied dryly and crossed her arms for good measure. It made Baldur throw his head back with laughter.

"What a firecracker you turned out to be. There are legends about you, Astra, of life and death bonding in a body," he said. "Legends that transcended the realm of the living and made it all the way to my curious ears."

"Baldur," Edda snapped, her voice thundering across the black woods.

Their obsidian leaves rustled with troubled clinking, like wind chimes made of glass. "Hrista has taken over a living realm. She will inevitably provoke the powers that be with such actions."

Suddenly, the humor vanished from his face.

There it was. The shock. The anger. It flared like nuclear sapphires beneath his dark eyebrows. "Damn that firefly. I told her not to do anything stupid," he grumbled.

Baldur had seen this coming. He'd at least suspected that Hrista had the potential to do something awful. We'd brought him bad news, and his fascination with Astra subsided as quickly as it had emerged. There were bigger problems to deal with, and finally... I saw the *real* Father of Berserkers, the force that Edda would need to help us. Our world was not yet lost.

UNENDING

I had lost track of time.

The claustrophobia was eating away at me, a stark reminder of my imprisonment on Visio. Granted, this was just a cell made of stone and iron. It was warded against all kinds of magic, yes, but it could still be torn down. A rune or a sigil could be broken. There was a solution to it. This was my way of avoiding despair. My own self-healing reasoning to stop me from going mad.

My darling Tristan was helpless. Hrista had taken the silver cube with all my memories. We didn't even have access to that. It wouldn't have helped, anyway. If I died, I died. If I shed this body, I would forsake everything. I would never be Unending again. I would shuffle right into Purgatory, my powers lost forever.

Hrista had done an impeccable job of destroying me.

"There hasn't been much movement outside," Tristan said after a long, heavy silence. He'd spent the past couple of hours observing the clones through the small window of our cell, expertly fitted with steel bars and more magic to keep us from escaping. "I assume we only have the two guards outside, by the door. I haven't picked up any other scents, either. No additional heartbeats."

I sat on the edge of the bed, knees under my chin as I tried to see a path forward through this awfulness. It was hard to shake the feeling that I had been incredibly stupid. What a ridiculous emotion to have, and the body just made it worse. Neither Tristan nor I could have anticipated this. We'd gone over the chain of events. The decision. Nowhere had Anunit given any hint that she wasn't who we'd thought she was. There was no room for me to blame myself. Well, actually... there was. I could have processed my anger better. I could've told Death about Biriane. She would've had enough sense to stop us, and the World Crusher would not have been released.

"But how was I supposed to know?" I murmured, hearing the tremor in my voice.

"What?"

Shaking my head, I got up. "Nothing."

"Unending..." Tristan replied, beckoning me to look at him. I could barely do it. There was hope in his beautiful eyes. And I could practically hear his pulse rushing, the enthusiasm thundering through his ribcage. He was itching to take out the guards and walk us out of here, but we both knew that wasn't an option. Hrista had planned well for this. She had spent a considerable amount of time building Anunit's rogue profile and grooming us. The real one had been locked up somewhere. We didn't know when exactly, but it made sense that she'd had nothing to do with Reapers being brought back to life. That was clearly part of Anunit's palette of awful deeds.

"I can't even shed this body," I told him, sounding utterly defeated. "I'm useless, Tristan. Even if I had my scythe, none of the death magic I can still wield would in any way be useful to our circumstances. If I die, I die for good, and we'll never see each other again. She upended everything, and I welcomed it with arms wide open." So much for not blaming myself.

"It's not over," he said, undeterred. I loved him with everything I had. I would've given my own flesh to believe his words to be true, but the facts were against us. "We're trapped here. Surrounded by clones. You saw the Berserkers through that stupid window, didn't you?"

His enthusiasm faded. Uneasiness settled in his gaze. "Yeah... I have no idea how to handle one of them if we ever cross paths."

"Let alone the dozen or so that are here. She may have even brought more of them over, in the meantime."

"So what do you suggest we do?" Tristan asked, raising an eyebrow at me.

I shrugged in reply, wishing I could be as strong or as resilient as he was. My own nature had been taken away from me. I had no Reaperhood to return to. My body was a hindrance, no longer a joy. In the blink of an eye, the dream I had been struggling to attain for so long had soured beyond repair. What good was a family if the world was destroyed?

"I... I don't know."

Hrista appeared out of nowhere beyond the steel bars. "Finally. A clueless Reaper. I thought I'd never see the day. Your kind is famous for being obnoxious know-it-alls... Oh, the delight!"

Tension filled our cell room in an instant. Her mere presence destroyed the last of my hopes—though I could no longer maintain any sort of optimism. I didn't like this state of mind, and I did not know how to get myself out of it. I had never had such issues as a Reaper before. But as a living being, I was at the mercy of my feelings.

"You have not defeated us!" Tristan snapped. "We'll find our way. We always do."

"Aw... that's so romantic," Hrista replied, mocking him. "I am totally rooting for you, Tristan. Believe it or not, I want you and the universe to prove me wrong. I want the power of love to defeat me. But I reckon the three of us already know that that's not going to happen. Had love been worth anything, it would have kept Spirit and me together forever. Instead, here we are!" Her humor faded. "I have The Shade. I will have the entire world of the living on its knees by the time I'm done. The realm of the Reapers will fall apart. Death and life will break... the balance will be gone, and the universe will shudder in my grip."

"And then what?" I asked, my tone flat. I figured the approach might work, since Tristan had effectively used it on me. "What will you do then?"

Hrista let out a full sigh, as if she'd just woken from a wonderful dream, and I'd nearly spoiled the ending for her. "I have no idea, and that's the whole beauty of this exercise."

"So, good ol' chaos. That's so boring and overdone," Tristan chimed in, picking up on my jabs. We didn't need telepathy to be on the same wavelength, it seemed. I'd almost forgotten. I'd been so caught up in my own misery, that I had neglected the very man who had set me free from my five-million-year curse.

I nodded. "It's actually quite the cliché. GASP has dealt with much worse."

"They have never faced me," Hrista shot back with a hiss. We'd insulted her immense pride, and I'd finally found a soft spot that I could poke until it bled. Pride had brought greater entities down. I'd figure out a way to do the same to her. "I'm a Valkyrie with flawless control over both light and darkness. I have been given the superior knowledge of Death's ancient magic, as well. I have made life, and I now claim the Earthly realm as my own."

Tristan clicked his teeth. "Is this supposed to be the official announcement? I thought you'd at least notify the ones outside The Shade. You know there will be hell to pay for what you've done."

He didn't need to know what she was capable of. He didn't require the historical details of Valkyries and Berserkers—Tristan only had what I'd given him from my readings of the World Crusher's book. Everything she had accomplished until now was proof that Hrista was a worthy adversary. I feared she was worse than the Spirit Bender. He'd never hurled Purgatory magic at us. He'd stuck to what he had known. Or maybe death magic had been all he could use. Hrista was clearly superior.

"I'd laugh in your face, but you're in a cell, your fate sealed, done and dusted," Hrista replied, regaining a sense of calm I hadn't seen in her since she'd played the part of Anunit, the rogue Reaper who traipsed across the universe helping Reapers become real little boys. "It would be cruel of me to rub it in your face. However, I see that you are doubtful. It's perfectly understandable. Life as you know it is over, and I'm trampling it without a single shred of mercy. I suppose denial is part of the process."

She was going somewhere with this. Hrista had not come here just to tease us. As if reading my mind—or at least the faint changes in my expression—Tristan inched closer and took my hand in his. He squeezed tightly, pouring all his love into this simple yet meaningful gesture. I had worked so hard to give us a family... and Hrista had toyed with us. I would never forgive her. Even in a living body, I would pay her back for what she had done.

That's it. The anger. Feed on it. You need it more than you need despair.

"Why are you here? Gloating is the mark of a weak and pitiful spirit," I said, raising my chin in defiance. There was something about Tristan's quiet encouragement that had given me an extra surge of strength. "Surely, you, the brilliant Hrista, the uber-talented Valkyrie whom everyone somehow underestimated, has a better reason to be here than to... gloat."

She almost smiled as she looked at me. There was hatred in those blue eyes. It burned cold, but it was unmistakable. "Your husband here has been around for what, some forty years? But you're ancient. Pretty much timeless, right?"

"Old enough to know that tampering with the universe will only come back to bite you in your Valkyrie ass," I retorted.

"That remains to be seen. But you're right about one thing, oh, mortal one," she said, once again in a dazzlingly good humor. The white silk poured down her back, the armor clanging whenever she moved. For a rebel of Purgatory, she seemed attached to her original uniform. It told me plenty about Hrista. "I didn't come here to mock you. There's no fun in that. I came here to let you out. There's something I want you to see."

As if summoned telepathically, Esme and Kalon's clones entered and unlocked our cell. Esme's double put a pair of charmed cuffs on me, just to be on the safe side, and Kalon's slapped a pair of solid steel ones on Tristan that he wouldn't be able to break out of. I didn't need any explanation, but it did give me a bit of comfort—there was paranoia involved, and they were willing to take even the most useless of precautions against me, just to be on the safe side. I was still a threat, in a sense, at least in their minds... I would've been a fool to tell them otherwise, wishing we could find a way to prove them right, instead. Hrista led our odd pack outside. As soon as my feet touched the grass, dew tickling my toes, I could tell something was different.

"Look up," the Valkyrie said.

We did. From inside the cell, our view of the sky had been obscured. But out here, we could see it clearly, and it caused my stomach to shrink into something small and painful. "No... What is that?" I managed, my throat suddenly dry.

"The first sign of change," she replied. "You see, Unending, Tristan... I don't give a crap about what you or your people will want to do to me. I have started something here. You cannot stop it. It's something otherworldly and of my own making. It's irrefutable and undeniable. It's absolute and infinitely better than whatever the universe threw together."

Red and green rippled across the night sky, swallowing the half-moon and the night sky. Flashes of white burst here and there, like ghostly thunder beyond a sheet of multicolored clouds. It wasn't normal.

The Shade's sky had always been a spell of night, courtesy of the witches. But something else had taken over.

Something had changed it. Something awful.

"What the hell did you do?" Tristan mumbled, his lower lip trembling. There was horror in his eyes. He didn't need to know what that celestial phenomenon was in order to realize it wasn't supposed to happen.

"I am a creator, Tristan," Hrista said, beaming with pride. "I have created, and now... all the realms will bow before me. But not before I topple their leaders, of course. Consider this," she motioned around us, "the hors d'oeuvre, I think you call them. The appetizer. The first stage of a cute little dinner party I'm throwing. The theme of the night is—"

"Chaos." I finished her sentence for her.

It was clear now. The sky. The Shade takeover. The clones. The release of the World Crusher. I had a full picture of what Hrista was doing, and "terrified" did not even begin to cover how I felt. Tristan squeezed my hand again. This time, there was fear in his eyes. Confusion. Grief.

I understood that my time to mope had come to an end. My husband was a strong man and a fearless vampire. But I was the Unending. *Hrista may have taken my body, but the spirit is still mine, bottled in this sack of meat and bones or not.* I owed it to him to stay strong. There were weak spots. Regardless of how the rest of her plan unfolded, I could still find the right buttons to push.

And I would push. I would push until I heard Hrista scream.

SOFIA

*L*aurel, Missa, and Ida were full of surprises. It became obvious when they guided us across the entire island and deep into the bowels of the fake Black Heights. Derek and I were still careful and ever alert, but we took comfort in having Haldor and Regine on our side. They'd bound the clones' hands with Purgatory magic—thin strands of darkness that could not be broken by anyone other than those who had cast them.

We had gone well past the known residences of the dragon clones. The upper cave system of the mountains had been left behind a while back. I checked my wristwatch, though I wasn't sure why. I had not recorded our entry time, and neither had Derek.

"How much deeper?" I asked.

The corridor ahead tightened some more, its eerily polished walls closing in. I'd thought I'd learned our beloved island by heart, yet this place proved that I had forgotten some parts of it. According to Laurel, at least, the Black Heights and their chambers had been made identical to the original from back home. "We're almost there," she said, leading the way. Missa and Ida were compelled to line up behind her, followed by me and Derek, then Haldor and Regine.

It was growing colder, the temperature reaching near freezing. As a vampire, it didn't bother me, but I still experienced the chills, my skin tightening as I watched my breath flower into playful steam clouds in front of me.

"And what is it exactly that you're going to show us?" Derek replied. "Forgive our distrust, but your people have done nothing but harm."

Ida chuckled. "I completely agree. We dared to demand independence and... well, here we are. Left behind to rot in this place."

"I could describe it," Laurel said, "but it's better if I show you. It saves me the additional explanations. You'll have plenty of questions, no doubt."

Haldor grunted behind us. "How come I never made it down here?"

"Oh, there are places in The Shade that not even the Berserkers know about. Some clone-made, others from the original designs. Hrista didn't want anyone to know about the lower tunnels," Laurel said. "The only Berserker who knew about them was destroyed by her blade. He's one of your shadow hounds now."

I looked over my shoulder and I recognized Haldor's expression. Shock and grief. Unmistakable, even for an entity of Purgatory. "I suppose you don't know who your shadow hounds are?" I muttered.

"No. They lose any form of individuality when their Aesir are destroyed," he said. "I suppose whoever he was, Hrista brought him over first, holding his Aesir hostage, much like she did with Brandon's Hammer. Only, in his case, there was no Haldor to hinder her evil plan."

"Do you always talk about yourself in the third person?" Regine retorted.

I could almost feel his eyes rolling. "Do you always insert yourself into conversations where you do not belong?" Haldor was a heavy hitter, clearly. Regine had found her match, but that didn't seem to bother her. On the contrary, she enjoyed the occasional jab, just to remind us that the Berserkers and the Valkyries were literal opposites.

"Just a little bit more," Laurel said from the darkness ahead. It swallowed Ida and Missa next. By the time we caught up with them, the tunnel had begun to widen again, a distant light casting shadows against the amber-colored walls. I ran my fingers over the surface, trying to understand how this place had been made.

"Magic?" I asked Derek, but he responded with a shrug. "It's strange. I could swear it's actual amber."

"It is," Laurel replied, slightly amused. "Hrista had her Berserkers scan

the entire island and study its depths, too. They came across this place."
The fact that the clones and Hrista knew more about our world than even
we did wasn't the greatest shock. They were already aware of Astra's genetic
makeup as a threat to the disgraced Valkyrie, and there was probably more
in their notes on top of that. "Some of the first dragons who came to
The Shade made these lower tunnels. They told absolutely no one, and
they used amber to mark this as their turf. Fire dragons. So, if ice dragons
accidentally stumbled upon these tunnels, they would know to stay out."

I cleared my throat, the chalky dust in the air making it harder for me to
breathe. "It irks me that you know more about my home than I do."

"Oh, we are just curious to a fault," Ida giggled. "Besides, the dragon
clones, as you call them, they were never that territorial. The rest of us
could go up the mountains of *these* Black Heights freely. The caves, too.
It's how Laurel found this place."

Finally, we reached the end of the tunnel, and my blood chilled—a
strange reaction to a sense of anticipation, I figured. This couldn't be a
trap, that much was clear. The enemies were gone, and we had a Berserker
and a Valkyrie with us. On top of that, the comms worked, so we could
always call for help. No, this was real, and it was happening, and I dreaded
learning the truth. We obviously needed it, yet a part of me didn't wish to
know it. *A childish way of hiding from the inevitable, I suppose.*

"Here we are." Laurel's words preceded the view.

Ida and Missa stepped aside, just in time for Derek and me to step into
the giant cave bubble. It had been carved into a cylindrical form, its walls
also covered with a thick coat of amber. The floors were the black stone of
the mountains themselves, and a peculiar light glowed from below. Only
then did I see where we stood—on the lip of a deep chasm, at the bottom
of which we could see about twenty odd-looking tanks. They resembled
the oxygen tanks used by firefighters in the Earthly dimension but made
of glass.

"What the..." my voice trailed off as my husband caught my wrist and
held me back. I hadn't even realized that I was still walking, nearly falling
over the edge and into the chasm. I would easily have broken something if
I had fallen to the bottom.

"Careful, my love," he whispered in my ear and pressed his lips against
my temple for a second. I smelled his fear then. Sharp and heavy, much like

mine, as we both looked down and saw the mingle of shimmering white and sickening black masses that seemed to wrestle one another inside each of the glass tanks. That was what illuminated the entire chamber. The war between light and darkness enclosed below.

"What the heck are those?" Regine gasped, her eyes widening as she followed our gaze. "That... crap, Haldor, look!"

"How is that even possible?!" The Berserker was equally baffled, and I had no idea what we were dealing with. I only knew that the dread I'd carried with me into this place had now grown into something much uglier and more difficult to control.

Laurel turned around to face us. "Unbeknownst to anyone, Hrista found a way to embed death magic into Purgatory magic. I reckon it had something to do with her innate ability to wield light and darkness alike. It helped her fuse the two together with a thread of Hermessi energy. The Spirit Bender had that harvested before the war."

"What are those things?!" I asked, urgency sharpening my voice. I was close to screaming, and my blood pumped so fast, my flesh felt like it had caught fire despite the freezing cold.

"They're called world seeds," Laurel said. "Hrista used some seriously awful magic to bind those elements together. But she needed Kedra's catalyst to make each tank into a viable world-maker." Upon noticing my confused expression, she briefly explained what Kedra's catalyst was, and my stomach just... dropped as the dots connected in my mind. Astra had told us about the black witch before—Hrista had mentioned her to them upon their first meeting just before the Flip. This was the same Kedra. My head hurt...

"Wait. What's a world-maker?" Derek asked, his brow furrowing as he tried to understand what they actually meant. I was inclined to take them literally, since Hrista clearly suffered from a deranged god complex.

"It's a magical organic compound," Laurel explained. "It's got light and darkness from Purgatory. It's got life from the Hermessi. It's got death from the Reapers' realm... and it's imbued with organic matter from The Shade. It works now, because Hrista activated the formula with Kedra's catalyst." She was talking about the cube that Isabelle's clone had stolen from the real island, the very object that Claudia's doppelganger had succeeded in bringing over to this place. Up until this conversation, none of us had known what that thing did. Now that we knew... good grief, it was terrifying. And to think it had been in our possession for so long, yet we'd had no idea. Isabelle's clone had stolen this from the witches' Sanctuary. Corrine and the others had been equally ignorant to its existence, yet Hrista had known it was there. "It has multiple uses, that object. This was one of them."

"What do these do?" I asked, suddenly shaking like a leaf.

"You don't want to know..." Ida replied, shaking her head slowly. There was fear in her eyes as she glanced down at the glowing tanks. I saw reds and greens bursting through the struggle of light and darkness, and flashes dancing across the entire mass. I saw blues and yellows and other colors, too... snippets of something so complex that it terrified me.

Derek shook his head. "But you have to tell us. We spared you for this!"

"Forgive Ida, she wasn't really sure if I was telling the truth, either," Laurel said. "I'm the only one in my village who knew about this. Since we were set free from our tasks, I took time to explore this place. I'm good at hiding, so I stayed out of the Berserkers' sight." She paused to briefly look at Haldor and smirk. "No one saw me. Eventually, I came upon Hrista and a couple of her loyal clones talking about the world seeds... I figured that was interesting, so I eavesdropped on that conversation, then came down here to see for myself. It's real. It's all real."

"You still haven't answered the key question," Regine warned, one hand gripping her sword. She wasn't the only one itching for violence. Derek was getting restless, too.

"One drop from any of those tanks, and a massive creation will take place. Like a seed of nature, it will touch the ground or the water where it's dropped. If you feed it and toss it into emptiness, it will flourish in the nothingness like this place did. It will grow, impossible to ever stop. It will develop land and water, trees and bushes and plants..." Laurel sucked in a breath. "A single drop will feed on its surroundings, it will build upon the life it encounters, and it will never stop spreading."

"This place you call fake... it started with a drop of that," Ida said, pointing at the tanks, "in a glass of water."

Hrista opened this pocket between worlds and let the drop of world seed grow into our Shade."

"*Your* Shade," I replied.

"Why did Hrista leave the tanks here?" Regine wondered, upset and confused. "It doesn't make much sense, does it?"

Laurel sighed. "I think she plans to use these tanks against another world. Maybe yours, maybe this one, I'm not sure. You see, one drop can make a world, but all these tanks set free at once? The forms will battle and consume one another. They'll eat everything in their path. You, me, every single Shadian still here... we will all be gone, and the world seeds will keep fighting to coexist, unable to get along... it's why you see them fighting in the tanks. The glass is powerful magic, it stops them from breaking out."

That alone was deeply troubling. The implications made me want to scream. We were stuck here with a bunch of literal ticking time bombs, and Hrista could come back at any moment to set them off and destroy us. "There is, of course, a lot more we still do not know," Ida felt the need to mention that. "Laurel says Hrista took a tank over into the real island."

My knees buckled. It was all I could do not to fall as Derek tightened his grip on me and moved us away from the edge. Haldor and Regine were baffled. Their expressions spoke of fear, too—they understood the implications as well as I did.

As did my husband. "You mean to tell me that not only are we at risk of annihilation if Hrista breaks these damn tanks, but that she took one of them into our realm, too?"

Laurel nodded.

"And you didn't think to tell us sooner?" I croaked, my voice breaking.

"I waited until after the Flip before I could explore these parts. As soon as I showed this to Ida and Missa, we came looking for you. At the villa," Laurel replied.

"I think the Daughters and Lumi will want to see this," Derek said, scowling at the tanks again. It was as if he couldn't believe what he was seeing, even though it was obviously and painfully real.

"That Soul Crusher guy, too," Regine added. "It requires the representatives of every realm."

It most certainly did.

This was insane. The odds were stacked against us even higher than we'd realized, and our most valuable fighters had not yet returned from their perilous voyage. Now, more than ever, I wanted to gather our children close, all three of them... to hold them tight and kiss them. They were the future. I could not let Hrista or anyone else destroy that.

ASTRA

*B*aldur was a ridiculously handsome Berserker. His features were designed to seduce, yet his nonchalance sort of killed his enticing allure. Perhaps he was too certain of himself. Or maybe he'd come on too hard, too fast—clearly a creature of Purgatory with zero social skills. Either way, it didn't matter. He'd creeped me out and there was no coming back from that.

Unfortunately, he couldn't stop staring. Smiling. Undressing me with his eyes. It became increasingly difficult to focus until Edda finished her account of the events so far, then smacked him over the head. "Focus, you old fool!" she snarled. "More important things!"

The Mother of Valkyries had quickly gone from untrusting stranger to much-needed ally, maybe even a friend. Order's disappointing behavior must have played a crucial part in the shift, but I welcomed it. We needed all the help we could get.

"Right. Hrista. Okay. What exactly do you want me to do about her?" Baldur asked, feigning disinterest while he blatantly stole glances at me. Brandon stayed close, the back of his hand sometimes brushing against mine, gently, as if to remind me that he was still here. That we'd started something. Not like I could really forget. Not when my heart was beating wildly in his presence.

"She's in the Earthly Dimension," Edda said. "It's obviously a problem, and Order can't handle it. You know that."

Baldur looked at me. "And you, missy? Do you want my help?"

"I think I speak for all of us when I say yes." My response satisfied him tremendously. "We were told that we will need the Mother and the Father to get Hrista back here. Only then can Order punish her."

"And since you're the only portal opener who can cross the realms like she can, she is keen to hear your last breath. Is she not?" he asked me. There was something in the way he framed his question that made me nervous. It was as if Baldur was the only one who truly understood my plight. He obviously wasn't, but he certainly had a way of worming his way into my good graces. *Good grief, you are such a weirdo...*

"She is, yes," I said.

He turned his sights on Brandon next. "And you, you miserable oaf... you couldn't even defend yourself before Order."

"I tried but she wouldn't listen—"

"Shut up! You didn't try hard enough!" Baldur's demeanor changed from courteous-bordering-on-sleazy to absolute-hard-ass in under a second. "You brought this upon yourself, Brandon, and I can no longer take you seriously. How can I still look at you and think of you as a Berserker, a son, if you got yourself kicked out of the very place you're supposed to serve?"

There was more to Baldur than met the eye. In addition to the smarmy charm, he also had a way of bringing someone as bold as Brandon to his knees. He'd almost faded, unable to hold the Father's stern gaze. "It's been a hard day."

"Yeah, tell me about it. And you wish to protect Astra like this?" Baldur was clearly not the forgiving kind. I wanted to speak up, but Brandon foresaw that and replied first.

"I will burn down the whole of Purgatory if I have to."

It made Baldur laugh. "How? One snap of my fingers, and you're out, boy."

"We need your help," I cut in. "Maybe leave the darkness measuring contest for later?"

"How can I help you if you're allied with weaklings?" Baldur shot back.

I wasn't sure where he was going with this, until Brandon stepped forward and straightened his back. The brief sideways glance he gave me spoke of his commitment—not only to our cause but to me. He had promised that he would keep me safe, and I still believed in him. Around us, the black forest with its obsidian leaves trembled and twinkled, chiming a chaos of faint notes that tickled my ears. The sound seemed to amplify my emotions, though it had taken a while to figure it out.

Baldur was feeding on the song of the leaves. He was growing bolder, perhaps bigger even. But Brandon wasn't backing away. No, he stood tall and looked Baldur in the eyes. "I'll fight you, Father. I'll fight you and prove myself worthy."

"I admit, I did not see that coming," the Father of Berserkers laughed. "If I beat you, Brandon, I will throw you out of here. You will never return, and you will never go near Astra ever again."

"And if I beat you, you'll come with us. Simple fight. No help from the Aesir," Brandon replied firmly. "Hammer wouldn't stand a chance against Briggel, anyway," Baldur sighed. "Fine. Let's do this. But remember,

Brandon, if I win—" I didn't even have time to process the conditions of this fight or duel or whatever it was supposed to be before Brandon rammed into him with the full force of his darkness.

I squeaked in surprise, and Hammer jumped back, growling and baring his enormous fangs. No one moved as Baldur and Brandon dissolved into thick wisps of liquid darkness. It turned out that the Father of Berserkers wasn't the only one who could work with such concentrated power.

A knot got stuck in my throat as I watched them. They dashed between the trees like mercurial shadows. One threw the other against a thick trunk. The shockwave of impact was so powerful that it fractured everything within a ten-yard-radius. Shards of obsidian rained onto the hard ground while the battle continued.

"Who's winning?" the Time Master asked Edda. I turned my head and saw Aphis following the fight with bright fascination. He likely fed on the violence. Most ghouls from Visio were peaceful once freed from the death magic spells that had kept them slaves to the Darklings. Aphis, however—as quiet and as gloomy as he was—clearly had an inclination toward aggression. Not necessarily to actively participate, but to watch. To draw something from it.

"I'm not sure," the Mother of Valkyries murmured.

All eyes were on the two shadows. They zigzagged in and out of the obsidian forest. They crashed into trees and split open the ground with their brutal thrusts. The darkness spread around them like a sickening mist, yet they showed no signs of exhaustion.

Suddenly, Brandon stopped about fifty yards from us. He looked at me for a split-second, just as a black shadow bloomed behind him, swelling and growing more menacing with each breath. I didn't even realize I was glowing all pink until I saw my light reflected in his burning blue eyes. *What a strange effect...*

I wanted to scream and tell him the Baldur was coming up behind him, but Brandon smiled at me and vanished in a puff of black smoke. The Father of Berserkers emerged, immediately confused as he'd hoped to deliver a crippling, defeating blow. He stilled and looked around a couple of times. Left, right. Left, then right again. Nothing. Darkness danced across the giant blade of his long-handled axe, itching to slice into Brandon.

"Come out and face me, coward!" Baldur roared, visibly satisfied with how the fight was progressing. His breathing was ragged, however. He'd been running around a lot. I imagined moving in black wisp form could not be easy. I imagined nothing about being a Berserker was easy, not even having to exist with the notion of once having been the worst of the worst.

A shiver trickled down my spine as Brandon's voice brushed over my ear. "Watch this, Pinkie." I froze, and a shadow blew past me. Baldur didn't see him coming until it was too late. His twin blades were out, and he revealed himself before the Father of Berserkers. But as soon as the dark wisps flew off him, I realized he didn't look like Brandon anymore. Baldur was stunned.

A pained look contorted his face. "No, you cruel bastard... not my son!"

"What was his name? Geralt?" Brandon showed no mercy, though I couldn't quite figure out what the play was, exactly—only that it worked.

The twin swords came down fast and cut Baldur across the chest. The Father of Berserkers shrieked and snarled in agony, then dropped to his knees. Brandon crossed the blades against his throat and waited patiently, still looking like... a younger version of Baldur? Yes, he was slimmer and perhaps a bit shorter, but he resembled him remarkably well. "His son," I whispered, putting two and two together.

"Baldur remembers only one thing from his life, but he remembers him vividly," Edda said. "His son, Geralt. When Baldur died, Geralt succeeded him on the throne of their kingdom. A man as bad as his father, truth be told. Baldur became a Berserker, handpicked by Order, and not long afterward, his son entered Purgatory."

"Yield, or I'll have your son cut you down," Brandon warned.

Baldur lowered his head.

"He was tasked with taking Geralt away and tossing him into the afterlife, where an eternity of punishment awaited him," Edda continued, shadows lingering over her eyes. "Baldur tried to bargain with Order to make Geralt into a Berserker, too, but she wouldn't have it. She said Geralt was mediocre, at best. Just a bad man trying to step into his father's shoes..."

I could see now what a hard game Brandon had played. I also knew what his ability was now. He'd promised me he'd show me some day. Yet another promise kept, much to my surprise.

"So, Brandon is something of a shape-shifter, huh?" Thayen muttered, understandably fascinated.

"I yield, you bastard," Baldur told the Berserker. "And screw you for stooping this low."

"I fight to win," Brandon replied and sheathed his swords, then turned around and found me staring. He left the Father behind and walked over with a hard face and white fire in his eyes. Nobody saw it coming. I certainly didn't, as he stopped a hair's width away, grabbed me around the waist and kissed me.

The moment our lips met again, the entire universe fell apart and recombined itself into something that simply worked better. This kiss lasted longer than the first time. I was able to take it in. To truly... take it in. Everything stopped. My heart. Time. The troubles with Hrista. Everything, as I surrendered to him and welcomed his embrace. Brandon held me tight and kissed me with all he had—his soul, his darkness, his fears and his regrets. I felt each piece of him touching my soul. The half-sentry in me was overly reactive, probably because Brandon didn't have a living body to shield him from me.

Our spirits twirled around one another, weaving a new path into the cosmic void. Mine sang a beautiful melody, and I let it ring in my ears long after Brandon politely pulled himself away and smiled. "Pardon me," he said, his voice a little raspy. "I couldn't help myself."

One quick glance around us told me our friends flustered. Not shocked, just flustered. This wasn't the time nor the place for a flashy romantic gesture, yet Brandon had managed to surprise everyone once more—myself included. Big eyes and slightly parted lips and the emptiest silence enveloped us for quite a while as I tried to find my words. Despite the persistent tingling in my extremities, I was able to move past this moment, though I wasn't sure how. I only knew that words were coming out of my mouth.

"Erm... You won. That means Baldur will help us, right?" I asked.

The Father of Berserkers let out a slew of expletives before he got up and put his axe away. It hid behind him in a sliver of black shadows. "Yeah, I'll help you," he grumbled, then pointed a furious finger at Brandon. "But I'll pay you back for using Geralt against me. I promise."

"I won, fair and square. Quit whining," Brandon replied bluntly.

Baldur would've liked nothing more than to tear him a new one, but Edda intervened. "Enough. You're like little children! Yes, Brandon won, Baldur lost, and that is where this conversation ends. No threats of retaliation." She glowered at the Father. "I expect better of you."

"Really?" Myst snorted a chuckle.

My head spun. We'd been on a constant rollercoaster ride since we'd stumbled into Purgatory. The walk here had been pleasant and calming, especially after our dismay with Order, but Brandon had managed to spice it back up again, leaving me flustered and breathless and feeling a million kinds of wonderful.

I had no idea where this would end. I only knew that Brandon was not the kind of person I could just walk away from. Furthermore, I doubted I'd ever manage to get him out of my head for the rest of this life. Or out of my heart. *My soul.*

Baldur took a deep breath, closing his eyes for a moment. Only then did I notice that Brandon had cut off some of his braids. I spotted them on the ground, scattered among the shattered black trees, snaking between shards of obsidian leaves. "I could ask for Order's permission to leave Purgatory," the Father of Berserkers said. "But that would mean admitting that I need her."

"She'd be a fool not to grant you passage," Edda surmised. "We're going after Hrista. She will want the girl captured and brought back, surely."

"Yeah, but why do it the easy way?" Baldur shot back with a cold grin.

It made Myst pinch the bridge of her nose. "You want to use Astra, huh?"

"Why, it's like you've read my mind!" the Father replied, his eyes reduced to venomous slits. They grew wide and sweet again when he looked at me. "Brandon may have stolen your heart, but I can still make your body sing." He paused for a second. "That came out wrong."

"You think?" Brandon blurted, blue fires burning angrily white for a moment.

"What are you talking about?" I asked, though his acknowledgment of Brandon's effect on me only served to amplify the feelings I had been dealing with for quite a while.

Baldur coughed lightly and offered an apologetic smile. "Hrista tapped into some very old energies to open up unauthorized portals. The same kind of energies that made you, darling."

"Okay, now I'm the one who's lost," Thayen replied.

"When darkness meets light, when death meets life, the impossible is achieved. The unimaginable is unlocked," Baldur recited, and Edda nodded in agreement. "Somehow, Hrista's spirit contains all four components: darkness, light, death, life. Astra here has three, for sure—life, death, and light. Three that I see clearly."

"Order said as much, more or less," Edda said, unsure of Baldur's direction.

"But she was wrong!" the Father laughed, downright thrilled to have outsmarted Order on this. "There are four in Astra, too! Though I cannot account for each of their origins. I mean, life comes from the Oracle genes, for sure. Light... I reckon that's the Hermessi thread that made her, and it's what might qualify her to become a Valkyrie beyond life. Or it could be both or the other way around! It doesn't matter. They're there." Well, we'd had that wrong until now, it seemed, but I was glad to get some clarifications here. "Death comes from the sentry side. And the darkness, I feel it, I'm sure Brandon feels it, too, though he could never quite put his finger on it." He paused to look at the Berserker.

"You're on to something," Brandon muttered.

"But I don't know its source! It is so weak... merely in its infancy. But it's there. Maybe that's why Order missed it. I guarantee you we're dealing with all four here. The only difference between Hrista and Astra, however, is that Astra's spirit is still wrapped in a meat sack."

"But wouldn't killing Astra heighten the girl's chances to become a Valkyrie?" Myst asked. "If I were Hrista, I'd try to avoid that."

"I'd try to avoid killing me regardless of the level of threat I pose to that crazy lady," I said. I did wonder about the source of my darkness. Where had that come from? Would I ever find out?

Baldur grinned. "That's the thing. Astra is a problem for Hrista with or without a body. It doesn't really matter. But by killing Astra, Hrista punishes her and her family by taking the girl away from them." He looked at me. "Now, let's get you back into portal opening mode, sweetie. I'm dying to grab a fistful of Hrista's hair and return her to Purgatory."

"You make it sound so easy," I murmured.

I'd accidentally brought us here while trying to get us back into The Shade. What were the odds that I'd succeed the second time around? Brandon had promised me that practice really did make perfect when it came to these powers, and I'd proven it with my steep learning curve and rapid development thus far.

"Have some faith in yourself," Brandon said, forever imprinting himself onto my soul. "I know I do."

That was the sweetest truth. The bitter one had Hrista waiting for me to set foot into The Shade. We all knew now that there was more to me than we'd thought. I found comfort in having Jericho and Dafne, Thayen, the Time Master, and Aphis by my side. I had Myst, too, and this enticing Berserker, Brandon, who'd turned my world upside down. And then there was Edda and Baldur, oh, the seemingly crazy Baldur with terrible manners but such intricate knowledge of how the universe worked.

In the end, my choices were simple. Run, or keep pushing. And I had no intention of running. Somebody had to defend The Shade and our way of life. If Hrista feared me so much, then I had to rise to the occasion and make those fears justified. As Brandon touched my hand, a fire was rekindled. My resolve burned brighter and hotter than ever. One way or another, I'd get us back into The Shade.

THAYEN

For a moment, I had found it hard to imagine that Baldur, this whirlwind of a Berserker with no end and no beginning might be able to bring out the best in Astra. And yet, despite Brandon's killer frown and Hammer's threatening growls, the Father pressed his fingers against the half-Daughter's temples and hummed softly, while she focused on opening a shimmering portal.

She had done it before, even though she'd gotten the destination wrong.

The first hint I got that something big was coming was when her skin lit up pink. Astra glowed intensely from the inside, her Daughter nature taking over. Nurtured by Purgatory's energies, it flared brighter than ever before. Baldur's influence was playing its part. "That's it," he said, laughing as he opened his eyes. The blue fires had turned pink, and I sucked in a breath, realizing that Astra was using the Father as some kind of conduit.

"Holy smokes," Jericho breathed, eyebrows raised in astonishment.

"You can say that again," Dafne replied. They had their arms wrapped around one another, waiting with childlike anticipation for Astra to come through and take us where we needed to go.

"Stay with that feeling," Brandon whispered in Astra's ear. He'd coached her before. I knew she would respond. Baldur cried out in what sounded like pain, his skin turning paler as a shimmering portal tore its way between him and Astra. Before its upper tip could reach their heads, Baldur grunted and pushed Astra back, breaking the physical contact.

The shimmering portal grew and widened, the pink glow now concentrated exclusively in Astra's hands as she tried to maneuver the damned thing. White light poured from inside it, an ocean of diamonds waiting to be crossed.

"There it is," Baldur laughed, clearly pleased with himself.

Brandon took Astra's hand in his with a determination I hadn't seen before. I welcomed it, after the earlier uncertainties. The Berserker had proven his intentions to be pure, and Astra surely benefited from his presence, from his attention and affection. It felt good to see them like this. She needed him, and I had a feeling he needed her, too, in his own way. "Come on, we need to go," he told her.

Hammer padded closer, giving him a faint whimper. It brought a tear to Astra's eyes. "Turns out he's choosing to come with you, after all."

Brandon had not made any effort to convince the Aesir to follow him, confident that Hammer would be able to choose freely once faced with the options. This had been his moment, and the dire wolf had chosen to leave Purgatory in Brandon's company. We had no idea what that meant for his future, but if his Berserker had gone rogue, Hammer would follow.

"You honor me," Brandon told the Aesir, who huffed in return and licked the back of his hand. It was a wholesome moment, a much-needed breath of hope. I imagined a future for them together—Astra, Brandon, and Hammer. I had no idea where the thought had come from, but due to the warm smile on her face, it felt right.

"Are you ready?" Myst asked, and I turned my head to find her gazing at me. She leaned forward, and for a moment, I anticipated something I knew I wanted. But it never came, as Brandon pulled Astra through the shimmering portal, Baldur jumped in after them, and Edda grabbed both Myst and me and took us with her.

"That was fun!" Jericho exclaimed as he and Dafne followed us through the passageway, swiftly joined by the Time Master and Aphis.

The enhanced team was complete, and we'd safely made it... "Hold on," I mumbled. "We're not in The Shade." "Oh, come on, seriously?" Time snapped, his chin jutting angrily. "Ah... now I see it. Well played."

We weren't in The Shade, per se. We'd made it to a small patch of dry land just outside The Shade, separated by less than a mile of water. The ocean spread all around us in its precious shades of blue, glimmering under the moonlight. "But we're home," I said. "Or home-adjacent, at least."

"Okay... I'm considering this an improvement," Astra replied, her breathing labored as the shimmering portal closed behind us.

"It is an improvement," Baldur said. His humor vanished as he turned his attention to The Shade. "But I don't think *that's* supposed to be there."

There was something wrong. Awfully wrong. "What did she do?" I heard Edda ask, though nobody had an answer, just a pile of questions, each stranger than the other.

The usual spell that cloaked our island had changed into something... different. A dome of black smoke now covered my beloved home. Reds and greens burst through it. Blues and yellows. Every other color on the cosmic palette joined them, occasionally interrupted by white lightning.

An electric charge filled the air. The kind of heavy humidity that I could smell. It told us a storm was coming, and we had landed smack in the middle of it. The ocean rumbled, its waters choppy as they attempted to swallow our little piece of dry land. It had been calm earlier, but it was changing. The Time Master made use of some of the swamp witch magic knowledge he'd acquired over the years to elevate it above the water. His lips moved, and I dared assume he was reaching out to Death, too. We needed help.

"I don't understand," Myst said, stunned by the sight before us. The dome crackled and moaned, swelling and growing, ever so slowly. It was obvious, though. It could not be denied. Whatever the spell cast upon our island was, it was spreading. "What sort of magic is this? It doesn't look like Purgatory magic."

"It's much worse," Edda concluded, covering her mouth.

"This is hybrid magic," Baldur said what the Mother couldn't, as the shock had rendered her speechless. "Like I told you, darkness and light, life and death. Hrista found a way. I'm willing to bet that the box of Kedra, the black witch, played a fundamental part."

Astra nodded once. "Okay, so what do we do?"

"I imagine Hrista will answer that question any moment now," the Time Master replied, drawing his scythe as he looked ahead. Before he could use his death magic, however, a bright white pulse smacked him in the forehead, and he nearly fell into the water. Aphis caught him and held him up, while the rest of us turned to see Hrista coming.

A jetty made of ice extended from beneath the hybrid magic dome. With each step that Hrista took, the frost expanded beneath her, creating a walkway for her to approach us. My blood ran cold as I saw the woman behind her. She had cuffs on, and she seemed... different. "Unending?" I mumbled, mostly to myself.

By the time Hrista reached us, Baldur and Edda had already assumed their combat positions. The rogue Valkyrie didn't seem frightened, however. Maybe amused, but certainly not impressed. Unending's hands were bound with threads of black mist, and her nostrils flared furiously.

"You've been a very bad girl," Baldur said and manifested his long-handled axe. Edda drew her shining trident, and they both lunged at her with everything they had. They glided across the water like birds, the moonlight dancing on their blades.

But Hrista disappeared and reappeared behind Unending with a sly grin, while the Mother and Father came to a screeching halt. Unending looked so downtrodden, it nearly broke my heart. "Don't bother," the Reaper said. "She's not really here."

"What?" Baldur needed a moment to get his thoughts back in order.

Edda held on to his shoulder for support, equally puzzled. "She's not really here?"

"In layman's terms, I'm projecting," Hrista replied, then looked at the Time Master. "I shot my disabling spell at you all the way from back there. I'm a sniper, do not mess with me."

She seemed like she was having fun. Unending, on the other hand, looked close to broken, and I couldn't understand why. "How... what happened to you?" I asked the Reaper.

It was Time who answered, instantly recognizing her new condition. "She has a living body. I don't know how, and I don't know why, but Unending, my dear sister, is stuck inside that meat suit."

"And something tells me this ray of twisted sunshine had something to do with it," Brandon concluded. He would've liked nothing more than to tear Hrista's head off, but there was no point. If we were dealing with a projection, it meant that she was well protected. She had come prepared.

Unending took a step forward on the ice, her foot slipping. She re-balanced herself carefully—having her hands bound made it more difficult, but she pulled through. "I'm a prisoner, and so is Tristan," the Reaper said. "For a particularly personal reason, I had myself fitted into a body, and now... I can no longer leave it. If I do, it will be through death only, and then I shall be automatically reaped and sent into the afterlife. Not even Death can change that. I will never be a Reaper again." Her voice broke, tears glazing her eyes—no longer galaxies but human-like pools of darkness and raw emotion. "I am here as proof that Hrista has a sure hold on me and my husband, as well as the entire island."

"There... See? It wasn't that hard," Hrista replied, enjoying every second. "Now, my turn." She looked to Astra first. "I knew you'd come, eventually. But I am generally well prepared, so this conversation already has an auspicious conclusion. You made it close enough, but you can never set foot inside The Shade. Ever again. I have locked all of you out. Every single Shadian, except for Tristan and his poor little wifey here, because there's nothing I like better than leverage."

Edda shook her head, making sure her disappointment was clear. "I don't understand what it is you're hoping to accomplish with this, Hrista. You don't belong here."

"I belong wherever I damn well please!" she retorted, immediately furious. I wasn't the only one who noticed, either. Unending was also intently focused on the Valkyrie. "And like I said, The Shade is mine, now. Try all you want, you are never coming back to it. I'm making it into something better, far superior and beautifully evolved."

"What the hell did you do?" I asked, horror unfurling in my throat.

"She took creation magic, and she perverted it," Baldur said. "My biggest concern is that she may be untouchable."

The projection claimed as much. Hrista had been able to fire a spell at the Time Master. She'd forced Unending out here to relay her message as a hostage. And she'd gotten her claws so deep into our island, I wasn't sure how we'd free it before it was too late. Myst looked worried, but there was anger in her eyes, too. It flared white and unforgiving, then dwindled into something soft and uncertain when she glanced at me. Hope, I realized. When Myst looked at me, she had hope.

"Say what you will, do whatever you want," Astra said, her hands still glowing pink—a shade I hadn't seen before. It was furiously intense and infinitely brighter, a mirror of her emotions, I figured. It was hard to even look at them as I waited for my eyes to become accustomed to that light. "I will get you out of there. One way or another, I'm going to come in there and drag your ass back to Purgatory where you belong."

Her bravery and determination made me feel like there was a light at the end of this peculiar tunnel. Sure, we'd stumbled plenty along the way. We'd won a few battles, lost some. Even so, we'd made it this far. The Shade was my home. It had welcomed me as a child, and now it needed me to protect it. It needed each of us who'd grown in its redwood embrace to come through for it.

Hrista was impressed. She wouldn't say it, but it was written all over her face, even in that projection form. Unending picked up on it, too. "Well, congratulations, Astra. You managed to open a portal. Whoop-dee-doo. You still have the entire population of The Shade to bring over. I assume you'll want your Reaper friends involved, too," she added, sneering at the Time Master.

Aphis was eager to rip her throat out, but the Reaper held him back. "You'll get your chance, just not now." "Maybe never," Hrista retorted, pointing a finger at Unending. "It's why she's here. Death is busy at the moment. I made sure of that. But you and the rest of your cohort might end up being a thorn in my side, so I figured Unending here would help even the playing field. If you so much as breathe in my direction, I'll lop her head off and throw it at you across the water." She looked at me next. I felt her hate coursing through me. Or maybe it was just mine, as powerful as hers. "And the same will happen to Tristan. Make sure you tell Esme that. I'll have her clone eviscerate him."

"Why are you doing this?" Myst asked the sister she'd once held in such high regard. I could only imagine how she felt in this moment. There wasn't much I could do, unfortunately, other than make sure that Astra would keep her promise.

"Because I can. Because I am better, and because I am tired of seeing the universe punish excellence and reward mediocrity. What happened to the Spirit Bender must never happen again. I will upend the balance, and I will rearrange the entire world," Hrista said. "And then, my dear sister... you'll be welcome to join me. Or, should you choose to be stupid, I'll be more than happy to reduce you and anyone else who dares interrupt my work into mere shadows of your former selves."

Myst had deliberately chosen to keep her Aesir out of this. So had Edda and Baldur, as well as Regine before them. The only one who was practically vulnerable in this current formula was Brandon. His Hammer was close, a potential target for Hrista's wrath. The dire wolf had chosen to come with him, though, and Brandon would never lose sight of him again. Yet the mad Valkyrie's statement stood out, basically implying that even with the Aesirs safely tucked away in Purgatory, she still had a way to get to them. Valkyries and Berserkers couldn't be killed or destroyed—but their Aesirs were not indestructible. And that was what Hrista was banking on.

"Time to head back, sweetie," Hrista told Unending, then flashed us a broad smile. "It doesn't matter what you do from now on. I already got what I wanted. I got your Shade."

She retreated, cautiously walking in front of Unending. The Reaper gave us one last look.

"The World Crusher is free," Unending said. "Death is probably with her."

"I thought I told you no talking without my permission," Hrista hissed.

In an instant, her projection vanished into thin air, and the ice jetty collapsed. Unending cried out and nearly fell into the water, but an invisible force held her up just above the surface, the waves splashing at the soles of her feet. She was dragged back, swallowed by the black dome with its ripples of colors and lightning before any of us could even react. Her words had troubled the Time Master. "What was she talking about?" I asked him.

"I'm not sure myself. Death will know. I'll have to ask," he replied.

"Crap," Jericho remarked, finding his voice again. "What do we do?"

"You two are kind of useless," Dafne said to Baldur and Edda. They both scoffed, clearly insulted and in no mood for any of this.

"We just need a better approach," the Mother of Valkyries replied.

The Father seemed a bit more doubtful. "And a hell of a lot more firepower. Hrista has really grown a lot since I last saw her."

"We'll get her out of there," Astra declared, her gaze fixed on the captive island. "We'll figure it out. One step at a time. One problem at a time. Sooner or later, in one form or another, using one or all the forms of magic known and unknown to us, we will..." her voice faltered, but she recovered quickly. "We will prevail. We will defeat Hrista. We will get our home back."

We certainly had our work cut out for us. The Shade was temporarily off limits, but we now had the ability to bring everybody else back from the fake one. The Time Master's death magic had been temporarily numbed, but he was still in touch with Death, though we'd yet to learn her response to this insanity. The whole World Crusher bit was an unexpected enigma, too. I wondered if it bore any relation to our problem here—it sounded like another Reaper, one of the old ones, though I only remembered ten. The First Tenners. Plus, her name was ominous... I shook my head, throwing the thoughts away and going back to my resolve. All was not lost. And we still had Edda and Baldur, who'd been unable to showcase their prowess because Hrista had come to us as a projection.

Which said a lot about her, I realized. Hrista was a coward. She had tricks up her sleeve, much like the Spirit Bender, and a sea of deadly venom in her heart, but in the end, she was a coward. I looked forward to telling Mom and Dad that.

"She will not win this," Myst assured me, and I felt the vibrations in her voice. She meant every word.

Brandon's stern look spoke volumes, too. Even the dragons were with us, though a little weary.

There was a lot we didn't know yet, but even so, we weren't out of options. The universe hadn't abandoned us. Our fates were still our own to make and bend as we chose. And Hrista would soon come to learn what it meant to piss off not one but all the Shadians.

DEATH

The land before us was dead and black and empty.

Life had perished here, and not that long ago. I thanked the universe for killing the local civilization thousands of years ago. I would have hated to see them die a slow and miserable death from the World Crusher's unstoppable toxicity. I'd thought the Black Fever had been bad, but World had surpassed Unending quite elegantly.

The six Ghoul Reapers walked ahead of me, spread out and sniffing the carbonized ground. Here and there, puffs of steam burst through the cracks. A volcano had erupted not that long ago. I assumed the heated rocks beneath my feet were a mass of cooling lava. Nature was truly savage and unforgiving. My brother's finest work, for sure.

"We're getting closer," Eneas whispered, as if afraid World might hear him.

"Relax, she won't be running from me," I told him. "She's done running."

Filicore shot me an acid sneer. "Right. She's just waiting for you, arms wide open, so that you can shove her back inside another book."

There was nothing as far as the eye could see, with the exception of a single smoking mountain. Streams of red lava were still snaking their way down under the ridges. I could smell the Sulphur and ashes from here. What a desolate realm. The perfect metaphor for how World must be feeling.

"She'll be ready for that. Your snark is poorly constructed," I replied dryly, choosing to focus on sensing my creation. She was definitely near. I couldn't feel her from afar, but down here, my senses flared. Either her cloaking magic didn't work as well as she'd thought, or she'd deliberately taken it off. It did not matter. An encounter was imminent, and I was about to face my greatest mistake.

How I handled her would dictate how the entire universe might fare, going forward.

As if to deliberately spoil things for me, the Time Master's voice came through, a beacon of anger and despair and confusion. "Death... please, tell me you're there."

I stopped walking. The Ghoul Reapers stilled, also, incredibly responsive to each of my gestures. I couldn't help but appreciate that. What had happened to them was awful. I'd caused it, and I would absolutely need to find a way to make it up to them. The best option was to send them into the nothingness and spare them this misery entirely. But that wasn't my only possibility.

"I'm here," I told Time.

"There's a Valkyrie wreaking havoc in the world of the living," he said, then proceeded to tell me everything from the moment he'd been summoned to assist with the clone attacks in The Shade and all the way down to the seconds preceding this telepathic conversation. The more he spoke, the more troubled I became. There was so much happening in the Word's domain, yet my brother still couldn't be bothered.

I'd certainly made my own share of messes, but the Word had responsibilities that he'd been skirting for quite some time now. It didn't feel right.

"Order is indeed useless outside her realm," I told Time. I couldn't shake what he'd told me about Unending. Damn it, I should've seen that coming, but I hadn't. Hrista... Anunit, she'd played everyone, myself included. Shame would've done the entire world a favor if it could just swallow me whole. I had been bested by a Valkyrie. "I owe her an apology, though. A while back, I mocked her creation for not being brazen enough. Look at things now..."

"What about Unending? How do we save her?" Time replied.

"I'm not sure you can. Not from her body, anyway. From what you told me, I might have a clue as to what happened to her, but everything else... I admit, I'm speechless. Worst of all, my darling, I have my fingers dipped in another, equally dangerous pie. I'm afraid I won't be able to immediately assist you with this."

Not until I get my firstborn under control. The World Crusher running loose made Hrista seem like a few scattered raindrops on a sunny day. Nothing we couldn't handle. The Time Master didn't appreciate my response, however.

"You've got to be kidding me," he said, the fury mounting in his voice. "You're leaving us to fend for ourselves?"

"No, I'm telling you I'm busy right now. I will come when I can, but in the meantime, you need to find the Word. Go through the swamp witches, summon the Hermessi, I don't care how you do it. Find a way to bring the Word to you. He might be able to help."

"How?"

The Ghoul Reapers all stood up straight at once. A moment later, they scuttled back past me, running as fast as they could while the volcano roared and spat more bright orange lava. But it wasn't the eruption that had scared them off. It was the one Reaper they'd been forced to share a planet with for too long. The one Reaper who had destroyed their souls and turned them into anomalies of their realm. The shame I felt whenever I looked at them was unbearable sometimes.

I finally saw her. A dark silhouette against a reddish sky, rippling against the heat that emanated from the hard, black ground.

"The magic that Hrista is using... it's hybrid, like you said. Life and death, light and shadow. You have all four elements through Astra, but she needs an extra kick from each to... activate her full potential." I'd always known what a fortunate blend of magic and supernatural genes the Daughter-Sentry was. I'd kept it to myself, because such power was rare, and it had to be nurtured in the right conditions. Alas, Hrista was forcing my hand now. I didn't have all the answers, of course, but I did have a general idea of what could be done to help lift Astra toward her full potential. "A Reaper of good repute such as yourself. That's death. Add the ghoul Aphis to ring a bell with her sentry nature, and you'll have a winning formula. Darkness and light, that means one of each of your special friends," I added. "A Valkyrie and a Berserker. The stronger, the better. She'll be feeding on your spiritual energy."

The figure grew clearer as she approached me. Every feature screamed with familiarity as I saw her for the first time in ages. She was beautiful. Angry and miserable, lonely and betrayed, complicated and still so woefully ignorant. Yet she was mine. My own. My first.

"And considering that Hrista's weird dome thingy sounds like a life-building spell of titanic proportions," I concluded, my gaze fixed on the World Crusher. "You will need the Word to pour his energy directly into Astra. She will need conduits and all the support you can give her, but I have faith in her. Don't you?"

"I had faith in you, once," Time replied. His words cut deeply, but looking at the World Crusher now, I understood that I deserved it. "But yes, I have faith in Astra. We all do."

"Then follow her. Build her. Nurture her." I exhaled sharply, bracing myself for what would come next. "I will join you when I can."

"Wait. Unending said something about the World Crusher. What are you—"

The telepathic connection was cut off. My doing. I would've liked to tell him more, but there wasn't much I could do until I brought my first under control. There were many things I'd done wrong with her, yet I dared hope it wouldn't end badly. I wanted to face him with at least one problem resolved.

"Hello, Mother," she said.

My whole being froze, the sound of her voice frosting my very senses. Oh, I was foolish to harbor such hopes. I saw that, now. *Foolish. Like a mother, I suppose.*

I would have to do better. If I was to return the universe to its true glory, if I was to restore its balance, I would have to do better. For too long, I had allowed my emotions, my selfishness, to get the better of me. Maybe I wasn't anybody's role model, and maybe I'd pissed off too many Reapers throughout my existence. There were so many of them, and only one of me.

"Hello, World."

~

ASOV 92: A DAWN OF WORLDS

Dear Shaddict,

See you there...
Love,
Bella x